Praise for The Quant

'A protagonist who complains about British weather is one thing, but one who feels the Thames would be much improved by a few crocodiles is something else!'

'Some genuinely laugh out loud moments plus a really engaging cast of characters, and a meta plot that has me hooked! Cannot wait for the next one!'

'…a fun take, with engaging characters and good writing.'

'… funny, bloody hilarious in places. Its characters are well written. I think, if the next one is as good, it will be the start of a bloody good series of books.'

Amazon

'A very entertaining, action-packed read with excellent characters and several good jokes - and no doubt some more I missed :) Reminiscent of *Ash* by Mary Gentle and the *Rivers of London* series.'

'…a delightfully fun read.'

'St. John does a great job of weaving in real history with fiction and an alternative history. So much fun!'

'It started interesting and just got better. The twists were unexpected and added to the story, can't wait for the next instalment.'

'Enjoyable and quirky.'

Good Reads

By Eva St. John

The Quantum Curators and the Fabergé Egg
The Quantum Curators and the Enemy Within
The Quantum Curators and the Missing Codex

THE
QUANTUM CURATORS
AND THE
MISSING CODEX

EVA ST. JOHN

MUDLARK'S PRESS

First published 2021 by Mudlark's Press

Cover art by Books Covered

First paperback edition 2021

ISBN 9781913628048
(paperback)

www.thequantumcurators.com

For Richard.
Ten

Day Zero - First Engineer

First Engineer glanced up from his desk in surprise. It wasn't time for the midday briefing, yet Second Engineer stood in front of him tapping a print-out against her thigh. An alarming item in itself. Files were only printed when the digital copy had been deemed so harmful that it had been completely wiped and a single hard copy made, to be filed or burnt at a later date.

'Report.'

There was no need for pleasantries. They were engineers, their job was to ensure a smooth running of society. Let the other departments clamour to be the best. Engineers were silent and knew the truth of things.

'This tripped our protocols as it ran through the security filters. It's a lecture for the neophytes.'

All staff who worked for the Mouseion of Alexandria started at the same place. Whether they would go on to be curators, custodians or even engineers, they all started as neophytes. Then their skills were assessed, and they were allocated to the correct departments.

'A neophyte lecture. What on earth could be in that to have triggered an alert?'

'It was written by Curator Strathclyde.'

First Engineer frowned and held out his hand for the offending transcript. When Strathclyde had first arrived through the quantum stepper, First had argued

1

vehemently that the man could prove to be highly dangerous. He had been overwhelmingly outvoted. The other departments had been charmed by Strathclyde and could see no threat in his friendly ways. They were treating him like a project or an interesting pet.

Despite First's objections, Strathclyde graduated as a curator. Now, he was being considered as an occasional lecturer in Beta Studies. First wondered when the rest of the mouseion heads would realise what a threat to the stability of their society Strathclyde was. Who knew what dangerous ideas he might try and inculcate? His eyes flicked across the paper.

Who amongst us hasn't wondered if we are not alone in the universe? He stared at Second and looked back over the paper, as he began to read aloud. 'If we can have a parallel existence between your Earth and mine, why not multiple universes?'

With a shaking hand, he took a match from his desk drawer and set fire to the paper, placing it in his bin.

'Do we know if he discussed the contents of this paper before he wrote it?'

Second shook her head. 'We've pulled all the audio files from any neighbouring wrist braces, and nothing was detected.'

First frowned. 'What about his own?'

'He doesn't always wear it. He's not impressed by the *wearing it for the common good* argument. Also, according to the notes, in his monthly assessment he commented, *that as it wasn't mandatory, he'd rather not.*'

'That's ridiculous.'

'In his defence,' said Second, 'he *was* tracked and spied upon through his wrist brace.'

'But that was unsanctioned. He would never have known about it if we had been doing it.'

'I don't think he sees it the same way. And, of course, he doesn't quite see the *for the good of society* the same way we do.

'This is not news to me, Second.' She flinched. Repetition of information was an unnecessary waste of time and unworthy of her rank. She waited to see what First was going to recommend. At this point, she felt her next suggestion would be at odds with his. She felt that Julius should be more closely monitored. He was an excellent example of a Beta mind and she wanted to study him.

'I have determined that Julius Strathclyde is a threat to society of the first order. He is an unresolved paradox.'

Second betrayed no emotion. First's reasoning was sound, but where Strathclyde was concerned, Second felt that First may be slightly conflicted.

'In order to protect the citizens of Alpha Earth, I will arrange for Julius to be removed from it.'

Second nodded her assent. She felt sure that they had lost a research opportunity, but First was within his rights. Julius Strathclyde must die.

Day One - Julius

It was one of those moments when you desperately try to take in every detail of your surroundings because you are trying to avoid one aspect of it.

I was standing in Sam's office. The air conditioning kept the room cool whilst the street outside sizzled, a clever breeze system meant that I could catch the scent of lemons and dust baking on the streets below. It was still only the morning, but it felt like today was going to be a hot one. I watched as a flock of yellow and green finches swept past the window. The view beyond the window looked over the library of Alexandria and the other mouseion buildings and on to the Mediterranean itself. I could have spent the rest of the day just staring at this beautiful alien landscape, but it was no good. The shouting was increasing, and I had to return my attention to the chaos of the room.

My partner Neith and our boss, Sam Nymens, were hurling abuse at each other.

Our friend Rami was showing more common sense and had wisely chosen not to pick a fight with the remaining person in the room; Asha Giovanetti, Head of Custodians, and scariest woman in Alexandria.

The sweet fragrances from beyond the window were being overwhelmed by that of vomit. At least two of my companions had thrown up, and now they were all

4

shouting at each other. Which in all honesty was better than the vomiting.

The object of their distress was a white man in his mid-thirties. He had a blond moustache and beard to match his long, flowing hair that just about reached his shoulders. In case his appearance didn't already scream *divine majesty*, he also wore a crown on his head.

Arthur, mythical high king of the Britons, had materialised in Sam's office and had somewhat thrown the cat in amongst the pigeons.

Standing in the same room as someone who thinks they are a god is a bit of an eye-opener. Honestly, I was getting a headache. My brain kept trying to see radiating glory, but my eyes were focusing on a wavy outline. The others had taken his sudden appearance far worse. I had initially tried to explain things to them, but it had all gone pear-shaped. I decided to try again. It was alarming to see my friends in such a state of distress. Neith appeared close to tears.

'Look, guys—'

Asha held up her hand. My voice trailed off.

'Enough, Julius,' she snapped, causing me to wince. 'If you can't keep your hysterical ravings to yourself, I will call for custodians to remove you.'

Hysterical ravings? Well, yes, the situation was extreme. I mean, a man had literally appeared out of thin air in front of us. They were all acting like he was a new type of curator or an anomaly. It was me that had leapt to

5

the conclusion of multi-dimensional universes and gods and the like. This had caused even more distress to the team than Arthur's actual appearance.

I was angry with Asha, but I had to concede that when it came to weird shit, they were way ahead of me. They had built a quantum stepper, after all, creating a bridge between my world and theirs. What did I have? Folklore and story books. The answer was bound to be some clever scientific explanation. I just liked my version better because I understood it. Mind you, last year quantum physics had also been beyond my understanding, and yet I had been relying on it for the past few months.

While we all stood and shouted at each other, Arthur leant against the wall and watched us with a puzzled smile. With a wave of his hand, the others fell silent. This didn't strike me as a positive development. If someone or something had the power to stop four people from talking or moving, it was clearly more than a *blip in the quantum field* as Rami had proposed.

'Arthur,' I began but his fury swept over me, and I dropped to one knee. 'My liege.'

Well, at least that stopped the headache, but now I appeared to be quaking with fear. And the minute I realised I was quaking with fear, it passed. Whatever influence this guy had over me, it didn't last long and was easily challenged. Still, in order not to receive any more negative attention, I decided to play along.

'You mentioned that you require our assistance in a wager. How may we oblige the great and wondrous Arthur, King of the Britons?' It was hogwash, but he smiled, and I realised that he bought it. He gestured benignly at me to stand up again, and I glanced across at the others in the room.

Neith was halfway through an expression. It seemed part awe and part *whatever you have done to me I am going to kill you*. Asha was similarly frozen. Her face was one of blank contemplation. Sam was thunderstruck, and Rami was still reeling.

'I need my sword back,' said Arthur. 'Some foul miscreants stole it from the Lady of the Lake, and I am here to rightfully reclaim it.'

I avoided Neith's eyes in case she put two and two together and realised she was the foul miscreant in question. Arthur hadn't recognised her, and I didn't want to draw his attention towards her until I knew how dangerous he was.

I tried to work out what was going on. If he wasn't someone from another multiverse, then what was he? Was this a quantum anomaly? Did these sorts of things happen regularly? Was this a side-effect, like splicing, that they hadn't told me about yet? If it was a known side-effect, it was a rare one. The others looked suitably stunned. Only Asha was keeping her cool, but I had decided that Asha could be standing on a rock in the middle of a lava flow, and she'd still have the same glacial

7

expression on her face. Maybe a small twitch of her lips to indicate her displeasure.

None of them had accepted my suggestion of Arthur being an actual person, and the idea of multiple universes had been almost vehemently denied. Normally they were dismissive of ideas that ran contrary to their teachings but this time their response had been extraordinary. However, the fact remained Arthur was standing in front of us, and they didn't appear to have an explanation for him. Arthur cleared his throat. It seemed I had been drifting.

'My lord, forgive me. I am overwhelmed by the honour. In order to complete this task, I will need the assistance of my companions.'

As I watched, I could see that all their expressions had started to change. Whatever Arthur was doing to hold them in limbo was slipping. If I allowed him to think that releasing them was his idea, he might be easier to handle.

'Very well.'

The air in the room shifted slightly and the four Alphas all started to shout as Arthur began to glow and radiate awe again. That was interesting. Whatever he was, his powers, as impressive as they were, were very limited. He was able to silence my companions, but not for long. He scowled at the four of them, and they fell silent. He scowled some more, but they seemed confused as to what they should do, and Neith gripped her head in her hand.

'My noble liege, tell me again what you need?'

Turning to look at me, I saw with relief that the others had relaxed. Arthur had clearly eased his grip on them. He placed his fists on his hips in a dramatic pose and began to declaim.

'That mighty sword, forged from the stars of heaven, crafted by the ancient blacksmiths of Albion. This noble blade…'

Worried that this might go on for some time, I interrupted him.

'Excalibur?'

Arthur glared at me, and I raised my hand quickly to cut him off.

'Neith. King Arthur wants his sword. I believe you may remember saving it once?'

I looked at Neith, willing her to play along.

'Julius. Are you mad? Call the bloody guards.'

Hmm. Not playing along then. Very well.

'Oh, Neith, you fine and faithful guardian. There is no need to fight on, your duty is at an end. Excalibur's rightful owner has come to reclaim it.'

'Over my dead—'

I cut her off. I wasn't sure what was happening. This Arthur figure could be a hallucination or reality. I was put in mind of my first few days waking up on Alpha Earth when I was in a permanent state of denial. However, what I did know was that uttering *over my dead body* was usually accompanied by *so be it* and a squishy pile of blood. I wasn't prepared to see how gory this hallucination could get.

'I'm sure you can remember where you placed it, for its continued safety and protection.'

The minute I saw her face pause in reflection, I addressed Arthur. It was time to test the range of his abilities.

'My liege, simply gaze upon my companion's thoughts. The sword's location should be easy to see.'

'Julius. Stop playing along. What do you think I'm going to do? Tell him where the artefact is located?'

'You can see it, though? In your mind's eye, so to speak?'

'Duh,' she jeered at me. 'He can't read minds.'

Arthur cried out exultantly and banging his fist dramatically on his chest plate, he disappeared.

***

Asha was the first to react. Calmly, she asked Neith for the sword's serial number. As soon as she had it, she called the custodians and told them to go and protect that section of the archives. She made a second call and asked whoever it was to join us immediately. There had been a pause in the call as she listened to a voice on the other end, and then simply repeated *immediately* and hung up.

I wondered who she had summoned. I didn't fancy their chances. Imagine making Asha Giovannetti repeat herself. The rest of us tried to follow her lead.

'Stay calm, everyone. We've all experienced quantum aberrations before. This is clearly stronger than normal, but we'll get through it.'

How typical of these people. Rather than meltdown and start wild speculations, they got straight to work dealing with the most pressing concerns first. I wanted to talk about what Arthur was. The others absolutely didn't. Each time I tried I was knocked back. I had thought the idea of multiple universes was an obvious solution. Asha thought I was hysterical, and no one was laughing.

'I'm not going to lie to you, butt. What the hell was that?'

Neith was pacing back and forth. She kept picking up a can of drink and then putting it down again without taking a sip. Even without her outward agitation, I knew she was troubled. When we had spliced the previous year, I got a whole slew of her tactical knowledge. She got my grandmother's Welsh idioms, blasphemies and a propensity to fold socks. I think I got the better half.

'Stressed much?'

She turned and looked at me then grinned ruefully.

'Fair play, butt.'

Butt was a term of endearment, just like *ach-y-fy* was one of disgust. They seemed completely normal to me, but I knew they still caught Neith out and she liked to know when she was veering off into the splice.

Sam, Neith and Rami still appeared shocked, and Sam had opened a bottle of brandy. At least he hadn't thrown up again. The vomiting was weird, he didn't look or act afraid, rather he appeared to be in pain or ill. He waved a glass at me and whilst I'd have loved a nip of something restorative right now, brandy was revolting.

Rami had picked up the chairs that had been knocked over when Arthur first materialised and we sat back down now, glancing at each other in consternation.

'Julius.'

I froze. I had done nothing wrong, but when the head of security says your name, it has the effect of making you doubt yourself. Had you been doing forty in a thirty? Were your library books all up to date? Asha continued.

'Well done. Whatever just happened, you kept your cool. First Engineer is on his way, and we should hopefully receive an explanation then.'

'But Julius just told that man where the sword is,' protested Neith, clearly still cross at having been manipulated.

'No, Neith. You did that. If, that is indeed, what happened.' She paused whilst taking the time to look us all in the face. 'All we know is that the vision disappeared when it thought it had completed its objective. As I said, First Engineer will know more.'

At the mention of the engineers, Sam had quickly placed his glass and bottle back on the shelf and offered a mint to Neith and Rami, who eagerly helped themselves. Whilst he and Giovanetti were a similar age and friends, she clearly outranked him, and he proceeded cautiously.

'Asha, do you think it was necessary to summon First Engineer?'

'Do you think I had an option? Some massive anomaly just turned up in here, rendered us immobile and disappeared again?'

'But First is an out-and-out psychopath,' protested Sam. 'Even his own mother would shrink in his presence.'

'It's just as well she isn't here right now, then.'

The voice came from a fairly inoffensive, slightly overweight man. He was wearing long desert robes. His mousy hair was receding, and he was sporting a crafty comb-over. He also had a pierced ear with a small gold loop. In short, he looked like an accountant who had turned up to pick up his kids from the disco and was likely to embarrass them by trying to say something cool to their friends. He certainly didn't remind me of a psychopath, but the way he had silently entered the room and even caught Asha off guard was unnerving. For the second time in under an hour, the four Alphas looked utterly shocked.

Ignoring Sam, who appeared to be sweating, the man closed the door behind him. 'Custodian Giovanetti, I take it *Immediately* is somehow connected to the "massive anomaly" you just mentioned?'

As he stressed the words, he used the same tone that headmasters did when they were asking someone if they thought they were being clever or funny. Sam, Neith and Rami had jumped to attention when he had revealed himself, but Asha had remained seated. I wasn't sure what to do, I began to rise, but as he glared at me I sat back.

'Were you all present?'

I said we were, but the others just nodded their heads. The cat had well and truly got their tongues today. As no one was going to talk, I decided to go out on a limb.

'Is it possible that the person who was just in the room with us is an actual manifestation of a mythical figure?'

First ignored me and addressed Sam.

'As head of the curators, you are responsible for the infantile bleatings of your team. See that in future, if they can't engage in an intelligent manner, that they remain silent.'

My face flushed, and I noticed that no one glanced my way, although I was gratified to see Neith was scowling fit to curdle milk. Having dismissed my suggestion, First continued.

'Very well. You'd better report, and then I'll have to decide what to do.' He broke off and tapped on his wrist brace. 'Send Second Engineer, and whoever is on anomalies duty, to Chief Nymens' offices.'

A few minutes later the door opened, and a woman about Neith's age walked in and nodded at First Engineer. She ignored all of us, so I assumed she was Second. I'd had the impression that all engineers would wear similar uniforms as the custodians did, but she was wearing a short skirt, high heels and a waistcoat. Her red bra was quite visible, so I tried not to look at her. Behind her, Jack walked in, and I was never so delighted to see a friendly face. Jack and I had graduated at the same time. He was something of a prodigy. Where I had been the oldest in the cohort, Jack, due to his outstanding intellect, had been the youngest. He had instantly been taken up by the engineers, home to the brightest of all the mouseion's employees.

Now, looking at him, I was shocked. The kid was exhausted. He gave me a weak, confused smile, and dropped his face into a blank expression, slipping something small into his mouth.

'Jackie!' I exclaimed brightly, inwardly promising never to call anyone Jackie ever again, and stepped forward to shake his hand. Damn it, I was so pleased to see him I might have even considered a hug, but he guessed my intentions and took a small step back.

'We do not refer to ourselves by our names, Curator Strathclyde,' said Second Engineer frostily, finally addressing me. I had long since given up being surprised that anyone knew who I was. Even without the mismatched eyes, I always stood out.

'My apologies, Jack. What are you? Seven hundred and fifty-eighth engineer?' I said with a fake laugh.

You see, this was why I didn't do small talk or try to break the ice. I ended up sounding like someone's overbearing uncle. You know the one. Whenever you're at a family occasion, he reminds you of the time he saved a policeman from getting run over. Everyone's heard the

15

story a thousand times and at the end can beat him to the punchline. Then later, after ten too many drinks, he would start a fight with the next-door neighbour about the correct way to aerate a garden pond.

At the moment I was still in the blustery bonhomie stage of the evening, but desperately working out how to shut up. I was really concerned about Jack's demeanour. He had been a lively companion and had always been ready with a quick laugh like any seventeen-year-old. Now, he acted like an old man.

'Pi has not earned the title engineer yet. For now, he is simply Pi-Jack.'

'Okay, sorry to have got it wrong, Jack.'

'Pi-Jack,' Second Engineer barked at me in the silence. Everyone avoided my eye, except for Neith, who was furiously trying to tell me something through her clenched expression. Asha broke the tension.

'First Engineer. Can we proceed? Time is of the essence for an accurate retrieval.'

'You are right, of course.'

What followed was a curious interview. Four of us were given mufflers to wear, whilst the fifth person was interviewed. First Engineer started off the interview asking me to recount exactly what had happened. Then Second Engineer asked me to recount the event again, only her questions were slightly different, and then Jack did the same thing. By the end of it, I was wrung out. Whatever Jack had slipped into his mouth worked; he was more alert now, but no friendlier. I put my headphones back on and watched as the same procedure was carried out on the four Alphas.

Eventually, the three engineers conferred quietly at the other end of the room, before returning to where we were sitting. One of Asha's fingers was tapping on the side of her thigh. She saw me watching her, and her hand fell still. Sam was shredding a sheet of paper, and Rami and Neith looked sick. I sat watching, trying to lipread. Whatever the engineers were saying, they seemed unmoved and in agreement. Surely nothing bad was about to happen. Jack would be more agitated, wouldn't he?

As they nodded their heads they returned, and First Engineer opened his mouth to speak. Giovannetti's wrist brace pinged, and she held her hand up, forestalling the engineers' decision. Neither she nor the engineers displayed any emotion about the interruption, though I couldn't help but think she was pleased, and he was annoyed.

'Hold on please, I will have instructions in a moment,' she said into her wrist brace, then looked at an engineer. 'It turns out that artefact DL278643 is missing from the archives. It went missing from the archives at 14:23 precisely. An alert was immediately established, and if I hadn't been incommunicado, I would have been informed then and there.'

Despite the theft of an artefact, both parties smiled for a second. The new system to avoid any future thefts from the mouseion had worked. I was impressed that they had acted on my idea of using the weight of an item and promised myself a pint if and when I got out of here.

Now, however, First Engineer was taking charge again.

'We were already aware that the sword had gone. As you summoned me, I received the report of the theft. It is unlikely that the two events are unconnected.'

Asha narrowed her eyes.

'Why did I not receive the report at the same time as yourself? We are of equal rank and the security of the mouseion falls under my provision.'

The man shrugged his shoulders as though her concerns were irrelevant.

'It was a failsafe. I didn't want you bothered with false alarms during the initial testing system.'

'Are you concerned that your engineers aren't able to build an efficient and accurate alarm system?' Asha's voice dripped disdain. 'I should have thought even your Pis could rustle up a foolproof system in their sleep.'

'We are still in the proto stages—'

'Of an alarm bell? It's not like you are employing any actual quantum physics here, are you?'

'No, but—'

'No buts,' said Asha sharply. 'Please ensure that I receive security notifications the instant they are triggered. I cannot do my job properly if the engineers are incapable of doing theirs properly.'

18

'Is that a threat?' asked Second Engineer casually.

I watched as Asha didn't so much as acknowledge the question but continued talking to First.

'Well?'

First tipped his head. 'I will remove the delay and hope that you are not too inconvenienced as the system beds down.'

'I have every confidence in the skill of the engineers that I shall not be bothered by false alarms.' Asha was back in control of the conversation and relaxed into her chair. The engineers remained standing, I hadn't been aware of a rivalry between the various departments at the mouseion, but it was clear that some sort of grudge match was playing out between the custodians and the engineers. I wondered where the curators sat in all of this. At the moment, the three curators in the room stood to one side looking deeply worried and angry. That's what I liked about the curators; you usually knew what they were thinking. In a world of cat people, they were the dogs.

'Now, First Engineer. I believe you were going to speak. Clearly, something has occurred. We are at your *limited* disposal as to how we may help.'

First muttered to Second as she quickly wrote a note. The woman flicked me a quick glance and carried on writing. I was not reassured.

'No one in this room is to speak of what occurred,' said First. 'Even amongst yourselves. I will run a detailed investigation and request that you all undergo a medical examination and brain scan.'

Asha nodded her head.

'Agreed, but there will be no sedation, and we will receive the brain scan without blockers.'

Sam swore and Neith moved forward to speak, but Rami grabbed her arm and pulled her backwards.

First shrugged his shoulders and gave a small laugh. 'As you wish.' Without fanfare, the three left. Asha sagged into her chair and exhaled loudly.

'Damn, that was close.'

Neith walked over to the sofa and slumped down. 'Can't believe you volunteered me for a brain scan without blockers.'

I didn't want to ask because I was fairly certain that I wouldn't like the answer, but I had to know. 'What do blockers do?'

Sam had been making mint tea and handed me a small cup. For once I was grateful for its sweetness as he gestured for me and Rami to join Neith on the sofas.

'When you get a full brain scan, it can be unpleasant.'

'Sod that, Sam,' laughed Neith, 'There's no "can be" about it. I had it done once after a massive explosion in Beirut. It was emergency repair work, and they had to find and fix the head injury as fast as possible. Absolute agony and days of weird neuralgic aftershocks. Synaesthetic malfunctions and constant vomiting.'

I knew I shouldn't have asked. I knocked back my tea.

'And the blocker prevents that?'

'It does, but it also means that without a blocker your brain can only be read, rather than also written on. Nothing can be erased or manipulated.'

'A blocker doesn't block manipulation. It blocks pain?'

'Correct,' continued Sam. 'Your brain resists change, a natural defence mechanism, so when we need to alter or speed things up, like when you had the tickle procedure to speed up your languages acquisition, we use the blockers. Like a sedative.'

'So this is like root canal surgery without anaesthetic?'

The team took a second to explain what I meant to Asha, who employed the usual Alpha expression of *Dear God the Beta's are basically savages* before Sam returned to me and shook his head.

'No, Blue, nothing like that.'

I have to confess I did sag in relief just a bit.

'It's far worse.'

Day One - Julius

After that rather gloomy announcement, Asha dismissed me and Neith but asked Sam and Rami to stay on. We headed out with the head of security's reminder not to discuss the incident with anyone, including each other, still ringing in our ears.

'So what in Bast's name was all that about?'

Neith stared at me, and I could tell by the way she was frowning, her folded arms and her tapping foot, that she might be slightly exasperated.

'What part of, don't discuss this amongst yourselves, was unclear? Seriously, Julius, you don't mess around with the engineers.'

I paused. I knew Neith, and I knew being told not to talk about something would be killing her, I just needed to find a way in.

'Am I allowed to ask about the engineers instead?'

Neith glared at me but unfolded her arms. 'Okay, but let's walk. We'll head out along the boardwalks.'

I was grateful for her suggestion. We were entering autumn, but the Egyptian heat was still something I wasn't used to even after all these months. I knew I would acclimatise eventually, but today I was glad of the sea breeze. The waves were rolling in and crashing onto the beach. Out on the water, people were zipping along on windsurfer boards their bright red and yellow sails flipping up into the monotone blue sky.

'That looks like fun.'

'Wait until you see some of the synchronised ones. Those are incredible. Ramin and I tried a few times, but on each occasion, we nearly drowned the other.'

'Curators do seem to go out of their way to find ways to kill themselves.' I grinned, knowing that Neith would like the compliment.

'It goes hand in hand with the personality type to make a good curator. Thrill seeker, adrenaline junkie.'

'Hardly what I'd call myself,' I said as we watched another windsurfer spin up into the air before landing back on the water.

'True, but you have other skills. I've been wondering lately whether a mix of personality types might work better.'

'You mean if there were more questioning or suspicious sorts in the curators, the thefts might have been spotted sooner?'

Neith frowned at me but continued walking. 'That wasn't what I had in mind, but I suppose you have a point. The thing is, it was spotted because we have such excellent custodians. Giovanetti and her team had been monitoring and waiting until they had enough proof to spring the trap.'

I thought about it, but that wasn't exactly how it had happened. Besides, there was another problem.

'If the engineers are so brilliant, shouldn't they have noticed the problem sooner?'

'Beneath their paygrade,' said Neith dismissively. 'Theft is for custodians.'

'What about when the stepper was switched off, and we were stranded. Why weren't the engineers all over that?'

'I'm sure they were. It's not in their nature to declare their presence, they are a behind-the-scenes sort. Notice that you never see them in the canteens or shared spaces. They all eat and socialise together. Like ants. You know their motto, "We never end", just like Pi.'

'They sound like a cult. First Engineer, Great Leader.'

'No, we don't do cults, remember? That's your lot. The engineers are just a bit extreme. I suppose they are the opposite of us curators.'

There was a large boulder ahead of us and we climbed up it and sat side by side, watching the yachts on the Med. This could be a very romantic moment, I thought, if I wasn't with Neith. I had been delighted to start working alongside her, and the more I got to know her, the more I liked her. When we had first met, I was crouched down in Charlie's bedroom in Cambridge. She had been terrifying and incredibly attractive. Fear does silly things to the male psyche, it's not a fact I'm proud of but it's there, nonetheless. Now, though, I could still see she was absolutely gorgeous, but the physical appeal had been passed over for sheer friendship. I could no more fancy her than I could Charlie. I could see how attractive Charlie was, but he was my best friend. And now I was beginning to see Neith in a similar light. Maybe as a sister. She nudged my knee with hers.

'You've gone silent.'

'Sorry. Just thinking about the engineers. You make it sound like they all have the same personality type, but they don't, do they? You told me that Giovanetti was once supposed to join the engineers but joined the custodians instead, and she's the watchful, suspicious sort. Whereas Jack—'

'Pi-Jack.'

'What?'

'Pi-Jack. That's his name now. That's what you should call him. Like Giovanetti rather than Asha, and Ramin instead of Rami.'

I blinked at the step-change. 'Neither of them minds. In fact—' I paused in reflection '—Asha asked me to call her by her first name.'

'I know. I was there. But she outranks you.' Neith was fiddling with her laces, and I had the feeling this had been annoying her for a while. 'Despite what she said, you should still call her Giovanetti to show honour.'

'And ignore a direct order?' I teased, but Neith just stared at me and shrugged her shoulders. I decided to explain myself to see if that would help. 'Back home, we tend to work on a flatter system of hierarchy. We all know where we stand in relation to each other, but we don't necessarily use our names to display it. In fact, we use the names in a slightly different way to show respect.' I stopped, trying to gather my thoughts. I found it painful to reflect on people that I might never see again.

'The provost runs the university. He is as senior as it gets. Yet we are on first name terms. I like him and he likes me. My students all call me by my first name, I respond in kind. None of us are confused by who is in the senior position.'

'So you never use surnames?'

'No, we do. All the time. Sometimes to show respect, sometimes for tradition, sometimes to show that we really don't like someone.' Neith was smiling. She loved the nuances of Beta Earth, and I was happy to explain. 'For example, the porters and cleaning staff like to go by their surnames. I've tried repeatedly to call them by their first names, but most of them don't like it. They like the tradition and the distance it gives them. Except for Tiff, she says being called Miss Fletcher sounds mad, so I call her Tiff.' I smiled. She made a rubbish cup of tea and I missed her. 'Then there's Double. An odious man, a lecturer in Modern French. Same rank as me, but I will never call him Bill.'

'So, how you use a name shows friendship as well as respect, but can also show societal privilege?'

It seemed a fair assessment, so I agreed, and she shook her head.

'That's why our system is clearer and easier to understand. We call her Giovanetti because she outranks us.'

'Except, I like her, and she asked to be called Asha. Just like I call Sam, Sam, and no matter how many times Soliman Alvarez asked me to call him Soliman, I always referred to him as Alvarez.'

'Oh,' said Neith, something dawning on her. 'I thought you called him that because you were finally learning how to recognise rank.'

I gave her an old-fashioned look, and she laughed. 'Fine, but seriously, you must call your old friend Pi-Jack, that's his name.'

'No, it isn't,' I countered. 'That's just his title.'

'No, not in the engineers. That's their name as well as their rank and designation.'

'See, that's another thing that's ridiculous. But my point is that *Jack* was proper curator material; loud, boisterous, and adventurous. Now he's popping pills just to stay alert. In front of his bosses, who didn't even comment, which suggests that they are fine with their new recruits taking stimulants to keep going. Which, frankly, is wrong. Jack isn't even eighteen yet. I don't know how you treat people over here, but back home we'd call that abuse.'

I knew I should be focusing on the sudden appearance of King Arthur, but I knew Neith would refuse to speak about that, plus Jack's appearance had shocked me. I honestly felt a duty of care towards him. If I had been back in Cambridge, I would have spoken to the teenager myself and got in touch with pastoral care. Child prodigies were not uncommon in Cambridge, and we did our best to navigate them through university life. Neith edged away from me and hugged her knees.

'I know it must seem odd to you, but you don't understand how tough a calling it is to be an engineer. Not only do they have to be brilliant, but they also are dealing on a daily basis with the quantum field. You know how it affects us, and we only travel through it once every couple of weeks. They deal with it daily.'

I was unlikely to ever forget that first sensation of the universe crawling through my skin, lice creeping through the follicles of my hair, tingly and freezing me down to my bones. My eyes were slammed with colour, every sound was a symphony, and then there was vomiting. It gets easier, but not a lot. And, of course, you can get quantum hangovers that are, quite frankly, terrifying.

'Pi-Jack is learning to deal with that, and he has the very best people around him, helping him to adapt and survive. I know the engineers have a high attrition rate but try not to worry. They will be doing everything they can to pull him through this.'

Until then, the attrition rate hadn't even occurred to me.

'If he can't cut it as an engineer, will he join the curators?'

'No, that wouldn't be possible,' said Neith gently.

'Because?'

'Because he'd be dead.'

I looked at her in alarm. 'Dead?'

'He knew what he signed up for.'

'But he's a child! 'I reminded myself that seventeen-year-olds didn't like to be referred to as children, but this was insane.

'He is a very rare and gifted individual. He was aware of the risks when he signed up. The chance to work the quantum field is the life dream of any scientist, as well as the chance to serve his society.'

'But what if he doesn't die, simply decides to resign instead?'

Neith shook her head. 'Well, I suppose that's fine. But no one ever has.'

'And that doesn't strike you as odd?' I asked, baffled.

'A little, I guess. But I can't imagine resigning from the curators. It's the best job in the world. Why would I leave? And Pi-Jack will feel the same soon. Remember how you feel in the stepper? He's coping with that on a far more regular basis at the moment. It's why they are such a funny bunch.'

It stank, but I decided to let it slide. The entire culture was different to mine. Every time I thought I had a handle on how they behaved, I realised I had made a subtle miscalculation leading to a massive social faux pas. This was not like being amongst Americans. These guys were as good as actual aliens, and I needed to remember that.

'On to matters quantum, could Arthur have been some sort of quantum hangover?'

'Julius, I am not going to answer that.'

Well, that was the truth. I needed to come in sideways and start extrapolating.

'Okay. Try this. Have you ever experienced the same quantum hangover as someone else at the same time?'

'No.'

'Have you ever heard of anyone else experiencing the same hangover as another person?'

'No.'

'Righty-ho.' I rubbed my hands together. Neith was prepared to play ball so long as I pitched the questions very carefully. I couldn't ask her about multiverses. That, at least, had been very clear. I was wrong on that score. A multiverse didn't exist according to their engineers, and they should know. Despite it offering a perfectly valid explanation to the Arthur manifestation. I persevered, 'Is a hallucination the same as a hangover?'

'Both are the result of a quantum journey.'

'Can you experience a hallucination if you haven't passed through the quantum field yourself?'

'I don't know.'

'And have you ever heard of someone having a hallucination, that has nothing to do with the quantum stepper?'

'I suppose, but that would be caused by their own biological brain conditions.'

Which would explain why we were all about to have our brains scanned. I continued.

'In this world, are hallucinations a common thing within the population?'

'No. We are able to treat and help individuals who are afflicted.'

'Are the incidents of hallucination around the QS facility increased?'

She paused.

'I haven't heard of that, but then—' she broke off.

'—but then you wouldn't, would you? Because the engineers would sweep in, tell everyone to say nothing, and take them away to have their brains examined.'

Neith pursed her lips. I wondered if I had pushed my luck and tried again from another angle.

'Here on Alpha, do you have the technology to appear and disappear at whim? I'd call it teleporting if I were back home.'

'Like in your sci-fi shows?' She smiled. 'No, we haven't worked out how to move matter through time and space.'

Well, that was patently incorrect.

'Except for the stepper, where you can actually travel to a parallel universe up and down its timeline? Doesn't it seem peculiar that your technology has developed in such a narrow parameter? I should have thought you guys would spend all your time teleporting here, there, and everywhere.'

Neith shook her head. 'No idea. Ask an engineer. Or rather, don't.'

31

I sat and listened to the waves breaking on the shore below. Despite the breeze, Neith was sweating, and I wasn't.

'Last question.'

'No more questions.'

'Hang on. Let me see if I've got this right. Hallucinations are rare. Mass hallucinations are even rarer. No two curators share a hangover. The technology doesn't yet exist for a person, not a hallucination, to appear and disappear. Is that correct?'

I was so close to an answer, but I could also see that it was disturbing my friend. To me, the concept of a multiverse explained everything.

'If you accepted that a multiverse was a reality—'

'No!' she shouted at me and slid off the rock, pressing her hand to her head. 'I have a splitting headache and your stupid, bleating suggestions are driving me insane.'

She held up her hand as I was preparing to argue back. Her smile had gone, and she was standing ramrod straight. 'Julius. Did you notice that Giovanetti said she gave the First Engineer *limited disposal* to proceed?'

The phrase had struck me as odd, but there was too much going on at the time, not least my own fury at having been called infantile. I nodded. I wasn't sure that, if I spoke, I would be able to stop myself from shouting at her. I don't think anyone had ever accused me of bleating or stupid suggestions, and I was steaming. Neith continued.

'Asha was reminding them that she hadn't granted full disposal. If she granted full disposal, that would have included their right to kill us.'

Now I jumped off the rock to face Neith full on. 'Kill us?'

'Yes, of course. Stop over-reacting. The custodians and engineers take care of society. They will give up their own lives to protect those freedoms and they regularly do. Look at how Pi-Jack is struggling right now or the red custodians that died at Soliman Alvarez's home, even your friend Shorbagy. They are all prepared to die to protect the rest of us. And sometimes, if they feel the need arises, they will take the first move to save an individual or society at large.'

'Are you insane? What about judge and jury?' My voice might have started to get a bit louder.

'For matters of life and death? Now who's being insane? Let a bunch of amateurs have a natter and then make their minds up based on their "gut instinct".'

She took a deep breath and tried a weak smile. 'Julius. You are not listening to me. The engineers aren't happy with you. I mean *really* not happy. And people that the engineers aren't happy with disappear all the time. You'll be a case note somewhere. Giovanetti will raise a complaint, which will be acknowledged and filed, the world will continue to turn, and you'll continue to be dead.'

33

I stared at her in horror and for the first time on Alpha, I felt truly scared. Certainly, the idea that someone was contemplating my death was alarming, but the fact that Neith was so resigned to it, terrified me.

'Enough. Last one back to the seafront buys the locusts.'

I watched as she raced off, but I decided my heart wasn't in pretending that everything was fine. I loved this world, but I was beginning to hate it as well.

Day One - Julius

I felt rude walking away from Neith, but I was still shaking. She was clearly trying to stop me talking about the engineers or Arthur, and I understood that she was trying to help. The trouble was that it made me feel like a child. I suppose storming off in a tantrum rather proved the point, and honestly, I was a bit of an ingénue over here. I had no objection to my ignorance. It was exciting learning new things on a daily basis. What I resented was not being allowed to research or explore ideas and events. If I was back home, I'd have already started researching Arthur and the concept of a multiverse. Instead, I was stuck in some sort of naughty corner. Worse yet, if I stood out of line or drew too much attention to myself, I could be disposed of.

I tapped out a quick apology on my brace and hit send. Then I started to head home. I felt torn. I had to investigate the Arthur appearance. A mythical figure had appeared in front of me, and everyone was telling me it was an anomaly. Do not discuss it. Do not think about it. Do not pass go. Sometimes I wondered if these guys had had every scrap of curiosity drummed out of them from day one. I was desperate to do something, but as I wanted to avoid the scrutiny of the engineers, I knew I would have to find something else to occupy my mind.

The other day, Neith, Rami and I had been discussing Soliman Alvarez's final words. "*Not* that *book, you idiot. The codex*". Almost as soon as he had said the words, someone had shot him. It had been the final act in a raid that had revealed Soliman Alvarez, head of the Quantum Division, had been running a black-market line in stolen Beta artefacts. Instead of being safely rescued and preserved in the mouseion departments, Alvarez had been smuggling and selling these precious artefacts to the highest bidder. So much for a perfect society.

I'd been following the subsequent press coverage and noticed that there had been no mention of a codex. That was a loose thread that I could safely investigate, plus codices were my happy place. I would research what Alvarez had been referring to. If there was a missing codex out there, I intended to find it.

Changing my plans, I headed towards the best place in the world to begin my research, the library of Alexandria, beacon of illumination and knowledge. As I walked along the pavements, full of resolve, laughter spilt out from an open door. I could hear chatter from within and the enticing smell of hops. So I went to the pub instead.

Settling down at an empty table, I knew I had attracted a few frowns from my fellow drinkers. The custom over here was to say hello to newcomers, strike up a conversation, make them feel welcome and at ease. Making small talk with strangers is as close to hell as I can envisage, so whenever I enter a new pub I smile and nod my head, then make straight to an empty spot and keep my head down. It's the height of bad manners apparently, and I'm doing my best to be more polite, but with so much on my mind, I knew I couldn't chat about the grain yield on the lower Nile if you paid me.

Determined not to think about Arthur or the engineers, I wondered about the last thing Soliman Alvarez said before he had been murdered.

The codex. As a lecturer and historian, I spent every day dealing with books and manuscripts, but there was always something exciting about the word codex. I'd tried to explain it to Charlie once, who laughed and said it rhymed with sex. He wasn't an utter philistine, but there were days when he put on a bloody good show.

Everything about a codex screamed rarity. What secrets did this one contain that Alvarez had died for? The investigation into the black-market ring was, as far as I could see, being dealt with openly. There were daily briefing reports explaining to the public what had been discovered that day, and who had been involved. The guilty parties were stripped of their rank and offered re-zoning to remote territories to farm. Or suicide. If they chose farming they could take their families with them if the families agreed. If they chose suicide, they had to leave their families behind.

The suicide option puzzled me. As did the fact that many, so far, had taken that option. It was viewed as a more noble decision. Death before dishonour. Or rather, Death before farming in the Outer Hebrides, seeing as how you had already dishonoured yourself. They were funny about death. They didn't believe in an afterlife, so they weren't eager to meet their maker. And they weren't mad, risk-taking, adrenaline junkies. The very thought. But they just seemed to have a more fatalistic view about it. We all are born, we all die. With suicide you get some say in the matter. As I said, an odd bunch, and I still really didn't have the full measure of them.

However, they did pride themselves on transparency. And whilst the concept of the codex was something worth killing someone over (suicide is fine, murder is an enormous no-no), I wondered if I could find some clues to the codex in the original footage and transcript of the raid. God knows, at the time I had been mostly hiding with Neith behind a sofa. I may have missed something.

Happy that I had a starting point and a mystery to unravel, I took a sip of my beer and sighed contentedly. The Egyptians were excellent brewers, and I had a new topic to study. The day was improving. Now, if I could just work out what the hell was going on with the Arthur appearance.

'Damn, but that *is* a good pint.'

I looked up to see Arthur sitting opposite me, wiping beer froth from his long blond moustache with the back of his hand. No one in the pub had reacted, and I wondered if he employed a perception filter like curators did when they first arrived in a location. Or maybe he was invisible, and I was hallucinating? Beyond the evidence of my senses, I really had nothing else to go on, but he seemed as real to me as any other person in the pub.

'Hey,' he shouted in the direction of the bar, 'two more pints of your finest over here, wench.'

'Not *wench*,' I hissed rapidly. Obviously, he wasn't a figment of my imagination, but I was beginning to wish he was. 'What are you doing here?'

Arthur thought about it, shrugged his shoulders and had another drink before answering. 'Maybe because you're the only Englishman around, and you were thinking of how good that pint was?'

Was it really that simple? He was a god, and I had summoned him? The brightest minds on this Earth had told me that was not the case. In fact, they had ridiculed me for this opinion. That said, I was resolved to think of him as real. Beyond that, I would let other smarter people work it out. I decided to channel Descartes. I thought; therefore Arthur was. Or rather, even if I didn't think, Arthur was. It was exasperating.

'You don't normally appear when I have a pint. Not even when I have too many.'

'Too many?' Arthur laughed loudly, and a few other tables turned round and smiled politely.

Oh God, I thought, please don't let Arthur be some manifestation of an English lager lout.

'To be honest, Julius, I don't know how this all works.' He seemed embarrassed and leant towards me. No one was listening to us, but I couldn't help but lean in as well. 'The thing is I'm not a totally proper god.'

He leant back and nodded his head, as though in response to my astonishment. Unfortunately, he saw that I was just staring at him blankly, and he frowned. The table began to vibrate slightly.

'Of course you're a god,' I rushed in quickly. 'Arthur King of all Britons, he who will return to save Albion in its moment of need.'

The table stopped shaking and Arthur was smiling again. I didn't actually believe I was sat in a pub talking to a god or even a mythological figure, but right now I had no idea what he was, so playing along appeared the easiest option.

'Well yes, to lesser mortals like yourself I know I seem truly godlike, but there are in fact levels. And I just don't quite make it. Anyway, some of the guys set me a challenge, reckoned it would help me with my divine status. Told me if I could get my sword back I might be taken seriously. The way they put it was, who trusts a king that lets his sword get chucked in a lake.'

'You were dead at the time.'

'Exactly my point, but the guys said death was irrelevant to a god. Which is true.'

It was true, I supposed, but it still felt like Arthur was being hazed. 'Who are these guys, then?'

'Great chaps. Loki, Lucifer and Lugh.'

Jesus, there was an unholy trinity if ever I heard of one. Loki, the Norse god of mischief. Lucifer, an angel with a chip on his shoulder and banished by his father to rule over Hell. And Lugh, an Irish deity, a youthful warrior, and smarter than the first salmon of spring.

'Occasionally Anansi joins us, but he's a very busy god. Takes great pride in his work.'

Oh, good grief. If I thought the trio was bad, Anansi was a nightmare. People who thought Loki was the trickster god had not yet discovered Anansi. The brilliant spider god, weaving misery, misfortune and pranks all in the same web. In folklore, Anansi didn't tend to go out of his way to start trouble, unlike Loki. But if trouble came looking for him, it would rue the day it did. Four of them together. Poor Arthur, he may as well hand over his pocket money straightaway if this was the playground he was dabbling in.

'So, what happened when you first tried to retrieve the sword?'

'I'm not one for details but I went back to the scene of the crime, so to speak, and saw a woman like a small dark otter slink out of the water, pulling my sword behind her. Another woman joined her, a tall mighty warrior with skin like coal. I was about to join them, and remove my sword from their grasp, when they disappeared. I investigated where they had been standing and followed them. I found myself in a strange place of white walls and the brightest light.'

41

This must have been when the gate first signalled a malfunction. Arthur, whoever or whatever he was, had been able to follow Neith and Clio's path home. Only when he stepped into Alpha, more time had elapsed.

'I couldn't sense the sword and I couldn't find the women, so I had a bit of an explore and discovered this world. Eventually, I got bored and left, but the guys convinced me to come back.'

'Tell me.' I was curious and trying to deal with the smaller details whilst my head tried to come to terms with the larger, mind-boggling stuff. 'Did you come through the stepper this time as well?'

'What's a stepper?'

'Did you follow anyone? Like you did last time?'

'Ah no. I just decided to be here. I did mean to ask about that. How do you lot have these godlike abilities to travel between the two worlds?'

Well, at least I knew that he was travelling in a different way to us. I don't know how that helped, but every nugget of information would be stored away and inspected later.

'We use a quantum stepper. It's a sort of machine that uses quantum technology.'

He stared at me blankly. I tried again.

'It's a chariot that traverses time and space?'

Arthur drank his beer whilst trying to look thoughtful.

'That does sound rather godly. Does Zeus know? He gets very snotty about people pinching chariots.'

'No, no, it's not actually a chariot.' I started whispering very quietly to myself not wanting to summon Zeus. I still didn't know if it was me doing this, and I really didn't want Zeus to turn up. As gods went, Zeus was something of a major arse. 'It's just quantum physics.'

'Explain,' demanded Arthur.

Explain quantum mechanics to a fifth-century folklore figure, dressed in the manifestation of a myth. I took a deep breath.

'I don't fully understand it myself, but a good way to look at it is using the Schrödinger's Cat analogy.'

Arthur sat upright, looking around alarmed. 'There's a cat involved?' His hand dropped to his hip, where I noticed Excalibur now rested.

'Sorry, I forgot about the cats thing. Anyway, Schrödinger put a cat in a sealed box.'

'Good man.'

'There's no way to see or hear what's inside.'

'I like this Schrödinger.'

'Yes, thought you might. Now the thing is, without being able to open the box, you have no way of knowing if the cat is dead or alive.'

'Does it matter? The cat is trapped.'

'Well, yes, but in terms of quantum physics the important thing is that the cat can be both simultaneously dead and alive.'

'But it's trapped. Yes?'

'Yes.' I sighed. On reflection, Schrödinger's Cat was a bad choice. King Arthur had once been nearly killed by the giant cat, Palug. He'd better not hang around Alexandria too long. He would find the Egyptian attitude towards cats tricky. I tried again.

'Shall we just agree that humans have to use a device to travel between the worlds, and you…' I paused, at a loss. 'And you do whatever it is, that you do.'

'Very well. And no more talk of cats?'

'Agreed. So, now that you have your sword does this mean you are now a god?'

'Maybe, but not here on this Earth. Very little juice for me to pull on here. Good shout, about back home though.'

And with that, he necked his pint and disappeared, leaving me none the wiser. I was pretty certain I wasn't projecting, because, as far as I was aware, I didn't have the ability to project fully formed human beings. Although his comment about there not being enough juice on this Earth did make me wonder. The old adage about mankind being created in God's image had often been reversed. We make our own gods. Was it possible that the gods did exist somehow? If enough people believed in them? Derrida, Gaiman, Pratchett amongst many others had all postulated the same thing. Maybe they were real? Sort of?

I ordered another pint and realised I had missed my opportunity to ask Arthur about himself. I had a feeling he would have been happy to talk at length.

'Sorry, did you say something?'

I startled and laughed as Arthur suddenly sat in front of me again.

'Did you want me to talk about myself?'

I shook my head and realised that he might actually be able to help me with my other problem.

'No, I was just thinking about your hunt for the grail. I'm embarking on the hunt for a missing codex, and it's going to be quite the challenge. I just wondered if you had any tips?'

Asking my imaginary friend seemed as good a place as any to start. He looked at me blankly.

'What's a codex?'

I pondered the question, wondered just how much he really wanted to know, and decided to keep it simple.

'It's a book.'

He yawned.

'No trust me. It's really interesting. A codex is quite simply the precursor to the modern bound book. The step between scrolls and books. A codex is a bound collection of handwritten manuscripts.'

Arthur examined his fingernails. 'Sounds like something a monk would get excited by?'

I laughed. 'It would. Do you know, I think it's the fact that you can see the author's actual marks on the parchment that makes it immediate and appealing? Little scribbles in the margins, crossings out, a stain from a drink. You can also watch as the author smudged his work, then swore and dashed off to grab a cloth to dab at the spill. Then there's the parchment itself. The skin of an animal from many hundreds of years ago, even a thousand. Sometimes, the hide would contain flaws, with holes in the skin itself, that the scribe simply wrote around. Some would even make a point of embellishing the hole, drawing attention to the imperfection.'

Arthur put his hands up in mock supplication. 'If I agree it's fascinating, will you stop talking?'

I nodded. He had a point; it was one of my pet subjects and I could be known to go on at length about them.

'What's it about then?'

'No idea.' I smiled and drank my beer

'Well, who wrote it?'

My smile got wider. 'I don't know that either.'

He paused and tilted his head. 'So, you are trying to find a book. You don't know where it is, who wrote it, or what it's about. Do you even know what it looks like?'

I was laughing now. 'No, I don't even know that.'

'Then, why is it so important?'

'Because when someone mentioned it, they were killed.'

Arthur's eyes widened. 'Forbidden knowledge!'

'Exactly.' I was pleased that he understood me so quickly.

'That, good sir, is indeed a perilous and noble quest. You are most courageous. This is worthy of my attention.'

He stroked his moustache, frowning deeply with his noble looks cast in studious reflection. I wasn't sure about being described as courageous. I had always thought that was spelt f-o-o-l-h-a-r-d-y. He sighed deeply.

'No,' he said, 'I've got nothing. But I will think on your endeavours and see if I can do anything to aid you. Now, you'll have to excuse me. They seem to be making films about me back home, and one includes giant elephants. I must say I don't remember the elephants. Or maybe I do?'

And with that he was gone again. The idea that Guy Ritchie was somehow powering up the Arthurian godhead could only make me grin, and I eventually ambled home. I dropped a note to Jack, inviting him out for a drink if he had any free time, and put in a requisition form to study the transcripts of the recent Alvarez Affair. I had the rest of the afternoon to myself and decided to spend it back in my apartment catching up on some reading.

Day One - Neith and Rami

'Neith!'

I turned around. Ramin was running towards me, and I was filled with an overwhelming surge of affection. As long as Ramin Gamal was nearby, the world was okay. The months where I had doubted him had messed me up to the point of wanting to quit the service. I couldn't reconcile a world where Ramin was a villain. I had tried to explain the dilemma to Julius once, and he'd just waved his hand around a bit and pointed out that I'd taken Clio's betrayal quite calmly. I suppose I had always known that Clio was a live wire. He said I was bound to have more of a crisis in confidence if I kept going around with such strong, certain opinions. I had explained to him, but he'd just said I should have more faith in friendship, then carried on reading. He did that a lot. Read, and make irritating pronouncements.

Working with someone from another Earth was harder than I'd thought it was going to be and seeing Ramin   reminded   me   of   that.

I stopped walking and gave him half my locusts.

'Where's Julius? I thought he'd be driving you mad with a thousand questions.'

'He was,' I said glumly,' and they were all about the engineers and the incident.'

Ramin crunched on a locust, and we walked on. 'Did you convince him to stop?'

'I think so.' I sighed. 'I'm not certain, but he might be sulking.'

'He's not really a sulker, is he?'

'No, you're right. I'm being unfair. I just always feel like I'm the one to blame when I won't answer his questions.'

Ramin grabbed my hand and squeezed it affectionately.

'Don't do that to yourself. He'll adapt, it will just take time. And it's not like he's like the other angels, out having fun in their retirement. He's working at the very heart of Alpha's society. Politically, economically and culturally.'

We walked on in silence for a bit. Ramin was right, angels, those beta individuals we used as emergency couriers, were generally old and happy to have a quiet life. But Julius was full of energy and questions. So many questions. And that questioning attitude was contagious. The responsible thing to do would have been to desist, but recently I always seemed to have another question. To anything. It was an annoyance. I choked back my question and tried to alter it to an observation instead.

'Maybe Julius would have been better as a custodian. They are the ones that ask questions. He couldn't stop going on about how Pi-Jack was faring, as though we were somehow to blame.'

Even to me, my statement sounded petulant. Ramin just smiled at me.

'So, what about that anomaly?' he asked, and I could have wept.

'Ramin. Are you mad? You know better than Julius. The engineers will take care of it. Sweet Bast, it's not the first time we've had quantum visions suddenly appear in the middle of a hangover.'

'But none of us were suffering from a hangover.'

'So what? So, this is something new. The engineers will sort it out. That's their job. Not ours.'

I wanted him to stop talking. If he talked like this in front of Julius, it might encourage him to speculate further, and I didn't know if I had properly impressed upon him how deadly the engineers were. They could justifiably kill anyone they considered a risk to society. They were excellent at protecting the many, they were just a little more cavalier about protecting the few. That was my job. And I would do all I could to protect my friends.

As we walked along, I could tell from Ramin's silence that he disagreed with me but was working out how to say it. If it had been Clio, she'd have pretty much slapped me in the face.

'You know, Julius might have a point. We are all a bit rigid in our concepts of personality types being better suited for one role or another.'

I glared at him. 'Don't you bloody start.'

'Well, look at us. We run in, we make lightning-fast decisions, fight, engage and acquire the object. We don't sit back and plan.'

'Of course we do. We can spend weeks on a live event, planning and preparing.'

'But only operationally. We don't stop to think. Should we? Or what might happen to the timeline if we do something else instead? Can we save the object and leave it in situ?'

'Because we know the item will be lost if we don't.'

I couldn't see what he was driving at, but he was beginning to annoy me.

'And how do we know that?' he challenged. 'It's certainly not because we've investigated the matter.'

'I do loads of research before I perform a step.'

'Your research is to ensure a successful mission.'

I threw my hands in the air. 'Of course.'

'Not whether or not the mission is essential, or if the object could be saved another way.'

I was speechless. This was silly, and I was cross. I had just spent my morning having one spurious conversation, but Julius didn't know any better. Ramin's words were just, well, they felt seditious, and I glanced over my shoulder.

'Worried someone may be listening?' said Ramin ironically. 'In our perfect society?'

I didn't reply. It seemed wisest. Certainly, the past year had rocked my world. I had a role in society, and I and my fellow curators worked towards the good of it. We enriched it by retrieving artefacts that the inhabitants of our parallel world were too careless to take care of.

The fact that some of these items were being stolen to order, and that factions were prepared to kill for those items had unnerved me. There were criminal elements in our society, and I had felt foolish and uncertain that I was unaware of them. The fact that they had emerged in the first place suggested an issue. Weeds can't thrive if there isn't water for them to spread their roots.

'You know Julius may have a point,' Ramin continued. 'Giovanetti has been thinking along the same lines. In fact, it was what I came to find you for. I have a new job. Sort of.'

I stopped walking and stared at him. After the Fabergé affair, Ramin had wrongly been placed on sand leave. By wrongly, they obviously made the right decision. He should have been put on sand leave. All the evidence pointed to him as being a potential traitor. However, now he had been properly vindicated, he should be allowed to continue as a curator.

'A new job! I'll go and talk to Sam. Come on.' I grabbed at his sleeve.

'Calm down. I'm still a curator, I'm still on active service, but now I report to both Nymens and Giovanetti. I'll attend both team briefings, and I'll let Giovanetti know if I am aware of any concerns I have within the curators.'

'Why?'

'Well, Giovanetti said I ask lots of questions. I see problems before other people do.'

'That's true.' I smiled.

'And, since being framed and placed on sand leave, I've become more suspicious as well.'

It made perfect sense, and I was proud that Ramin had been chosen for such a radical role.

'You know,' I said, slowly. 'This questioning thing must be infectious.'

Ramin grinned at me. 'What did you have in mind?'

'Before Soliman died, he shouted out something about a codex—'

I broke off as Ramin started laughing. 'That's my girl. I've already requested the documents of the investigation to look at over the weekend. Care to join me?'

I was relieved that Ramin was on the same path as me. I knew I would feel better when that last strand was tidied away. It had been bugging me. Leave the engineers to their work, and we'd just tidy up this little thread, and all would be well.

'Yes. This is what we do. We are curators, let's do what we were meant to do. A hunt for a missing codex, only this time it's going to be here, on our home turf.'

I was almost giddy with relief and purpose. Quantum anomalies and black-market racketeering were not my concerns, lost artefacts were.

'Shall we invite Julius?' said Ramin. 'He does have a unique way of seeing things?'

I wanted to, but his questioning of the engineers worried me. 'For his own safety, shall we leave him out of it? Besides which we have the brain procedure tomorrow. He'll want to spend the weekend recovering from that.'

We looked glumly at the empty packet of locusts. It probably wasn't wise to eat anything else now. We'd only be throwing it up in the morning.

'True enough,' Ramin said with a sigh. 'Come on then.'

As we headed off, he turned to me.

'Go easy on Julius, though. He has a lot to offer. And who knows, some of what he says may even be right?'

I thought about it but was suddenly feeling sick again and realised I was already worried about tomorrow's brain procedure and decided not to think about anything at all.

Day One - Julius

My brace pinged alerting me to a Personal Update Status Change. I was readying myself for the following day's trip to the custodian archives and already regretting storming off and leaving Neith. She had only been trying to help.

I looked at the Status Change alert in surprise. I'd had one of these when I had been granted citizenship and another when I graduated as a curator. They only tended to notify of significant events, and I wasn't aware of anything occurring. I opened the message.

Under Consideration of Permanent Removal by order of First Engineer for reasons of stability.

Was I was being fired? I had no idea what the message meant and was about to call Neith when my brace pinged, and I saw it was Sam.

'Curator Strathclyde. Could you come to my office right now?'

I listened to his formal tones. Maybe I was being fired?

'Sir, is this about this text I just received from the engineers? Have I been fired?'

I waited for him to relax and assure me there was nothing to worry about, instead he told me to take a scooter to get there. Skipping food, I headed downstairs and walked over to the quantum buildings. Whatever this was I wasn't in the mood to hurry towards it.

When I entered the office, Sam ushered me over to the sofa, but I noticed that he referred to me as Curator Strathclyde again.

'Sir, what is this about. What does *permanent removal* mean?'

Sam had been sitting but now stood up and walked over to the window. I sat quietly and watched as he paced around his office before sitting down again on the sofa opposite.

'The thing is Julius. Nubi's balls. This is just wrong.' He broke off and jumped up and walked over to the drinks bar and put some mint in a teapot. I sat very still. Whatever this was it was worse than I expected.

Sam sat down again and placed his hands on his knees and looked me squarely in the face.

'Permanent removal means death.'

We stared at each other in silence whilst my mind scrambled to catch up.

'I'm to be executed?' My voice might have squeaked.

'No,' said Sam hurriedly. 'At least not yet. The motion is being *considered*. It's a formality that the engineers need to notify every one of their current leanings.'

'And I find out about this via a text!? What have I done? How do I appeal?' My voice was now not just squeaky but also panicky. It wasn't my finest moment. I wanted to be able to sit there and nod sagely, whilst laughing in the face of danger, before manfully striding out of the office doing my finest Butch Cassidy

56

impersonation. Instead, I appeared to be channelling Benny Hill at a works tribunal.

'Appeal?' Sam shook his head. There's nothing to appeal. The engineers have all the information they need. They have judged you to be a threat to society. At the moment they are simply alerting you to your current situation, and of course, you family and work colleagues.'

'This is insane.' My face prickled and I knew I was turning red. I may have also started shouting. 'Do you mean everyone has been told about this?'

'Only those directly impacted. Anyone else would have to be looking at your files to see the notation.' Sam smiled sadly. 'It's all above board.'

'Well, that's alright then? Jesus. Do you mean Neith has been informed as my work partner?' I knew I should have been more scared but honestly, at that moment, I was more mortified. This was just so embarrassing.

'Curator Salah will have received notification at the same time that I did. One minute after you were notified. It's important that the recipient of the notification is told first.'

I laughed. 'Yes, those sixty seconds make all the difference.'

'So, what will Neith do now?'

'Nothing, she'll have more sense than to get involved in engineers' business.'

The door slammed open and Neith stormed in.

'Nubi's balls, Sam! Julius, sweet Ra, you're safe.' Turning back to Sam she carried on shouting. 'This is a total dick move. Sam, what are you going to do?'

Whilst she was shouting at Sam my brace pinged again and they both stopped and looked at me.

'Opposition Registered. Archivists.' What does that mean?

Sam looked pleased and nodded his head whilst Neith went and poured water on the mint leaves.

It means,' said Sam, 'that someone is prepared to stick their neck out but it's not helpful. The archivists don't have much sway in these matters.'

A moment later both their braces pinged. I looked at them hopefully, but it was simply the same update as my notification. Just a minute delayed. Neith handed me a cup and I blew away the steam and looked at the bright green leaves. How the hell had it come to this. What had I done? And how could there be no appeal process? My brace pinged again, and I put down my cup.

'Temporary Opposition Registered: Custodians.'

'Yes!' cried Neith, and Sam let out a sigh of relief.

'That's a lot better.'

I wanted to agree with him, but I was so far out of my depth that if I drowned now my body would never be found.

'But it only says *Temporary*?'

'Better than nothing,' said Sam. 'Trust me, that's huge.

'So, what does *Temporary* mean?'

'It means that the custodians want more information but currently they are leaning in favour of your existence.'

I shook my head and was pleased to see that my hand wasn't shaking.

'What about the other departments?' My voice had also steadied itself. Could the engineers proceed even with these oppositions?'

'Yes, but it will probably have to go before a hearing to justify their actions.'

'You mean their decision. They haven't actually done anything.'

'No, after your removal, there would be a hearing if objections were still on record. They'd probably receive a small censure note, honestly though it's such a bureaucratic rigmarole that most people tend to go along with the engineers' decision.'

'Hang on. Wait. But I'll still be dead?'

'Yes. But it's not all bad news.'

'Nubi's balls, Sam. How is any of this good news?'

'You are swearing quite a bit Curator Salah?'

'Sorry, boss. Slightly agitated.'

'I understand and I am too.' He drummed his fingers on the table. 'Julius, I like you. A lot as it happens, and I don't intend for the engineer to just switch you off. Happily, we do have a few things in our favour.' He put his cup down and leant forward. 'You don't have any family here and no head of department. No one as yet has replaced Soliman Alvarez. It's a piece of minutiae but someone who represents you needs to officially sanction the engineers' actions. As you don't have anyone they could be tied up for months in paperwork. I think they'll want to avoid that.

'Well yes,' I said sourly. 'We don't want them inconvenienced.'

Sam waved a hand at me and continued. 'Secondly, I will ask Giovanetti to recommend your permanent removal, if it were to go ahead, to be your return to Beta Earth with a memory wipe of the past year.'

I sagged. Sam was smiling and I knew it was better than nothing, but I looked at Neith and knew she was no happier about that option than I was. A death sentence where I currently lived or lose all knowledge of this Earth and of the friends I had made and the things I'd done.

'But what have I done wrong? What's caused this? Is it Arthur?'

Sam and Neith looked at each other troubled.

'Unlikely,' said Neith, 'otherwise we'd all have been under consideration. No, it has to be something else. Have you had any other interactions with the engineers at all? No matter how small?'

I could think of nothing and sipped my tea whilst the other two looked at me expectantly. My life was in the balance, and I didn't have a clue why.

'Could we ask them?'

They both scoffed and I carried on thinking.

'My lecture notes were rejected but it can't be that.'

They looked at each other and shook their heads doubtfully. 'Seems unlikely. What was the reason given for rejection?'

'That's the funny thing. I have no idea. I simply got a note from the engineers' department saying topic extraneous, all files removed. And they had as well.' I laughed remembering. 'Even the files on my personal terminal had been deleted.'

Sam and Neith recoiled. 'That's it.'

I tutted. 'Unlikely, it was simply a lecture on-'

'Stop.' Sam jumped to his feet and Neith covered her ears. 'Do not say another word. Whatever the subject matter of that paper, do not discuss it with another person or you subject them to the same removal consideration.'

I looked at them stunned. How could a paper aimed at students about alternative Earths be so problematic? I was standing on an alternate Earth for God's sake. They knew all about ours. What was the issue? However, Sam and Neith weren't kidding. I had inadvertently stumbled over something that had effectively signed my own death warrant and I was at risk of signing theirs as well.

I felt sick. 'What now?'

'Now, you wait,' said Sam. 'And don't put a toe out of line. I'm going to remove you from teaching duties so that you can't accidentally trigger the same issue. I'll also talk to Asha and see what she suggests. For now, I think you are reasonably safe but just tread carefully and don't draw attention to yourself.'

Day One - Minju

Minju Chen, Head of Antiquities for the Mouseion of Alexandria, pushed away from her screen and sighed. She was working on her own in the Roman acquisitions room. Tucked away at the far end of a very long subterranean corridor, she sat and plotted. Since the utter fiasco following the discovery of the stepper being used in a black-market trade, business had been slow. At first, the quantum steps had been cancelled altogether. Now the protocol allowed one step a week, and each one was being monitored to within an inch of its life.

It was more imperative than ever that they find the plans to build their own quantum stepper. She was furious that Soliman had been killed outright as he started to rant on about the codex. It wasn't his death she regretted, but the speed of it. For alerting the engineers like that, she would have happily flayed him, starting with his toes. Her hunt for the stepper's schematics had been the most covert aspect of her operation, and Soliman just blabbed it out to all and sundry. From what she had seen, the engineers had not missed his announcement and started to take active counter measures.

Without her own stepper, her plans to re-organise this world into a new order would be hard to bring about. She didn't care about the treasures the way others did. If they wanted to drool over priceless artefacts, then so be it. In fact, it made them easier to manipulate towards her own goals. It was just as easy to whip up anti-Beta Earth sentiment. Those narrow-minded bigots were just as easy to steer, and between the two factions, she and like-minded Haru could guide this society to a new dawn. Except now, her plans had been derailed.

It was galling, and she could feel her tail begin to sway at the injustice of it. Taking a deep breath, she ran through the verses of Marcus Aurelius and found the inner calm she needed to still her agitation.

Nothing good came of letting your body display your emotional state. Of course, Aurelius had never had to conquer a tail, but Minju wouldn't complain. When she had first spliced with a snow leopard, she had despaired. Her body felt disfigured. She had to manage strange, wild thoughts and impulses, but slowly she learnt to see the splice as a sign. The animal was a perfect foil for her inner beast, and she gradually learnt to embrace the alien warrior she had been gifted. Before, she had been brave and fast; a quick and clever curator, although a frustrated one, watching the foolish behaviours of her seniors. Their pacifism wasted the resources of the stepper, but what could she do? After the splice, she had learnt how to stalk, to use patience and guile to achieve her goals, and so she began to plan.

Eventually, she had grown an entire network. She was beginning to make policy changes, or at least get others to make them for her. She had money, power and influence, and no one saw what she was doing. To her, the tail showed she was a predator. If others chose to see a fluffy cat, that was on them. They had their one chance. She wouldn't give them any other clues. Her tail stilled completely, and she smiled again, pleased once more that she had dominion over her anxieties.

There was a knock on the door, and Haru Giovanetti walked in. Her offices were one of the few places where she could talk at liberty, and Haru was one of the few people who knew most of her ins and outs.

'I thought this might amuse you. Asha has been scheduled to have a brain scan by request of First Engineer.'

Minju looked at him in surprise. 'I take it this isn't routine?'

'No, and she's not the only one. They have also requested that curators Nymens, Salah, Gamal and Strathclyde join her.'

Well, that was curious. What had that little group done to draw the attention of the engineers? Both parties were an irritation to Minju, but they both had values that she appreciated. The engineers were single-minded and incorruptible. She admired that, although it made them impossible to infiltrate. That little group of curators were also noble in their own way. They may be emotional and conflicted, but they cared for each other and showed the true ethos of brotherhood. True *optimates*. It was a weakness, but a noble one. She wondered, if pitched against each other, which side would win. Haru was still waiting expectantly.

'There's more I take it?'

Haru opened his eyes wide and nodded his head. 'I'll say. Asha has insisted the scans are done without blocks.'

Minju tilted her head and worked hard not to stretch and smile.

'A brain scan without a block? What on earth is your wife thinking? Do we know what happened?'

'No, she isn't talking and—'

'—neither are the engineers.'

One of Minju's greatest frustrations was that she had never managed to infiltrate the engineers.

'And you really haven't managed to get Asha to give you even a hint of what's going on?'

'As if. You know Asha. Sworn duty, blah, blah, blah.'

Minju had always admired Asha. At training college, she had seen her as a potential ally, but it became clear to Minju that her friend was as determined to protect this society as Minju was to change it. Still, she could see that Asha was going to be a powerful citizen, and she kept close to her. When she married Haru, Minju was astonished. For such a smart woman she seemed to have fallen in love with a weak-willed, vainglorious sociopath. Just Minju's type. It didn't take much to convert him to her cause. Now he was just where she wanted him. Head of Medicine and sitting by Asha's right hand.

'Ask her after the procedure if it was worth it. She'll be in pain and weakened. You might get her to let her guard down.'

Haru picked up a jewelled hairpin and started to play with the clasp. 'Already on it. If Asha is doing this without blockers, she must really fear the engineers.'

'And you have no idea of what's happening?'

'Nothing. You're close to that Beta,' said Haru, waving the hairpin at her. 'Why don't you ask him? I bet he'd just blab the whole thing out.'

Haru was right. She would invite Julius over for a pot of tea. Unlike Asha, he was refreshingly open and naïve. He'd probably just tell her all about it without her having to ask. There was something to be said for someone who was completely free of this planet's indoctrination.

'I wonder if poor Julius knows what he is about to be subjected to.'

'That fool? He's probably nodding and smiling as we speak.'

'You mistake him for one of our Britons. Whatever Julius is, he is not quick to temper, nor does he take umbrage at petty slights.'

'Don't you find all those silly little questions and smiles annoying though?' He was waving the hairpin around like it was a baton, and it was beginning to annoy Minju, as was his criticism of Julius.

'No, I find them dangerous.' She snapped her fingers and held out her hand and Haru returned the hairpin.

'Dangerous?'

'Before he arrived, the system worked and had done for years. Within a year of his arrival, our enterprise has been exposed, layers of administration have been torn open and shattered. Society is questioning how the QS is being used, and there is a low-lying sense of unease in the population.'

'But he didn't do that?'

'No, but I think his *silly little questions* played a large part in it. And I'd be a fool to dismiss his impact. Julius is an Englishman. They have empire running through their DNA. We must watch him carefully and even now he could be planning to overthrow us.'

Day Two - Julius

'Oh, my god.' This time the vomit came out of my nose as well as my mouth, and I thought I was going to die.

'Did you call?'

The pain in my head was indescribable. I looked up at Arthur and was utterly unsurprised to see tentacles streaming out of his mouth. They matched the ones that were creeping down from the ceiling and along the edges of the hospital bed, I flinched away from him.

Black mucus dripped off the tentacles, I tried to shake my head free of the vision, but a shrieking sound split across my ears. I scratched at the side of my face, my nails tearing at the skin, anything to distract from the noise. Of course, the minute my fingers touched my face, the skin began to blister and burn. I threw up again for the umpteenth time.

Throwing up made things worse if it were possible. The medics recoiled when they discovered, after the procedure, that I had had what I like to refer to as a full English. They had no idea what I meant until I told them and after that, they went from appalled to horrified in a matter of a few seconds. At that point, they rushed off to find a doctor. Someone who was presumably going to have me put down. Frankly, I wouldn't have raised any objections.

Whilst I waited for my misery to end, I now had to try to deal with the egotistic self-serving conundrum that was Arthur, who was smirking at me.

'You are not my god. Go away.'

'Yet here I am. And why wouldn't you worship me? I am the undisputed High King of England. You are an Englishman. The matter is simple.'

There was no denying we had some sort of bond, but even so, this was ridiculous.

'You are not a god.'

Even if he was real, whatever that meant, he wasn't a god. He was a myth. I groaned. Nothing made any sense.

'I am so.'

'Prove it.' I was too ill for this conversation and just wanted him, or my symptoms, to disappear. He looked at me with a puzzled frown.

'How?'

'Make me better.'

'Like this?'

And, suddenly, I felt excellent. Not just good, but fresh-as-a-daisy good. The good you feel after plunging into cold water. Alive and tingly. I laughed. I couldn't help myself, and the screen was dropped as a nurse came rushing forward. Arthur had gone again. Was it his choice or had the act of making me feel better depleted his resources? He and I needed to have a good sit-down to try to work out what he was. Engineers be damned. In the meantime, I had to deal with a very concerned nurse who'd called for a doctor. When she arrived, she and the young nurse were discussing my vitals. He seemed concerned that I might be experiencing hypoxia. The doctor shook her head and, after prodding me a bit and peering at me intently, which appeared to be a universal medical trait, pronounced me good to go. As I passed the other cubicles — Neith, Sam and Rami were in various stages of looking dreadful — only Asha was sitting in her chair, rather than still in bed. She was sweating, and her hands were gripping the end of her armrests. Her eyes flicked to me briefly. She gave me the tiniest fraction of a nod, then continued to fight her demons. I left feeling somewhat guilty.

I quietly called out for Arthur, but he didn't materialise. Surprising myself with a sense of disappointment, I decided to continue with my research into the codex. My carrel was booked, so I may as well get on with it. Half an hour earlier, I had wanted to die. Now, I was full of beans. Yesterday's threat of termination was still worrying me, but so long as I avoided the engineers and anything to do with my lecture paper, I should be safe.

The custodian offices were on the back edge of town. A lovely shiny edifice with landscaped gardens. The joy of not being crammed between the sea and the mouseion buildings meant that a place had room to stretch. The architects had been able to design a structure that looked aesthetically pleasing, not designed to primarily squeeze into.

I walked alongside the building. It was clearly a popular location; ahead of me, a party of school children were snaking towards the entrance. As they walked, they trailed their hands along the curved, opaque glass walls. Where their fingers touched the glass, its apricot tones traced their patterns in lines of yellow and pink. Some children drew little pictures. One girl stopped to draw something quite rude, and I had to hide a smile as her teacher rushed back and wiped her palm across the surface of the glass, a sweep of rose covering the child's graffiti. Having nodded her head in acceptance of her punishment, her teacher moved back to the head of the line, and the little girl quickly stroked her fingers across each other in a gesture of disavowal. I grinned. There was a curator in the making. The girl realised she was the centre of attention and stared at me boldly, challenging me to report her. Instead, I stuck my tongue out at her. She took a whole step back, looking shocked, then laughed and ran to catch up with the rest of her class.

I slowed my pace and ambled along. I didn't want to arrive at the same time as a school visit, plus the weather was lovely and I felt alive. Copying the little girl, I stroked the glass wall, watching as the colours ebbed and flowed under my hands. Looking up the wall, where the breeze was cooler, it was a paler shade of yellow. In summer, the walls glowed red as the building rolled and undulated. I

71

didn't know how they engineered glass like this. It was so strong and fluid. I was used to sand in building constructions — it was how you made cement and bricks after all — but in this Egypt, they had refined how to use sand and had made glass into something truly wonderful. I had mentioned it to Rami, who simply pointed out that there wasn't a shortage of sand. Why not use it? Plus, it was easy to break down and re-use, rather than a reliance on petrochemicals. I couldn't help feeling that the last part of the sentence was a commentary on my own Earth. As usual, I found myself in the uncomfortable position of trying to defend the indefensible.

The glass turned translucent as I reached the main foyer. Like all public buildings the reception area was open and light. The glazed atrium roof let the sunlight in, but not the heat. And the lush planting from outside continued inside. There was no main desk as at the mouseion buildings. Instead, scattered across the atrium were various desks and sofas where groups of custodians congregated, either sipping tea or working. A welcoming sign proclaimed the custodians' motto "We Care", and I was reminded of the Ministry of Peace. It was unfair to compare this place to an Orwellian nightmare, but I did like the way "care" could be interpreted.

There was a friendly buzz, nothing threatening or unwelcoming. As I entered the foyer, one of the custodians stood up and walked towards me. Her primrose robes had a single star at the neck. I had been hoping to see Shorbagy, but instead, I smiled at the woman as I outlined what I needed.

Following her, I was set up in a carrel. Once I confirmed that I would do nothing to bring harm or dishonour to the records, the institution, or society, she entered an access code. The holo-screen sprang to life, and she left. I took in the small booth. There was a desk and a holo-screen with a voice interface. In a corner of the room was a haptic suite where I could don gloves and visor and immerse myself in a simulated reality of the video footage. In addition to the research facilities, there was a small drinks-making area, although they only offered mint tea or cold water. The ablution facilities were at the end of the outside corridor. The custodian had also mentioned that there was a tributary of the Mareotis flowing through the building, and I was welcome to swim in it if I wished. I was also invited to join the custodians for lunch.

It would be fair to say that I had never been in a police station anywhere quite like it. I wondered if miscreants got the same service. Maybe a manicure before their fingerprints were taken?

I cleared my throat then asked Tiresias to download what I needed. Tiresias was an intelligent Google. It acted as a search engine, as well as a depository of knowledge, but the trick to Tiresias was that it was an intuitive engine. It paid attention to how you searched and what you considered a suitable answer. After a few weeks, it began to pre-empt what you were searching for and would just give you what you needed. Depending on your research style, you would still get interesting additional results. Tiresias and I had come to a sort of grudging standstill. It provided me with what I was looking for, but I was forever poking and prodding to see if there was anything else I had missed. I liked the synchronicity of random ideas. Tiresias had an algorithm for that.

Still, in the first instance, there was no denying it was ridiculously fast and accurate. I sat back and flicked the video and watched the last few minutes of Soliman Alvarez's life, frowning. That wasn't how I remembered it.

'Tiresias, is there a transcript only of this event?'

Text showed up on my screen, and I read through it. I then asked for an audio only followed by the VR walk-through. Tiresias reminded me that I had just had a mind scan and that a VR walk-through might trigger a headache or nausea. That gave me pause, but I was so concerned with what I had just seen, heard, and read that I wanted to check every angle possible.

'Tiresias, are my searches being recorded?'

'Yes.'

'Can I turn that off? Put up a privacy screen?'

'Why?'

Good question, Tiresias. When I had first started wearing my combat suit, it had been fitted with an automated voice powered by Tiresias. The voice they had selected for me had been HAL 9000 because they thought that might be comforting. Whilst the Blitz rained down upon my head, I had the voice of a psychotic computer whispering in my ear. Since then I had requested a few different voices and had settled on Joanna Lumley.

'Because I don't want people to watch what I am doing.'

'Why?'

'Basic privacy?'

'Are you planning on doing something illegal?' Joanna was beginning to sound like HAL 9000 again. It wasn't the tone as much as the suspicion.

'No. I want it to be a surprise for a friend. I would hate for them to accidentally stumble on what I'm doing.'

'This is acceptable.'

'You'll shield these files?'

'These files? No. Other files, yes. The Alvarez Affair is a matter of public record, there is to be no privacy on any of these files or any associated ones.'

'You mean I can see what everyone else has looked at as well?' That made me pause. I might be able to discern something from other people's search patterns.

'Of course.'

I thought about it. 'If I use the VR will it cause an alert at the medical lab?'

'No. But if you become ill, the information will be presented for your wellbeing.'

Seamless, efficient, creepy?

'Launch the VR.' I crossed my fingers that it wouldn't make me ill again, but whatever Arthur had done had utterly restored me. I hoped I wasn't about to undo that. As I had watched the standard video, I realised the footage of Alvarez talking had been altered. I needed to see the scene from every angle.

For my own safety, I could only move about in a proper VR room. In this limited VR suit, I just got to stand in a corner and watch the events play out in front of me. Finally, I removed the gloves and helmet and placed them in the sanitising basket. Like the video, the 3D version had been altered.

'Tiresias please can I see the original files?'

'These are the original files.'

I tried again.

'Was the transcription I read from a live feed or from a later recording?'

'From the live feed you just watched.'

Hmm. I was going around in circles, but I didn't want to voice my concern out loud. I pressed the help button, and a second later a disembodied voice of a custodian answered my query.

'Hello, Curator Strathclyde. May I offer some assistance?'

I explained what I was after.

'Was Tiresias not able to answer your question?'

'Probably, I just wanted to run it past a human for a faster answer.'

There was a laugh before the custodian continued.

'A human, faster than Tiresias. How funny.'

And I thought we were too reliant on computers back home.

'Am I disturbing you? Would you prefer I asked Tiresias?'

'Not in the slightest. My job is to serve, I just fear I may not be able to help you as well.'

'Very well, I'm trying to view the original files of the Alvarez event.'

There was a pause, and then her voice filled the room again.

'You already have the original files.'

That didn't make sense. I had obviously asked the question incorrectly. What I was after were the files that were first uploaded from everyone's braces. The master copy, so to speak. I assumed the master copies would be held securely, and that copies had been taken for the purpose of general inspection. They couldn't risk damage or wear to an original file.

'But what about degradation?' I tried again and was met with surprise.

'Why would they degrade?'

I sighed. Of course they'd have solved degradation of data sources. I gave it one final stab.

'How many people have viewed this footage.'

'Approximately fifty million people.'

I was staggered. That was an enormous figure.

'Do you normally get so many views on a case file like this?'

Again with the laugh.

'Not so big, usually. But this was a murder, which is extraordinary. People like to watch from the safety of their own homes.'

Ghoulish, but unsurprising in a society where crime rates were so low.

'And after all those views, there has been no back-up or restoration of the original video footage?'

'No. Is there a problem?'

'No, not at all. Just impressed by the thoroughness of it. It's just I remember it differently.'

'Ah yes, observer bias,' she said kindly. 'It's a well-known phenomenon.'

She wasn't wrong. Back home eyewitnesses could apparently make terrible observers.

'Would it help you to see your own live feed and your witness statement?'

Now it was my turn to laugh. That hadn't even occurred to me.

'Excellent, just ask Tiresias and it will take care of everything for you. Can I help with anything else? Would you like to join us for lunch?'

I thanked her but decided to push on, and she said she would arrange to have some food sent to me. Once she signed off, I requested my own files and had the bizarre experience of re-watching events through my own eyes, but second hand.

I watched as I stepped cautiously into the main room, Neith in front of me. Everything was as I remembered.

The sense of disconnect was strongest watching it again through my eyes. Very clearly, I watched as Soliman said *book*. Never once did he say *codex*. I listened to my audio file as I relayed what I had witnessed, and when it came to repeating Soliman's final words on the tape, I also said book.

Every single recording, from every eyewitness, said *book* not *codex*. The obvious thing was to admit that I had remembered it incorrectly, but if that was the case, so had Rami and Neith. Us three, or the entire society. I knew who I believed.

I called up the custodian again and told her I was done. I assured her that I was untroubled by my findings and that everything was in order. The med lab told me that Neith and Rami were still under observation, so I went for a run to process my thoughts. We had a major problem on our hands. Despite everyone's reassurances, the enemy was still very much within.

Day Two - First Engineer

In an office across the city, another meeting was taking place. This time, all was order and control. Every subroutine and variable was checked, assessed and evaluated. Pi-Fuad stepped forward, approaching his superior's desk. Pi was covered in holographic tattoos, wavering all across his skin. Like every engineer, he took pains to draw attention to his appearance. It was a mark of disdain. The more a person was judged by their appearance, the less worthy the person making the judgement. The idea that outward appearance gave any indication of inner capacity was a notion that engineers found very droll and liked to play with. However, today, there was little to laugh at.

'First Engineer, I have a report here that Curator Strathclyde spent three hours reviewing the death of Soliman Alvarez.'

First looked up from his work and swore, making the junior officer flinch. So many people viewed those files that he wasn't interested in monitoring them himself, but certain names, ranks, job titles or repetitions would register a small alert. An algorithm would run a micro-subroutine to see if any links could be ascertained. Anything of note was then glanced over by a human.

'What in the name of Pythagoras is he doing with those files? And why was his brain scan rescheduled? I wasn't informed.'

First had been sat there all morning waiting for the results to come in. Now it seemed there had been a change of plan, and he hadn't been notified.

The engineer checked his notes. A slight tremor in his hands shook the report. 'According to the records, he had his scan first thing and experienced an intense reaction, due to eating a large breakfast. He proceeded to make a very fast and full recovery and left after half an hour. Additional notes from the medical team suggest investigating if eating a large meal can speed up the healing process.'

'Waste of time,' dismissed First.

'I concur.'

'Because?' Any opportunity was an instructional one, and First liked to make sure all his staff were capable of drawing quick and accurate conclusions.

'We have the evidence from hundreds of brain scans, with or without blockers. These all result in heavy vomiting and other symptoms if food has been ingested within the previous six hours.'

'Does the sample size categorically rule out food as being a negative experience?'

Pi tapped his keyboard and pulled up the figures.

'No, sir, but the sample is certainly large enough to suggest that food shouldn't be ingested. Everyone who eats food prior to a scan has a negative experience. However, just because we haven't yet had an individual who doesn't recover quickly, doesn't mean they don't exist.'

'In addition?'

'In addition, Strathclyde is a Beta individual. It is that, more than anything else that is likely to have had an impact.'

'Correct,' nodded First, pleased that the junior engineer hadn't missed the obvious variable. 'Suggestions for future investigations, were they to be permitted?'

Pi stood still, running through a few ideas, and continued. 'We need to test other angels. Perform scans on them and see how they respond, having just eaten a large meal.'

'Variables?' drilled First.

'Age of angel. Time spent on Alpha. Underlying health condition when they joined Alpha. Any subsequent brain procedures.'

'Ethically?'

'Ethically, we are not permitted to do this. This is a hypothetical reality only.'

'Very good Pi...' First paused, gratified that he couldn't recollect the engineer's name. He watched in displeasure as the engineer smiled. First tutted. 'Pi-Fuad. Now I remember. Your smile reminded me of your early years with us. Never mind.'

Pi-Fuad stared straight ahead. No evidence of disappointment or annoyance. He had let himself down by smiling, revealing his personal pleasure at having been forgotten. A perfect worker did not wallow in emotional indulgences.

First nodded. Pi-Fuad was very close to being assigned a number. For now though, he needed to focus on the job rather than himself. Dismissing him, First returned to the details of Strathclyde's investigations.

The Beta had examined the moments of Alvarez's death from every possible angle, in every possible medium, and then frowned. Only this section of the tape had been re-written. First knew there was no flaw as he had done it himself, obliterating every trace of the word codex. He wasn't permitted to alter eyewitnesses' brains, but he could certainly do everything else so that they would be cajoled into accepting that they misheard Alvarez's final words. Except that from the way that Strathclyde had gone through the files, it didn't look like he was convinced.

First sighed in frustration. Humans had far too many variables. They were much easier to deal with on the macro level.

Tapping his brace, he called up Haru Giovanetti, Head of Medicine. A second later Haru instigated a hologram projection that First slapped down. The last thing he needed right now was Haru's dreadful smiliness.

'Greetings, First, how can I help you today?' Even his jolly cheer-up voice grated.

'I'm waiting for the results of the brain scans on four individuals. I understand the scans were taken over three hours ago. Why am I still waiting?'

'Let me find out. Ah yes, here we are. They are next on my list. Let me write up the results and—'

First cut him off. 'I don't need you to write it up. I'm perfectly capable of reading the raw data. And may I remind you that these files are classified? I don't want some written report bandied all across the servers.'

'I am very well aware of that.' Haru's voice lost any sense of pleasantry. 'If I can remind you, we had to run these tests with no more input data than the fact that the individuals had experienced a group hallucination.'

'And you weren't tempted to ask for more from the patients themselves?'

'I don't like your tone, First. You gave me a set of instructions, and I followed them perfectly. The procedure was carried out without a blocker, and the only questions asked were those you requested.'

'Excellent. I am always suspicious about husband-wife bonds.'

Haru overrode the hologram veto and was now glaring at First. He still wouldn't be able to see First, but he was making sure that First could see how angry he was.

'Asha and I have always, *always*, respected the rules and regs of each other's departments, as well as those of other departments. You asked for this to be treated as a classified operation, and the suggestion that either Asha

84

or I would not have complied is repugnant. I shall be filing an official complaint against you to the pharaoh. You overstep your bounds, First.'

First yawned loudly enough to ensure Haru could hear him.

'Send me the files now, then do whatever you want. And if those files aren't here within five minutes, it will be me submitting a report for your incompetency.'

Finishing the call, First leant back in his chair. After three minutes and forty-two seconds, the files arrived, and he called for Second.

He pulled up the medical reports of the four curators and the chief custodian. Nothing appeared to indicate a brain abnormality. As he had feared, they had not suffered a group hallucination. He tapped on the reports and altered the findings until it was apparent that the five had suffered a group event. He then altered the files to indicate that the sword was still in place. It wasn't perfect, but for it to be perfect he needed to erase the five individuals. And, for now, Asha was too powerful. She was also too bloody clever, any attempt on her would likely backfire.

Dammit, why couldn't people realise that all he was trying to do was protect society and keep it running smoothly? Killing a few people in order to meet that goal should not be considered a bad thing.

For now, he rested his chin on his fist and began to wonder what this "Arthur" manifestation indicated.

***

Second entered the room without knocking. First nodded his approval, not that she looked for it. She knew he didn't fully approve of her, but then she considered him prone to emotional outbursts that clouded his judgement. She didn't think she was devoid of emotions; she just didn't let them interfere in her job.

He handed a printed document to her, which she flicked through and returned to him. As suspected, none of the five subjects had experienced a hallucination or a quantum echo. First frowned at her in surprise when she returned the document.

'Have you had time to properly evaluate it?'

'Yes.' No equivocation. No request for a second glance. She wondered if she had digested the intel faster than he had. Again, he could be ridiculously competitive. As if it mattered. He burnt the paper and looked over the flames at her.

'I also received another report regarding Strathclyde this morning. Following an unprecedented recovery from the brain scan, Strathclyde visited the custodian archives and interrogated the evidence as pertained to Alvarez's final words.'

Second looked alarmed. 'The part where he mentioned the codex?'

'That bit alone, and he examined it from every angle and every source of evidence.'

'He won't have found anything.'

'I know that, but the question is why is he investigating?'

The room fell quiet as Second processed this new piece of information. She broke the silence with a sigh.

'Maybe it would have been better to have him disposed of, after all?'

'We have to go through the proper channels.'

Second noted his peevish tone and replied carefully. 'No, I meant maybe we should have eliminated him the moment Curator Salah pulled him through the stepper, as you requested? Maybe we still should?'

First's utter hatred of Strathclyde was going to waltz the engineers into disaster if he kept fixating on the Beta. For now, Second tried to placate him, wondering if she should call on the Council of Ten to re-evaluate First's position.

'It is frustrating to be proved right when your solutions were not enacted. Now we stand at the abyss.'

'The abyss?' Second raised an eyebrow a fraction. This was the exact sort of language she wished to avoid. Soon he'd be using metaphors.

'Yes. Look at the evidence. A curator is investigating the erasure of the word codex. The same curator is wittering on about multiverses to whoever will listen to him. An anomaly broke into our world and removed an artefact, and the five witnesses did not experience a hallucination. Everything the Ten have sworn to protect and conceal is unravelling in front of our eyes. Mere anarchy stalks the plaza and boulevards.'

First cleared his throat. 'The point is, we need to do something.'

'I agree. I think the time has come that, as a Ten, we have feared for centuries. We are not alone, and we have been found.'

First tried to take control of the conversation. 'Solutions?'

Second walked over to a chair in the corner of the office. First liked people to stand in his presence. Second was breaking in a new pair of high heels and was blowed if she was going to discuss quantum physics whilst a blister was forming. She picked the chair up and placed it in front of his desk, enjoying his blank expression.

'I think we must monitor their every move. Either Salah or Strathclyde, or both, have attracted the attentions of an entity that does not exist on either of our planets. I believe this could be the first evidence of the hypothesised multiple universe theory.'

First nodded. What other conclusion was there?

'Potentially, but without examining it ourselves how can we know? It could indeed be some form of quantum aberration that we also don't understand. If only the workbook that we had from Leonardo was complete.'

That was the crux of the issue. They were working blindfolded since the original codex had somehow been lost.

'We were fools to ever allow a rumour of a missing codex to reach Alvarez's ear,' growled Second. 'He could only think of it in terms of financial gain. Whereas we know it will reveal the true working of the quantum stepper. Not the jerry-rigged stepper that we have built over the centuries. We are close to a breakthrough, I know it. Maybe this manifestation is the catalyst we need to develop a properly functioning stepper?'

'That, or it will cause us to collapse all of reality.'

Good grief thought Second. Maybe she shouldn't delay convening the Ten? They were sworn down through the generations, since the death of da Vinci, to safeguard and develop his work. And if they had to safeguard it from even First of Ten, then so be it.

As Second left the room to set up a surveillance protocol, First pondered if she was going to make a play for his position. It seemed the most logical thing for her to do, given that she was at odds with his viewpoint. Killing her was a waste of a very fine brain. He would just need to convince her that this Arthur manifestation was simply a quantum variable somehow created by Strathclyde. It may even be evidence of another Earth and a traveller setting across from there, but what it absolutely wasn't, and couldn't possibly be, was some sort of pan-dimensional being.

Following the appearance of the anomaly in the curator's headquarters, First had been forced to delay the removal of Strathclyde. An accident right now would seem suspicious. Not that they had any problem justifying what they did, and they would be given a clean slate. It was just easier if their hands moved silently through society. People were happier when they weren't asking questions.

Day Three - Julius

'I have a question,' said Rami. His tone was outraged, but there was no genuine hostility in it. 'Exactly how did you make such a miraculous recovery, yesterday?'

I scanned the room, but no one was sitting within hearing range. I had chosen the farthest seat from the bar, which ensured no passing traffic. It had been two days since I had received my new status notification from the engineers, and whilst Sam had reassured me that nothing would happen quickly, I was still jumpy. Neith and Rami joined me for lunch on the terraces of The Last Bar. I had always enjoyed the view from here. Meeting out by Lake Mareotis felt unnecessarily clandestine, and as I had evidence of further skulduggery, I didn't want to tip anyone off. My calling up the files had probably already raised a flag somewhere.

'Arthur showed up and fixed it.'

Rami groaned. 'I shouldn't have asked.'

Neith scowled and grumbled about figments of my imagination. I'd have been crosser, but I knew she was scared about the power of the engineers.

'He is not a figment of my imagination,' I said and tried not to sound too testy.

'Then what is he?' Rami said with a sigh, earning himself a second scowl from Neith.

'I have no idea. Back home he is a mythological figure. He isn't even worshipped. Although, he is idolised, like

91

some perfect embodiment of England. Which is a laugh, as he started out as a Celtic warrior opposing the Saxons, but don't get me started on the misappropriation of national figures. St George, anyone?'

I laughed and laughed alone. They had no idea what I was nattering on about.

'Ignore that. The thing is, he isn't a god back home, nor has he ever been known to walk amongst us. I honestly don't think he's from my Earth. I think something about your gate has made him stronger.'

'Or something about you,' said Neith.

I paused. That didn't feel right, but I was well out of my depth.

'So, you accept he is real, and not a hallucination or quantum hiccough?'

'Julius, please.' She looked wretched. 'I don't want to talk about him. I don't know how or why he is connected to you. I just know that his presence puts you in great danger.'

I was glad we were talking about this. Maybe Rami's presence gave her a sense of protection?

'Do you know, Neith, he first appeared after he saw you? He told me he watched you and Clio retrieve his sword, and he followed you both back through the stepper.'

Neith's face froze in fear, and I realised I had gone too far. This society had undercurrents that I still hadn't fathomed. My crashing about in search for answers was alarming my friends and potentially bringing trouble down on their heads. I changed tack on to what I hoped was a topic of less drama.

'Shall we ignore him for now? We have other pressing issues.' And I went on to explain what I had discovered at the custodial offices.

'No one can tamper with those files!' said Rami with astonishment and a small measure of delight. This was the sort of puzzle that he revelled in. Unbreakable safes, indecipherable codes.

I was just relieved they both remembered the word codex. I'd been beginning to doubt myself.

'Neith and I were also going to look at the files today. Seems like great minds think alike.' He grinned. 'We were also curious about what Alvarez's final words meant. But I think we should tread carefully. If someone went to such lengths to manipulate the files, they will certainly be monitoring them.'

'Do you think I'm in trouble?'

'More than usual, you mean?'

'Hey.' I mean, he wasn't wrong, but really. I hadn't told him about the death threat, it was too embarrassing plus I didn't want him somehow contaminated. He wasn't long out of sand leave himself. The problem was I just didn't see myself as a troublemaker or rebel. I still viewed myself as an academic. A lover of puzzles contained within the pages in a library. Not a lightning magnet for chaos and destruction. 'I am not an albatross.'

The reference sailed over Rami's head. Neith sat down with three drinks and placed them in front of us, before explaining.

'Sailors believed they were harbingers of bad luck. Coleridge wrote about one. Had to research him when we saved that collection from fire.'

'Was that the incident with the swans?' said Rami, laughing.

I was desperate to hear more about the swans, but Neith huffed and changed the subject. I would have to ask Rami about swans another day.

'So, someone is trying to keep the issue of a codex a secret? Excellent. Who exactly has the technology to alter all those files?'

'The engineers is the obvious response, but it's clearly not them,' said Rami, thankfully.

I raised an eyebrow. 'Why obviously?'

'Because they aren't interested in codices. The engineers are at the cutting edge of technology. No, this must be something rare and valuable. Something that was stolen.'

'Which means our thieves are still in play if they can cover their tracks like this.'

'But Alvarez's ledger had so many names in it, I was sure that they were all ousted. I mean even the former pharaoh was revealed.'

'Well, maybe someone eluded capture?' said Neith thoughtfully. 'But whoever it is, we need to step carefully.

They think they have got away with it. Let's not alert them. Ramin, can we trust Giovanetti? Should you mention this to her? Your first step in inter-departmental co-operation?'

I was confused by Neith's words until they explained Rami's recent promotion. To me, it sounded a bit like snooping, but they both thought it was excellent news so, when we finished our drinks, I ordered something a little stronger to properly celebrate. With a delicious lunch and a bottle of beer, I had to confess I was feeling replete. It was a great word, one that suggests all is well in the world, even when it's not. I was out enjoying the sunshine, chatting with my friends and, for five minutes, not stressing about underground cabals and people trying to kill us. The world at that moment was pretty perfect.

'Hail Geezer!'

A tall, shaven man in a leather waistcoat worn over a naked and well-defined torso, shouted out to us. As he raised his fist in salutation, I could see his entire right arm was covered in snake tattoos. He was wearing leather trousers and what appeared to be motorcycle boots.

Neith looked at me, concerned. 'Did he just say *Hail Caesar?*'

'No, it's worse than that, I'm afraid,' I said.

'And it is Arthur, isn't it? I mean, he looks nothing like Arthur, but I still know it's him. I don't understand.'

'Nor do I, but I think the explanation is filed somewhere under divine majesty. He is Arthur, and he's not trying to hide the fact that he's Arthur, therefore we know it's him. It doesn't matter how he appears.'

Arthur now strode towards us, pretending to punch and wrestle some of the nearby curators. It was excruciating to watch as they buckled under the growing strength of Arthur's influence. As he reached us, I noticed Neith run her fingers through her hair and, a second later, slap herself. Hard.

'If you spot me acting like an idiot around this person just smack me, okay?' She glared at Arthur. 'You there. Arthur. Stop that, do you understand? I will not have my feelings manipulated in this way.'

'Is this fearsome maiden with you, Julius?' He gave her what can only be described as a bold smile, and I decided to nip things in the bud quickly. I wasn't sure what would happen if you launched an assault on a proto-god, but I didn't want Neith to find out. I shook my head at Arthur. He had clearly forgotten that he had met her on more than one occasion.

'Think Nimue.'

He took a rapid step back from Neith and bowed deeply. 'But I think even Nimue would be swayed by my mighty godhead.' He winked at me, and I groaned as I heard Neith take a deep breath.

'Did he just imply—'

'No! At least I don't think so. Let's just see what he wants. Then he can return to whatever film set he's been hanging around.'

When I turned around, Arthur had already moved on and was now preening in the mirrored glass. Liking what he saw, he smiled at the curators, who all started to gravitate towards him. He was getting stronger.

'Arthur?'

He turned round and looked at me, pained. He swung his arms out wide and tilted his head.

'Would it kill you to call me King Arthur?'

I thought about it and decided it wouldn't. Plus, and more importantly, it might if I didn't.

'King Arthur. We are delighted to see you again. Can I invite you to join us for a drink?'

I had no idea what I was doing, but I wanted to try and understand what he represented. Spending some time with him might help me understand what was happening.

'I have a plan!'

Neith and Rami were concerned, but honestly, that might also have been because he had just placed his foot on the seat of the chair and struck a heroic pose.

'Go on?' Playing along seemed the easier option.

He swung the chair around and sat down on it, leaning his elbows over the back.

'I've only seen people sit like that in Beta movies,' said Neith to Rami in astonishment.

'No, remember that guy from finance that used to do it and pretend he was a Beta stockbroker.'

'Oh yes. Doesn't really work on bar stools though, does it?'

They continued to whisper and giggle until Arthur cleared his throat and did the shake-the-table thing, which startled them into silence.

'Julius here told me of your plans to find a codex.'

Rami shook his head, and Neith gave me daggers. So much for keeping it a secret.

'And I, that is we, have devised a quest for you to undertake to recover your lost object.'

Arthur stared at us, waiting for applause and frowned when none was forthcoming.

'What?' said Rami. 'Do you know where it is?'

'Of course. What do you think omnipotent means?'

'It means all-powerful,' said Rami helpfully. 'Do you mean omniscient? All-knowing?'

'Whatever I say, is what I mean. It is not down to me to explain things to tiny minds.' Arthur was getting pissed off. This didn't seem to be going the way he had expected. I picked my beer up off the table.

'Yes, of course,' hurried Rami. 'I just meant to say that if you know where it is, could you just tell us?'

Arthur placed his hands on his hips, tipped his head back and roared with laughter, wiping a tear from his eye. It was a Hollywood performance.

'Where would be the challenge in that? No, look, as I said, we have a plan. I—'

'I think Giovanetti and Sam need to be part of this,' said Neith, suddenly cutting Arthur off. Picking her bottle off the table, she hurriedly apologised to Arthur.

Can we include a few more people?' Addressing the others she suggested that we meet back in Sam's office.

Poor Arthur. I almost felt sorry for the way Neith had dismissed him. But he remembered my warning to pretend she was Nimue, and he gave her a gracious bow and disappeared.

'Now what?' asked Rami, looking at Neith.

'Now we gather the team and hope that we can get through the next hour without alerting the engineers or our enemies. I don't know what Arthur is, but I'm beginning to agree with Julius. This Arthur figure has agency. He is the cause of our problems with the engineers, and potentially the solution to finding the codex. We must proceed very, very carefully.'

I tried not to smile to myself. It wasn't a total vindication of my theory regarding Arthur, but it was nice to finally have Neith on my side. We had been at odds recently, and that had left me unsettled.

Day Three - Julius

We were sitting at the conference table in the room adjoining Sam's office. Neith had called Sam and asked him to get Asha with all haste. Now, the pair of them were sat at the same table glaring at us.

'You were told expressly to ignore this quantum anomaly,' snapped Asha.

'Respectfully—'

Asha glared at Neith, but she ploughed on. 'I do mean respectfully, but the thing is Arthur has been turning up a lot in the past few days. I don't think he's a blip.'

'Indeed, I am not a blip at all,' announced Arthur, doing his regal manifestation thing and making everyone jump. 'The fearsome Neith asked me to delay my intentions until you were all gathered together.' He sketched a bow in her direction. 'If everyone is assembled, I am eager to share my plans.'

'I think you should just say what you want, and then go away,' growled Sam. He turned and looked at me. And, I must say, as Asha was already glaring at me, I was finding the attention uncomfortable.

'Julius. Is this—' Sam waved in Arthur's direction '—something to do with you? Because I am not about to have my brain scanned for a second time in one week.'

'Do you think *that's what I want?*' I asked. 'This has nothing to do with me, but instead of pretending this is a hallucination that we are all experiencing, why don't we try and ask Arthur a few questions and see if he knows what is going on? Maybe invite First Engineer over as well to experience the hallucination?'

I didn't want to make a habit of getting confrontational, but I really wasn't welcoming the idea that Arthur was somehow my fault. Particularly when it was Neith and Clio he'd followed back through the portal. And I was trying to dodge a death sentence.

'I am a god! Attend me.' The room started to shake, and we all turned back to Arthur who appeared to have swelled in size. A darkness hung around his shoulders, and the air crackled with electricity. The four Alphas had taken defensive positions and were preparing to launch an attack. None, as far as I could see were carrying weapons, but I knew that they were all trained in physical combat. This needed to stop.

I hurried over to Arthur and leant in so the others wouldn't hear me.

'Except you aren't actually a god are you, Arthur? I'm happy to keep that to myself, but I doubt you can do much more beyond shake a few tables. How about you calm things down? Tell us what we are here for, and let's start again.'

I was using the tone I reserved for students that were making a spectacle of themselves at closing time outside the pub. Shouting about Pliny and also the fact that the landlord was watering down the beer. I didn't want to embarrass Arthur, and I was pretty certain he wasn't a

101

god. You know, not least because gods don't exist. But he was something, and we needed to work out what. He cleared his throat.

'I am swayed by the supplications of my loyal acolyte here that I should be more lenient towards you, and so I shall forgive your behaviour and explain why we are all here.'

I tried not to look at Neith, but her smirk was so wide it would have been impossible to miss. *Loyal acolyte.* Honestly. Arthur and I needed to have a proper sit-down.

'We have decided to help you find your codex.'

'What codex?' asked Sam.

'Who's "we"?' said Neith.

Arthur ignored Neith and smiled at Sam.

'The one your engineers are hiding from you.'

We all stared at him in astonishment. Then everyone was shouting at once. I knew I should want to know more about the codex, but it was Neith's question about *We* that had caught my attention. Arthur never used the royal we. I was praying this was simply a new affectation. I absolutely didn't want to think what it could mean.

'Right. Let's calm down,' said Asha, quickly taking control of the situation.

We were in one of the conference rooms with a long table running down the middle. We gravitated to one end. Asha sat at the head until Arthur stood with his hands on his hips, looking nobly out of the window whilst the floor shook. Asha stood up and moved down a seat. She didn't seem annoyed, so much as trying to work out the new parameters. It was like watching a toddler playing with a knife and a scorpion. You know you need to step in, but you don't have a clue which to deal with first. For now, she and the others were playing along and, personally, it seemed like a good call for me as well.

'Tell me about the codex?' said Asha.

'Do you really not know?' asked Arthur, puzzled. 'The other side do?'

'The engineers?'

'No, your enemy.'

'The engineers are my enemy?' Asha sounded exasperated. I was already lost.

'No. The *enemy* enemy,' said Arthur with a sigh, as though speaking to a child. 'The engineers are just trying to hide the codex. The enemy is trying to find it. And you lot are running about in the dark. So, I thought, well, *we* thought, it would be fun to step in and help out. Like a challenge. And if this quest goes well, I will be elevated into the first rank of the deities.'

I really didn't like where this was going, but the curators continued to focus on the codex.

This time, Sam intervened. 'Let me see if I've got this right. There's a codex out there whose existence the engineers are trying to keep quiet. There's also a group of people, probably connected to the recent series of thefts from the mouseion, that are trying to get the codex for themselves.'

'Yes.'

'In which case,' said Sam to Asha, 'we haven't fully cleaned out the rats' nest. We need to dig deeper.'

'Agreed, but maybe we should call in First Engineer to see why he's interfering in a curatorial matter?' Asha tapped her wrist brace when Sam held up his hand.

'Before we involve the engineers,' said Sam, 'let's talk to Arthur a bit more. This Arthur-is-a-quantum-hallucination theory seems to be getting weaker and weaker. And, personally, I don't want to invite the engineers over for them to fix things, because I think I know how they will fix things. For the good of society, you know.'

Asha looked at Sam, and she placed her hand back on the table.

'Now, Arthur—'

'King Arthur.'

'Okay, King Arthur, what is this codex that the others seem so excited about?'

'It's one of da Vinci's.'

Well, that caused a stir. Who amongst us isn't instantly intrigued when we hear the name da Vinci?

'Do you mean the Leicester Codex?' I asked. 'That isn't missing.'

'The Leicester Codex? Eighty pages on how to move water about the place. Leave it out.'

The Arthur as Cockney motif was really beginning to bug me. Maybe if he was tapping into a collective mindset,

I should work harder on seeing him as some sort of blond-haired Teutonic hero. The dark Celt thing was horribly mangled with Guy Ritchie at the moment, and I didn't have time to unpick it.

'Tell me, sweet prince, what does this codex refer to?' I knew I was laying it on thick, but I was getting the hang of Arthur and he certainly liked the attention and adulation.

He smiled and nodded at me, and I'm not ashamed to say that I suddenly felt all aglow. King Arthur with Jedi mind tricks. That was something to keep me on my toes.

'The codex, my lord? If its purpose is not to inform us how to move water, what is its aim?'

'Well, how to move time and space instead. It is the blueprint of how to build one of your quantum chariots.'

At this point, it's fair to say the crowd went wild. As wild as they get, anyway. The four of them were now talking amongst themselves, arguing that the engineers should be summoned immediately, and, at the same time, that on no account should the engineers be summoned.

'Calm down, everyone,' said Asha. 'If there is indeed a missing codex detailing plans on how to build a quantum stepper, then we must secure it before the enemy does.'

'First, we need to establish who the enemy is,' said Neith. 'Julius has been doing some preliminary investigations and found that all mentions of the codex on the night of Alvarez's killing have been scrubbed clean.'

'Only the engineers have the technology and the ability to do that.'

'Then they are the enemy,' said Sam, glad to have someone to target.

'No,' said Arthur. 'The engineers are trying to keep it from both sides.'

'Well, who is the enemy?' demanded Asha. 'Are you here to help us or tease us?'

It was all getting tense, and I could sense that Arthur was getting fed up with the lack of deference. He had drawn Excalibur from its sheath, and he was carefully studying its blade.

'Sweet prince, you said something about a quest?'

Honestly, I had a bad feeling about this, but at the same time, I was excited. This was something new, and I loved new.

'Yes. A quest indeed,' said Arthur, putting Excalibur back in its scabbard with a dramatic flourish. 'For you shall be tasked to find and retrieve this hidden codex. There will be two teams, the defenders of truth and justice, those who uphold honour and the chivalric code.'

I took this to mean the "good guys", and I further hoped that this meant "us".

Arthur continued, 'And the scourge of humanity. The lovers of greed and despair, those that exist without honour.'

It wasn't too much to assume these were the baddies, or "them".

'And what are the rules?'

'Rules?' Arthur looked flummoxed.

'Yes, there are always rules in a quest set by the gods.'

'He's right, you know,' said a disembodied voice.

The five of us jerked our heads, startled.

There were two more men sitting at the table. This time there was none of the wishy-washy pull that Arthur presented. This time there was total awe and radiance. We sat silently transfixed, inwardly I groaned. My worst suspicions were confirmed. The gods were at play.

'Too much, Lucy,' said the man with the blond hair to the dark-haired man who apologised, and suddenly we all relaxed.

'Forgive me. Allow me to introduce myself. We are here to help our good friend Arthur earn his way up into the celestial pantheon. We thought a quest would be just the ticket. Then he'll need a few miracles, genocide, and a film franchise and I think we're good to go.'

The blond-haired god looked at his friend and cocked his head.

'Are we still going with genocide? I thought we'd agreed on plague or famine?'

The dark-haired god lightly slapped his hand on his forehead and shook his head.

'You're quite right. My apologies. Plague or famine it is.' He was about to start talking when he paused and turned back to his comrade. 'But accidental genocides are acceptable aren't they?'

'Oh, absolutely.'

'Excellent. Now, where was I? Ah yes, introductions. I am Lucifer and this is Loki. Shall we begin?'

Day Three – Julius

The gods were real. I was stunned into silence. My entire academic career was crumbling around me. How would I ever be able to discuss faith-based systems and man's desire to find himself within the world, when one of mankind's apparent tormenters was currently pouring everyone a glass of water? I shook my head again. The gods were real, and this changed everything. We had gone from what if there are hundreds of Earths, to what the actual…

'Julius are you okay?' asked Neith. 'You seem to be croaking.' Neith of course was still on the quantum aberration page of the handbook. At some point, this entire society was about to massively freak out. In the meantime, I had questions. Theoretically, I was the expert in the room. I had better get into gear and stop floundering.

I coughed politely, drawing everyone's attention to me.

'Can I ask something?'

Loki and Lucifer conferred, and Lucifer waved at Loki to proceed.

'We like questions, go ahead.'

I nodded, paused, and took a deep breath.

'In your world, wherever you come from, do you have — well I'm trying to think of the tactful way to say it — do you have God?'

Lucifer snorted and Loki started to rant.

'You walk on water and suddenly everyone goes mad. I mean what the hell? Zeus appears as a shower of golden rain, and everyone just raises their shoulders. God parts the Red Sea; the crowd loses their mind. And was he gracious about it? Was he hell? All that preening. Remember?'

Noticing that Loki and Lucifer were getting wound up, I cleared my throat again. Talking to gods was a minefield.

'So, can I check? God. He's definitely a man, not some beatific gender fluid or female divine spirit?'

Loki laughed and shook his head.

'Ah, I think you mean Gaia.'

'Oh, she's wonderful,' said Lucifer. 'That reminds me, I need to send her a thank you letter for some homemade fudge she made.'

'I love her fudge,' gushed Loki. 'Isn't she lovely?'

As the two gods went off on a tangent, I tried again. I knew it was off topic but how often did I get to talk to someone that thought they were a god? And might, in fact, actually be a god? I could tell I was already trying to rationalise what these people were.

'May I ask another question about *that* God?'

Lucifer and Loki didn't seem terribly keen to continue but nodded.

'Is he the Muslim God or the Christian one, or is he the same?'

'My, that was a masterpiece wasn't it?' said Loki. 'A great PR move. So, for years he'd been a perfectly happy god out in the desert and had a really great line in burning bushes. And, all credit, parting the Red Sea was cool.'

'Yes, okay, that was cool,' agreed Lucifer

'And I loved the whole angel thing he was working,' said Loki.

'Thank you.' Lucifer gave a quick bow.

'My pleasure. Then Anansi comes along and thought he'd play a joke on God and suggested that he expanded. Remember when Zeus started sprouting Athena and the like? Well, God discussed it and he thought it was a good idea, and he thought it was a bad idea. So he said he was going to do it and he said he wasn't going to do it.'

We all looked at each other in confusion. The sentence didn't make sense. I interrupted.

'Wait, I don't understand. You keep saying *he said*, then contradicting yourself.'

Loki raised an eyebrow and tutted. 'It's not my fault your language is so primitive.'

Lucifer nodded his head in agreement.

'Hang on, Loki, let me have a go.' Lucifer turned towards us. 'More my area, anyway. Now then. God was in two minds and was discussing it with himself? Any better?'

I nodded. 'Like Janus, the two-faced god?'

Lucifer shuddered.

111

'Really, don't compare Janus to God. It will only make Janus more big-headed. Anyway. God decided to split. He would carry on as before, and he would create some additional gods and that's where he played a blinder. He went for the whole trinity concept. God the Father, God the Son, and God the Holy Ghost. I mean. Hello! Genius. He sort of replicated himself three times, instantly making himself three times as powerful, then he roped in Mary as well to catch the female market. It was awesome. We just stood and watched in amazement as his star grew and grew. And, perversely, his God solo act also began to swell until he totally trademarked the God title. And the rest of us have been relegated, under the shade of the Abrahamic shadow.'

I was utterly enthralled.

'So what did Anansi make of his prank?' I asked agog. 'Did he think he was foolish? Was he cross with himself?'

'No,' said Lucifer very quickly

'Oh, no. Absolutely not,' agreed Loki. 'I would never say that to his face.'

'Or behind his back.'

'Indeed. It's fair to say that, as a prank, it massively backfired. He is still really sore about it.'

Oh dear, this didn't sound good. I decided to clarify quickly. 'Is he likely to turn up here?'

'Who? Anansi?'

'No, God.'

'Not a chance,' said Loki. 'He's far too busy with his billions of followers. Jesus is a good egg, and the Holy Ghost is a hoot, but they really are too busy to play.' Loki raised an eyebrow. 'Is that a problem?'

Even in my enthusiasm to talk at length about the roles of the gods, I could see I had annoyed the ones closest to me. I started to make amends.

'How could it be a problem when I have the all-powerful Lucifer, Lord of the Nether Kingdoms, and Loki, god of infinite cunning and cleverness, in front of me? This one meeting has been the crowning moment of my life, and I will forever talk to my children, and their children, and all that I meet, and tell them of the glory of meeting some gods in all their raiment.'

Loki and Lucy smiled and nodded. I breathed a sigh of relief; disaster averted. Which, of course, was when a third voice joined in. I hope it wasn't Lugh, I could do without the brilliant Irish god. A minute later I'd have given anything for it to be him rather than who we were now facing.

'Did I hear someone mention my name?'

A tall, dapper man was lounging in the corner of the room. At first glance, he was no taller than me, but something about his legs and arms suggested greater length. His fingers appeared to be in a state of constant motion, but when I looked at them directly, they were still. His skin was as black as a mole but nothing about him struck me as soft or endearing. This was not someone who hid in the shadows out of fear of the light, this was someone that drew everyone's attention.

He wore a blue waistcoat covered in a thousand tiny mirrors that reflected my every move. Everything about him made my small monkey brain scream in terror. I reminded myself that mankind had evolved past its basic fears and looked him in the face. There was something disconcerting about his eyes. The pupils were overly large, with only a thin blue band for an iris; beyond the blue, the eyes turned black again. Every contradiction put me on edge. Those terrible eyes stayed on me as he moved too close, nostrils flexing as he sniffed, his hands patting the air around me. Loki and Lucifer grimaced at each other but remained silent.

'Hello, Julius. Why do you feel different? I'm getting a hint of a believer. It's not much, but it's a lot more than the others in the room. Why are you different? I like a puzzle. I'm Anansi by the way.'

My heart was beating like rain on canvas. I was never going to outwit Anansi. I figured if I shared some information with him, he may be inclined to share some with me. After all, Loki and Lucifer were acting out of some archetypal gods' playbook. Maybe Anansi would as well? In the meantime, one of them might slip up and I could work out who they actually were. Real gods. Or people who thought they were.

'I'm not a local. I come from the other Earth.'

'Ah, so you know who I am. I get the impression that your poor foolish companions don't know me.' He paused and smiled at me. 'If you would be so kind.'

'Of course.' I cleared my throat nervously. I had no idea who any of these people were but pretending to play along with them wouldn't hurt. 'May I introduce you to Anansi, the spider god. On my Earth, Anansi is a popular figure in African and Caribbean heritage. He is well-loved. If the three of these gods have anything in common, it's that they are cleverer than most of their kin and they bore easily.'

'Which explains where we come in, or rather where they come in,' said Lucifer with a dramatic sigh. 'I will have to love you and leave you. As much fun as this is, I need to keep my skin in the game. People to terrify, unbelievers to torture, that sort of thing. Honestly, this seems like much more fun.'

'The price of your success.' Anansi smiled unkindly.

'Take care of yourself,' said Loki with a surprising amount of concern, and then Lucifer was gone. I'd like to say in a puff of brimstone, but there really was nothing. One minute he was there, the next he had gone, once again startling the others.

'Right,' said Anansi, rubbing his hands together. 'Loki has brought you all up to speed, but we know this has thrown you. The gods are real, shock horror, who knew? So, we are going to give you twenty-four hours to adjust to this fact, and we will all meet back here tomorrow, and

I will let you know how this quest is going to run. Oh, and between now and then we will display constant evidence of our existence just to help drill it in. Okay, ciao ciao.' And with that, he and Loki disappeared.

Day Three - Julius

For the first time in my life, I understood the term deafening silence. It felt like everyone had held their breath, and all I could hear was my own heartbeat pulsing in my ears. I turned to see how the others were reacting, to find four somewhat hostile faces glaring at me.

'What?'

'What?' said Sam, echoing me in disbelief. 'What in the name of Bast just happened?'

Asha chimed in, 'Julius, who were those people?'

Why did she think I knew what was going on? This was her world, not mine. In my world, we didn't have hallucinations, or a quantum stepping machine, or science that presents like magic. I shrugged and said as much.

'No, but in your world you have gods,' continued Asha.

'Not like that,' I protested. 'They're not actually real, you know.'

I wanted to suggest another option. That, rather than actual gods, or coming from either of our Earths, they came from another Earth. But each time I'd mentioned multiverses, I had noticed that whoever I was speaking to became distressed. They would become short-tempered or distracted. Sometimes they developed a headache or became queasy. It struck me as curious that a society that wholly embraced the reality of the quantum stepper and my Earth never discussed the concept of other Earths. I

117

was going to have to investigate that further, but whilst they were all deeply shaken by this encounter, it didn't feel like the right time to inflict further misery on them.

'Those people just now seemed pretty real to me,' muttered Neith, and Sam and Rami quickly agreed.

'Exactly,' I said. 'Which is why they have nothing to do with me. Our gods aren't real. This has to be something from your side. Some glitch in the quantum machine. I don't know.'

Talking about quantum mechanics took me to the deep end of the pool very quickly. Honestly, I was on safer ground with non-existent gods. I knew I was rabbiting, but having four very angry, confused people staring at me as though whatever had just happened was my fault wasn't a pleasant feeling.

'So what do we do now?' demanded Neith. 'Pretend this never happened, simply because we don't have any answers?'

'That is precisely what we are going to do,' said Asha, taking control. 'Sam, carry on with the scheduled steps. Rami, I want you to come with me. Neith and Julius, go home and get some rest. I don't know if anything is going to happen tomorrow, but I want to be ready. I didn't like their comment that they will be offering lots of signs. I want us on full alert but act as if nothing is happening. Until we know what we are dealing with, I don't want to start a full-scale panic.'

'Shouldn't we inform the engineers?' asked Sam. The idea of another encounter with First filled me with dread, but I could see his point.

'We are not calling the engineers,' said Asha, her eyes narrowing. 'If we did, I suspect we might suddenly disappear from the public record.'

I felt some of the tension leave my body. The way First looked at me made me question how many days I had left on this Earth. His expression suggested very few.

'I disagree.'

I stared at Neith in amazement.

'Do you, Curator Salah?' Asha's tone remained icy. 'Since when do you get to disagree with the head of the custodians?'

'Since four figures appeared in front of us,' said Neith as she ticked the points off on her hand. 'Since they started talking about Leonardo da Vinci and his codex and threatened to create a demonstration that we won't be able to ignore. Every single one of those aspects is engineer territory, and they need to be informed.'

'And you're prepared to risk your life for that? You're not concerned that they won't just sweep you away while they fix the problem? Need I remind you what happened to your parents?'

Neith blanched, and Rami quickly held her hand. I had no idea what that was about, but it was clearly traumatic.

'I have a suggestion.' No one was looking at me. Rami was trying to hold Neith together; Asha was watching her, waiting to see if she would explode or something. And Sam was watching the three of them.

He smiled at me sadly. 'Go on, son.'

I took a breath and continued. 'What about we do inform the engineers? As much as it makes me shudder, it sounds like Neith is right. This is their playground. But I also agree with Asha. I trust them as far as I can throw them. What if we tell all the department heads at the same time and make it clear we've told everyone?'

Neith grinned, nodding her head. 'Like when we came back from fifteenth-century France, and you sent texts and photos to everyone to show we were home? No one could quietly kill us.'

'Precisely.' I smiled back. 'Safety in numbers.'

Sam agreed and, whilst Asha's expression didn't seem to change much, she rapped her knuckles on the table and turned back to Neith.

'Very well. We will do as you suggest. For now though, go home and rest, but keep this to yourselves and let me know the minute you see anything odd happening. Gamal, I need you to stay with me, and help me choose the right words to inform all departments that the sky is falling in.'

He was still standing by Neith's side, and I could see he was about to refuse.

'Salah will be fine. Don't underestimate her.' Asha's words were for Neith as much as for Rami, and I watched as Neith took a deep breath and smiled at her friend.

'Go on and help Giovanetti, but if I were you, ma'am, I'd avoid the expression sky falling in. Might scare the horses you know.'

As we left the offices, Neith crossed her arms.

'I know you are going to ask, so; my parents were engineers. They both died in the line of duty. And that is all I'm prepared to say on the matter.'

Her face was resolute, and I knew I wouldn't be circling back to this fact for some time yet, even though it explained a lot about Neith's devotion to her society. I wondered how old she had been when they died. She nudged me in the ribs.

'Now, tell me about these gods of yours. Do you think they can do any actual damage?'

Day Three - Asha

'Unit Five, with me! Watch out for the frogs.'

The downpour of amphibians had started ten minutes before and was making it slippery underfoot.

Giovannetti's comments about a full-scale panic, only a few hours earlier, had been woefully prescient. The first signs of trouble came from reports suggesting a disturbance in the ancient monuments section of the mouseion. A family had been taking pictures of themselves by the statue of Anubis. A second later Anubis himself, seven feet tall with coal red eyes and a jackal's head on a man's body, wandered over and suggested a group selfie.

A custodian was dispatched to see what the screams were about. When *he* started screaming, a whole team of custodians arrived and were staggered to find the ancient Egyptian god of the dead offering two-for-the-price-of-one to the underworld.

No sooner had the custodians called back to command than other strange accounts began to flood in. Taps were pouring with blood or wine. No one was prepared to find out which. A custodian had approached a crouched figure that had the temerity to be scribbling graffiti on the walls. Shocked, the custodian challenged the individual and was startled as the figure uncurled itself and a ten-foot-tall snake wavered up above him. In his hands he carried two spray cans. He then winked at the custodian and, dropping back down to the floor, he slithered off along the street.

'I don't know,' said the custodian into his wrist brace. 'I have no idea what *two legs bad, no legs good* means.' He paused. 'Did you not hear me say it had arms? A snake with arms and a bad attitude.'

Another squad of custodians was dispatched to the scene.

Back at the custodian's briefing room, Giovanetti was watching a live-stream map of the city. It had been three hours since the men calling themselves gods had disappeared, and reports of events were beginning to light up the map.

There were multiple accounts of a woman with eight arms playing tennis with a horse with eight legs. Both were the height of the science lab, and they were using the globe that used to sit on the top minarets as the tennis ball.

Giovanetti shouted to a division to evacuate the area to sector three.

'Sector three is currently under water,' called out another custodian from his workspace.

'Why isn't it on the map?'

'We're having trouble keeping up with all the reports,' shouted someone from across the room.

'Captain, there's a man walking down Cleopatra Plaza, and he's handing out cigars. As he passes, people are dying.'

Asha slammed her hands on the table, and everyone jumped. No one remembered the last time they had seen her lose her temper. Giovanetti had been trying to contain the situation, but if her citizens were dying, she had to engage. She pressed the intercom buzzer.

'All red custodians. Onto the streets. Defend the citizens and get them to their homes.'

Half an hour later it got worse, as the custodians — both red and yellow — struggled to get a grip on the situation.

Ramin stood beside Giovanetti, watching a live holo-screen as a group of red custodians engaged a single man who was whistling to himself

'That's not going to work,' muttered Ramin.

'What did you say?' she asked, distracted, as she too watched the screen.

'The power balance is wrong,' he replied.

'I know.' She watched the screen intently. 'I don't understand why he's smiling.'

'No, I mean he's the one with the power. This is why the custodian's approach won't work.'

A moment later, they watched in disbelief as the squad was picked up and hurled down the street. The man was walking towards them, puffing out his cheeks and blowing them towards the water's edge until the entire cohort fell into the water. As the last custodian dropped into the harbour, the man brushed some dust off his sleeve, wandering off the way he had come. He looked like a child in search of a new playmate.

'Ramin,' said Giovanetti, having ascertained that her custodians were relatively unharmed.'How did you know that wouldn't work? Could you see his power?'

'Yes and no,' said Ramin. 'I mean I couldn't see anything unusual about him. But he knew he was going to win. That, I could see. Being a curator, you get a sense for situations going wrong quickly.'

Asha stared at him for a second, then tapped on her wrist brace.

'Sam? How quickly could you deploy your curators? I want them out on the streets fighting alongside the custodians.'

Sam's voice shot back as clear as day. 'My curators aren't trained for Alpha combat.'

'And my custodians aren't trained for this level of chaos. Yours are.'

There was a pause. Sam continued. 'Okay, they're yours. What do you need?'

'One pair per red custodian cohort. I need your curators to help assess the situation and suggest alternative methods of engagement.'

125

Disconnecting the feed, she jabbed Ramin in the shoulder. 'This. This is why you are here. To think in new ways.'

Ramin watched in horror as he realised he had just volunteered his friends to go and fight the gods.

'I should be with them.' He made to leave, but Asha stopped him.

'No. Just as your friends will be helping my custodians, you will be helping me. You are staying put and that is an order.'

'Ma'am, if Neith were to get hurt—'

'Stay with me and watch over her from up here. She has Julius by her side. They have each other's backs. Now you need to make sure that you have theirs.'

Ramin paused. When Giovanetti and Sam had first approached him to develop new collaborative working patterns, he had been thinking along the lines of days out and dinner swaps. A large-scale movement of people caught his eyes.

'What's happening in yellow quadrant? Why are the people running?'

'It appears to be—' She broke off in wonder. 'Good grief, it's a dog with three heads. I think after today, I will be drinking the bar dry.'

'You and me both. Hang on, I have an idea,' said Ramin, grinning. 'Where is that man with a lion's head?'

'He was last seen in Pyg's Bar buying drinks for everyone that hadn't fainted.'

Rami watched the screen; a devious smile crossed his face. 'With your permission?' Asha waved her hand towards the unit, and he pressed the toggle.

'Unit three. Split your team. Get one half to tempt the lion man out of Pyg's and onto the street. Get the other half to engage the three-headed dog.' He paused, listening to the reply. 'I don't know. Sausages? Get him to follow you onto Pythagoras Avenue. Once our cohort is reunited, and both creatures can see each other, get out of there as fast as you can.'

'What do you have in mind?' asked Asha.

'An experiment. Let's see what a dirty great big dog does when he sees an even bigger cat.'

Within minutes the two had been lured onto the avenue. As they saw each other, they leapt forward. Claws and teeth engaged as they ploughed into the front of a café. The window shattered around them, and citizens ran out of the café screaming.

'Not a perfect situation.'

'No, but at least no one is getting killed.'

Day Three - Julius

I was running along the street beside Neith. We had been teamed with a cohort of red custodians, and I was happy to see a face I recognised. Luisa Githumbi was the Chief Red Custodian and had saved my skin during the raid at Soliman Alvarez's place. Luisa and Neith nodded at each other, and I got the impression that Luisa had specifically asked for Neith for her detail. Now we were trying to evacuate a group of citizens who were currently being terrorised by a single woman.

'Apparently, it's a snake issue,' said Luisa to Neith.

'What?' asked Neith. 'Has she graffitied them to the spot?'

We had all heard the earlier reports of the snake with the spray cans, and whilst graffiti wasn't the best thing in the world, it certainly shouldn't be terrorising a bunch of adults.

'No,' replied Luisa. 'It's a normal woman, but her hair is made of snakes. What kind of a splice is that?'

'Not one I've heard of,' said Neith. 'Do you think these creature-people have come through the stepper spliced?'

'That's HQ's current hypothesis.'

'Right,' said Neith. 'They are probably feeling nauseous with a headache. We can use that.'

I had been quiet as the two women discussed tactics. I hated to interrupt, knowing I was the least important person in the squad in terms of combat readiness, but I really needed to find out about the snake hair.

'How are the citizens being detained?'

'Ossification, apparently.'

'Ossif– do you mean turned to stone?'

'Yes.'

I roared at the cohort to halt. Luisa clenched her jaw, but she had been briefed to take advice from curators, no matter how dishonourable it seemed. Not running to save civilians seemed pretty dishonourable indeed.

Relieved I had their attention, I brought them up to speed. 'She's not a spliced individual suffering from a recent ordeal. She's Medusa, and she is probably having the time of her life. Or she is utterly enraged. Either way, you must not engage directly. If she makes eye contact with you, you will turn to stone.'

Luisa had stopped scowling at me and was now glaring in open hostility. I could see she wanted to protest. She was not trained to engage in make-believe. But she was the best custodian there was because she knew how to adapt.

'Cohort visors on. Black mode. Guide civilians to a place of safety. Do not engage with the Medusa. Also, avoid her eyes. The infrared visor should be fine, but let's not push our luck.'

As we rounded the corner, I watched in awe as a woman was sharing a bottle of wine with a satyr. The satyr was a dumpy little fellow, about three foot tall, standing on goat legs with a hairy torso, heavy beard and two small horns. Even from where I was standing, the stench of sweat prickled my nostrils. Medusa seemed unaffected by the smell. She was taller than him, but still short, maybe a little over five foot, in a white Greek pleated gown. The dress was sleeveless, and Medusa's arms were adorned with golden bangles that rattled as she waved the bottle of wine about. Around her head swayed the snakes, each reptile moving independently of its companion and looking around the courtyard. A long red and yellow striped snake coiled itself around her neck like a choker. Its tongue darted in and out as it smelt the air around it.

As we arrived, she turned to look at us and I nearly wet myself. This was Medusa, to make eye contact with her was certain death. Instead, I looked at the group of crying citizens. One of the women was trying to shake a statue, tears running down her face as she sobbed and called out a man's name.

The group saw the custodians and started to run towards us. We shouted at them, warning them to avoid eye contact as they stumbled around the overturned tables and chairs.

As they ran Medusa called out and one of the men stopped. I shouted at him to keep running but even I found her voice compelling. In fact she sounded sad. She was so lonely. She didn't mean to hurt anyone. She just wanted company. Intelligent company. A handsome companion. I felt sorry for her. Hanging around with a smelly goat was no life for her. A woman like her deserved better company. Talking to her wouldn't hurt. All you had to do was avoid her eyes.

I took a step towards her and was surprised when Neith kicked me very hard on the back of my calf. I stumbled and as I swore, I momentarily stopped listening to Medusa. It was like a pail of icy water being dumped over my head.

'Helmets on everyone. Block all external audio.'

Luisa's instructions brought me to my senses, and we quickly guided the crowd towards us. The man who had stopped to listen to Medusa was now walking towards her, his face down. As he got closer to her I saw him turn to look at us and laugh and then he turned back to Medusa. He was within reach of the snakes now, but he showed no fear. He held out his hand in wonder as they all reached out towards him, their tongues darting in and out.

Medusa's head was bowed but she was still talking. The man was replying and laughing. From his posture, I guessed he was boasting.

'Julius,' said Luisa, through my earpiece. 'Are you certain she's dangerous? I'm still listening to her. She's giggling for heaven's sake. That buffoon is boasting about how fast he can run a mile. I'm not convinced she's anything other than a good time girl; simpering on the side of the varsity matches.'

Medusa. A good time girl. I was dumbfounded. As I tried to formulate a reply, she held out her hand and the man briefly allowed her to touch him. He flinched and then laughed when nothing happened. She put her hands on her hips and shook her head, as if to say *see, I'm completely harmless*. In horror, I watched as he reached out and cupped her chin tilting her face up to him.

I yelled a warning, but he didn't hear me. She gazed up into his eyes and he smiled adoringly back at her as her snakes writhed around her head. And then his face began to crack. We watched his skin become tight and then brittle. He was still smiling but now he was still as his entire body became stone. A flaky limestone statue dressed in a pair of red shorts and a pale blue polo shirt.

Medusa laughed and sat back down, resuming her conversation with the satyr.

'Shit,' said Neith. Which summed up how we were all feeling. We had just watched a man almost willingly walk towards his own death. Dear God, the statue's smile was dreadful. I shuddered and reminded myself to buy Neith a very large drink later on.

Luisa called across to me. 'Is the goat a threat?'

How did I know? There were mythological creatures and gods here that I had never even heard of. I was reminded of open house parties at a student dorm, where a mass invite had been sent out. Suddenly the place was heaving with revellers all intent on having a great time with no care for the host.

'I don't think so. Also, it's a satyr.'

132

Her expression as she glared at me was priceless, and I was reminded that we were operating very much on a need-to-know basis. Pulling out her laser-powered baton, she approached Medusa.

'Medusa! Stop and leave.'

Bemused, the gorgon began to make small talk. Whilst the two women were engaged, Neith and the custodians guided the shaking citizens to a side street. I was hanging back, keeping an eye on the satyr and trying to offer Luisa cover. Whispering instruction to Tiresias, I told him to let me listen to their conversation. If he thought Medusa was talking to me or I was responding to her voice he was to cut off comms and administer a small shock to me through my suit. Hoping I was properly safeguarded I began to listen to Medusa's beautiful voice.

'And you are in charge? All these men do as you tell them?'

'Violation three. Subsection forty-two. I am arresting you for knowingly bringing harm to another individual.'

'But he asked for it.' Medusa sounded confused and a little hurt. 'Luisa, you are too good for this nonsense. Here—' she poured a glass of wine '— join me in a drink. I miss female company. Men are so boring and boastful. It's been years since I've had a good old-fashioned girly natter.'

'If you refuse to come willingly, I will detain you forcibly and this will be noted on the charge sheet.'

Medusa took a sip of wine and held the glass out. I realised I was very thirsty and took a step forward when my helmet filled with a deafening roar of bagpipes and I recoiled, all exterior sound switched off.

'Julius! What in the name of sweet Bast are you doing?' snapped Neith. 'Focus. Can we save the stone ones?'

I was panting. That was close.

'Maybe. But only if we cut off her head. I'm not sure if that always works.'

Luisa didn't need to hear that twice. She had been playing along with Medusa's questions, trying not to pay attention to the level of seduction in her voice. She wanted so desperately to have a peek at the beautiful snake lady's eyes. A tiny glimpse couldn't hurt? Thankfully, whilst she was listening to Medusa's soft beguiling words, she could also hear the coarser tones of Julius Strathclyde. Flicking a toggle on her laser, she turned away from Medusa, swung back and, without warning, lopped Medusa's head clean off her shoulders.

There was a moment of stunned silence as Medusa's dulcet tones fell quiet, then her head landed with a thump on the polished marble floor of the plaza. The satyr walked over to the head, swigging a bottle of wine, then started to kick the head down the street.

The team stared at the statues, desperately willing them back to life. When it was clear they were not going to revert, Luisa ordered that they be carefully removed to the infirmary in case something could be done for them.

'Well, at least she can't harm anyone else,' said Neith still in awe of Luisa's brutal beheading.

'Not true, I'm afraid. You need to recover her head. Her eyes can still turn people to stone.'

Luisa looked at me in horror. 'But she's dead.'

'Even so.'

'That's preposterous. Her head has been removed from her body.' Luisa was almost pleading with me. This wasn't how a battle was supposed to take place. You crushed your opponent with overwhelming force, then sent their family a bill for damages. You did not go running down the street after a drunken goat playing football with a woman's head covered in snakes.

'Julius, go get the head. Bag it up and for god's sake don't look at the eyes.'

Day Three - Julius

'Julius. Are you drunk?' Neith peered into my face and reeled back. 'You smell of booze and goat.'

'His name is William,' I said importantly. 'We got chatting. Said I owed him a drink if I wanted Medusa's head. To tell you the truth he was a bit miffed that Luisa had lopped his friend's head off.'

'Billy the Goat?' Neith looked astonished and perplexingly, very angry.

'Yes. Bloody good bloke actually. We were having a great chat about Dionysus. You would not believe the tales he had on that god! Wowee.'

I shook my head and remembered the sack in my hand. I waved it at Neith. 'Sorry, forgot this. One head in a sack. Snakes dead. Eyes still very much alive.' I giggled. I didn't mean to, but it was funny. Neith was now tapping her foot.

'Luisa.' I watched confused as she called out to Githumbi, woman of the hour, slayer of gorgons and all-round good egg. 'Can you override Julius' suit consent functions and administer a restorative? My brace is recharging.'

The two women looked at me. They appeared to be swaying which was funny because I didn't remember getting on a boat.

A second later I felt a flush tingle through my limbs and an overwhelming desire to throw up. Clasping my hand over my mouth I ran to the loos. A few minutes later I returned and sheepishly handed Medusa's sack over to the curators who placed it quickly into a solid metal container.

Neith and Luisa appeared to have forgiven me as I sat at the table and grabbed some food.

'I-'

'Forget it, Strathclyde. You got the head. That's all that matters.'

I tore off a bit of pitta bread and dunked it in the hummus. I was embarrassed that I had got drunk whilst on service and wanted to do better in their eyes. We'd be on the streets again in a minute, but Luisa wanted all cohorts properly rested. This battle was alarming more than it was lethal, and she wanted to pace her troops.

My brace vibrated with the next general set of briefings. 'No one is to use hovercars. Some guy is shooting them out of the sky with lightning bolts.'

I leant across and signalled to Luisa.

'Make sure no one engages with the lightning thrower. I suspect it's Thor or Zeus. If they are here, they are dangerous and highly volatile. They need to be left alone.'

'How do you know all this?' asked Luisa

'How do you not?'

'Because we didn't take a degree studying this stuff,' snapped Neith.

'Every five-year-old back home knows *this stuff.*' I was embarrassed to say that I also snapped in reply. The things

I was witnessing were making my head spin. My entire postgraduate thesis was an utter farce after what I had witnessed today, and I wasn't handling things well.

'Julius, Neith. Engage.' Luisa was listening to a report and signalled me. 'Julius, we have a group trapped by a flock of magpies. Any suggestions?'

I ran through some ideas. 'Tell them to curtsey. Lots of good manners, that sort of thing.'

I watched as Luisa relayed my message in bemusement. It worked. The birds flew off. While she had been talking, I had an idea and spoke into my wrist brace for a few minutes testing out a theory. I stood up.

'Hello, everyone.' I felt silly making a public speech, but this hopefully would work. 'Tiresias knows what to do. I've just been interrogating the database. Alert every citizen to describe whatever they are seeing to Tiresias. It will be able to suggest ways to placate the anomaly. But be sure to ask it to look up Beta mythology and folklore.'

Soon, reports were coming in that some attempts were working on the smaller infractions.

***

'Why are we going this way?' asked Neith, as Luisa turned right at the next intersection. Instead of heading back to the custodians' HQ, we were running towards the waterfront.

'Davit Plaza is blocked.'

'Dare I ask?' said Neith and shook her head in wonder as Luisa replied there were reports of very heavy golden rain falling in just that section.

'Oh, that should be avoided at all costs,' I warned.

'Is it poisonous?'

'No, but it might make you pregnant.'

Four startled females all stared at me. I squirmed and felt a blush prickling my neck. 'I don't know. It could be something else. But there's a god called Zeus that likes to inseminate women in showers of golden rain.'

One of the women was standing in a puddle. She very quickly stepped to one side. Her companion, curiously, didn't. I made a note of her name, the last thing this civilisation needed in nine months' time was an influx of demi-god babies. God only knew if anything could be done about it, but it was best to be prepared. Not everyone appreciated babies with divine abilities. Especially this society. I followed Luisa as we headed towards a group of tourists trapped sheltering in a food kiosk near the seafront.

A man was sat on a park bench with a gaping wound in his side. It didn't seem to be causing him any distress. In fact, he was pulling bits out of his body and throwing them at the tourists. As the body parts hit the kiosk, the blood splattered across the window. Inside, the tourists could be heard screaming. But, apart from being terrified, I didn't think they were in serious danger.

I didn't recognise the god or creature but being able to pluck away at your entrails wasn't a local talent.

As we arrived, we were aware of another group of people off to one side. Bizarrely, they appeared to be taking notes. We ran towards them, shouting at them to take cover. Our initial assessment of Medusa had completely underestimated her threat level. We were not going to make the same mistake again.

'Citizens, leave now. We don't know how safe this area is.'

One of the four turned and looked at us. One sighed, two looked bored and one looked annoyed.

'Captain Githumbi. We are engineers and we are studying the anomalies. We have been making good progress across the city, testing our hypothesis. Watch.'

The engineer who had sighed dismissively when we arrived now walked calmly towards the man with the hole in his side. She was an older lady and had pink hair tied back in a plait that hung to her waist. She was wearing a rara skirt and wellies. I swear engineers get dressed in the dark. In fact, they were all wearing wellies.

As we watched, she started to make copious notes. The man began throwing entrails at her. Within minutes she was covered in blood, but she kept on typing as though nothing was happening. I watched in morbid fascination as he started to shout at her and noticed that, for a brief second, he disappeared. His shouting increased, and suddenly her hair shot up in flames, the blaze growing to engulf her head before she fell to the ground. She screamed and writhed on the ground, her skin igniting from within and as her scream trailed off her body stopped shuddering and a smell of burnt flesh drifted towards us on the sea breeze.

Neith was talking furiously in Welsh and repeatedly making the sign of the cross. I grabbed her hand and gave her a quick hug as much to console her as myself. We had all been in combat situations but few of us had witnessed anything quite so brutal or spontaneous. Two of the engineers threw up, their vomit splashing on their boots.

The people in the kiosk were screaming even louder now as the man returned his attention to them and continued to pelt them with body parts.

Luisa and her custodians all fired at the man, but the laser fire just seemed to fizzle away as it touched him.

The engineers strode forward together, walking towards their fallen comrade.

'Get back, you fools,' shouted Luisa as she ran towards them.

The engineer who had first spoken to us paused as the three of them turned and sneered at Luisa. They were pale and shaking but their chins were high.

'This is our battlefield and our fallen comrade. We will retrieve her when we have completed our experiments, and you will not stop us.'

'Sodding idiots.' Luisa marched back to us and instructed the custodians to be ready to engage physically if the man tried to set anyone on fire again. She stabbed at her brace.

'Giovanetti, did you know we have engineers all across the city running experiments? They claim they are finding ways to beat some of the anomalies. We've just witnessed one being burnt alive.'

We watched as the three of them approached their companion and walked past her, not even looking in her direction. Like her, they continued taking notes and readings as they approached the man. Once again, he started shouting at them. His annoyance as they ignored him was clear, and I winced, ready to see them all burn. I wasn't the only one. We all braced, and I could see Neith watching the scene with her head slightly tilted away.

Suddenly, I remembered who it was. Or, at least, who it could be.

'It's Prometheus,' I shouted across to them. 'Leave him alone and it will be fine.'

As I called out, I saw him smile. He stopped shouting as he threw some liver our way. A splat of flesh slapped me on the side of the neck.

'Well done, Strathclyde,' said Luisa, making me wince. An hour before I'd been desperate to redeem myself after the Medusa incident. Now it just felt hollow. 'Draw his attention from the engineers. Everyone call out his name. Let's divert his attention. And get those tourists out of there.'

One of the custodians sprinted over to the kiosk, and ran with the tourists, guiding them along the seafront away from this shitshow where ancient Titans were setting people on fire. Prometheus was now happily pelting us with blood scraps and, while not terrifying, it was pretty unpleasant. The engineers jogged back to us, looking furious.

'You bloody fool.'

I have to admit I was a trifle put out. I had just saved them from incineration. Did the engineers have a death wish?

'We nearly got rid of it.'

'What?' I said incredulously. 'You were about to be burnt alive.'

'No, we weren't. We were about to delete the anomaly. Did none of you observe how it wavered when Pi-564 had been analysing it? Are you lemurs really that dumb?'

I knew he meant I was the lemur, but the rest of the squad stiffened their backs. This was a new insult to me. One evolutionary step down from a monkey? One to think about later. For now, I needed to focus.

'I did see him disappear,' I said thoughtfully.

'Then why did you give it a name and acknowledge it? You instantly strengthened it. You have observed it and given it mass,' hissed the enraged engineer.

'You were observing him too.'

'No. We were studying a phenomenon.'

The rain of body parts was getting heavier.

143

'See, it's loving the attention.' The engineer had now decided I was beneath contempt and started speaking to Luisa. 'Captain. We want to try again. Can you all promise to stand back? And it would be best if you all looked away. Put your fingers in your ears as well.'

'How will we know when to turn round?'

'I'll tap you on the shoulder.'

'And if you don't?'

'Well, then you'll probably be able to smell us.'

Luisa spoke to Giovanetti via the wrist brace, then called the cohort to attention.

'We have our orders. Do as the engineers request.'

With one final glare in my direction, the three walked back towards the man and we turned our backs on them.

'Captain, this is wrong,' muttered one of the custodians.

'Agreed. But Giovanetti says we are trying out some new thinking. Just like having the curators with us, now, apparently, we are going to listen to the engineers on a battlefield.'

The derision in her voice was blatant, but she turned and instructed us all to engage our suits and lock into a partial sensory deprivation. All senses off, except for touch. And smell.

I stood in silence and tried to focus on the time I bought my first single by Blur. I'd played it repeatedly and tried to style my hair like Alex James. All had gone well or so I thought until—

Someone tapped me on my shoulder, and I disengaged my suit.

Looking round, the three engineers stood smiling at us. There was no evidence of blood on them or on us. The man was gone, but sadly the body of the pink, now blackened, woman remained on the floor.

'That took a little longer than we had hoped but the hypothesis held.'

'If the blood has gone, why is your colleague still dead?' asked Neith.

'We don't know. But we can see the kiosk still has broken windows, although the body parts have gone.'

'Could it be,' suggested Neith, 'that anything emanating from the anomaly disappeared at the same time, but for anything here that interacted with it, the results still stand? Something dented the cabin and, while the something has gone, the dent remains.'

The engineers nodded their heads.

'Agreed, that's a hypothesis that has merit.'

'Have you any advice or conclusions?' asked Luisa, eager to be able to put any field knowledge into action.

The engineers looked at her, appalled.

'We are still gathering data!'

Luisa ran her fingers through her hair in exasperation. 'This isn't a science experiment. This is happening in real time. Tell me how you got rid of the threat.'

'We just didn't believe in it.'

'But he was standing in front of you,' protested Luisa.

'Engineers know better than to believe what they can see,' replied the lead engineer tartly. 'Curators know this as well.'

Neith nodded. 'They're not wrong, butt. Your senses can be terribly unreliable.'

I liked it when Neith said "butt", it reminded me of my nanny. I smiled at the sudden head spin. Here I stood on a foreign Earth being lectured to by scientists about my reckless behaviour, whilst Neith's splice reminded me of a safer, simpler lifetime.

Day Three - Julius

'How long will this go on for?' asked Luisa.

'Loki and Anansi said they wanted us all to believe. So, I guess until enough of the population has been terrified,' replied Neith.

'Surely, the best thing would be one massive event in that case?' queried Luisa. 'Not all these small incursions.'

At that moment, everyone's wrist braces vibrated and flashed red. Giovannetti's voice called across the devices.

'All civilians away from the harbour. Everyone else, get down there now!'

We began to run towards the docks as Neith patched through to Ramin.

'He says an octopus is attacking the lighthouse.'

Luisa looked over her shoulder. 'An octopus?'

'A big one, apparently.'

A shadow passed over our heads as we watched the Lighthouse of Alexandria cross the skyline, it was in the grip of a gigantic tentacle. As it waved in the sky, the tentacle unfurled and flung the eighty-foot building inland towards the fields of wheat beyond the city.

Hordes of people were screaming and running past us as we pushed our way onto the harbourside. Boats lay crushed on their moorings or swept up on the roadside. Broken timber lay everywhere, sails flapped sluggishly as they lay on the ground. In the centre of the harbour, a mass of tentacles and eyes pulled itself out of the water.

147

'Retreat,' bellowed Luisa.

'Nubi's balls, Julius. What is that?' screamed Neith.

'I think it's an elder god. I'm trying to see if it has wings.' I shouted back at her.

'How do we defeat an elder god?'

'No idea. I haven't studied them much.'

'What does it want?'

'Live sacrifices, I think? I don't know. But I don't think they're benign.' I paused and examined the creature. 'Phew, we got lucky, it's just the kraken.'

Neith looked at me in horror. In fairness it was hard to imagine that anything might be worse than what was hauling itself out of the water. Above the screams from the harbour, a deep wail began. At first, I thought it was from the creature, then I realised it was a siren.

'What's that?'

'It's the long wave warning. Although, we tend to use it for sandstorms.'

Giovannetti's voice rang out from the loudspeakers above the wail and through our wrist braces.

'Everyone take shelter. EVERYONE. Close your eyes, block your ears. If you have access to sedation, sedate for eight hours. Repeat. Stay in shelter for eight hours. Sedate if possible. The siren will stop when the danger has passed. Everyone get to shelter and sleep. Ignore any anomaly. Do not engage. Shelter and sleep. All citizens. Curators, engineers, custodians. Shelter and sleep.'

Her voice stopped broadcasting as the siren continued. And then her message began again on a loop.

The entire population was in retreat, stumbling over each other and fallen masonry in their flight away from the harbour. Gods and beasts were chasing them along the street, adding to the chaos, their laughter rising above the screams.

We ran back to the accommodation blocks. Neith grabbed some tourists and told them to follow her. I did the same, as did the custodians. These tourists had nowhere to go. As we ran, I saw people clambering over broken windows, finding places to hide under tables and counters.

Neith split off down the boulevard towards her flat with her tourists, saluting me as she left. Her face was determined, and I knew she would get them all to safety.

I turned to my group to reassure them that we were nearly at my place when the older of the two men took one look at my eyes and yelped.

I looked over my shoulder in alarm and then realised it was me he was yelling at.

'Sir, I'm Curator Strathclyde. You are safe with me.'

A woman stepped up to her husband's side, clutching his arm.

'Get away from him, Joe. He's that filthy angel. He's probably in league with these monsters.'

The man squared his shoulder. 'It's alright, beloved. Stay back, he might be dangerous.'

I looked at them in bewilderment. 'I am not dangerous. I'm trying to help you.'

'Don't listen to him, Joe. He's a monster. You're disgusting, you are,' she shouted at me. The siren continued to wail over our heads. I was getting angry now. These stupid people with their ridiculous fear of me were beyond the pale. That they couldn't distinguish between me and a mythological nightmare was the final straw.

'Look, madam-'

'Madam?! What's that then? Joe, he's saying weird words. He wants to kill us!' she appealed to her companions who were all panicking now and looking at me in terror.

'Honoured citizens, I-' Which is when Joe punched me clean in the face.

I sat on the floor where I had fallen and watched as the small group ran away. I checked my nose, then lay back on the marble pavement, looking up at the blue skies. A group of Valkyries flew past in pursuit of some harpies.

I swore in anger, then winced. My nose hurt. This world was mad, and I wanted to go home.

A wet nose nudged my hand, and I looked up into the coal red eyes of Black Shuck.

'Good doggy.'

I was too angry and too sad to be scared. A demonic dog was licking my face. Why not? I noticed a melon by my hand. A fruit and veg stand was shattered, its goods scattered across the street. Pulling myself up slowly, I picked up the melon and waved it at the mighty hellhound. He wagged his tail.

Which is how we headed home, me throwing the fruit as a ball for the dark shadowy dog. The sirens wailed, and the kraken clambered over the harbour buildings until we made it back to my apartment. Shuck lay down at the foot of my bed, and I had to nudge him a few times as he sprawled across the sheets until we were both comfortable. Taking a sedative, I fell asleep.

Day Four - Julius

I woke in silence with a strange sense of loss. Shuck's comforting presence against my leg had finally gone. Despite the sedative, I had slept badly. The siren kept permeating my mind, and I dreamt of bombs falling, and women looking for lost children amongst the broken masonry. Each time, I would be standing across the road unable to reach them. The rubble I was standing on would begin to shift and slide and, as I looked down, the stones morphed into bones, and I began to sink into them. I would wake up screaming and clutching the covers and then Shuck would be there nudging me with his wet nose and giving a little concerned whine until I calmed down enough for sleep to claim me again.

Now, in the morning sunlight, the siren, the nightmares, and the dog had gone. I felt alone.

Yesterday had been a life changing day, and I knew it was going to take me a long time to think it through. I reached over for my brace. The instant I activated it, a series of alerts and alarms told me my presence was required at a full emergency meeting at noon. Was I about to be reprimanded for shouting out Prometheus's name?

A shower was needed, followed by a decent breakfast. I wanted to track Neith down and check she'd made it home alright. My nose was still sore, and I noticed the man's ring had cut me under the eye. Cleaning up, I was tempted to blow off the meeting. I was sick and tired of these people and couldn't trust myself not to lose my temper. I didn't feel ready to explain myself, given that for the second time in a year, my world had turned upside down.

My door chimed, which was an unusual courtesy. Fellow custodians normally banged on the door. Maybe this morning no one wanted any more loud noises or sudden surprises? Opening the door, I saw Neith looking shattered but smiling weakly, and I suddenly realised how much she meant to me.

'You are a sight for sore eyes,' I said, pulling her in for a big hug. We stood and just held each other for a few seconds before each gave an embarrassed laugh. Yesterday had been hell, but there was no need to go overboard.

'Whereas you seem to be a sore eyed sight,' joked Neith.

I groaned. It was a rubbish pun, but at least worthy of acknowledgement.

'Which monster gave you that?'

'Just a regular Alpha citizen, who took one look at my eyes and decided I was either a monster or he knew who I was, but considered me a monster, anyway. Whatever. He lamped me and then he and his family ran off in another direction.'

'What an idiot,' said Neith. 'Although, in the circumstances, I suppose it was understandable.'

153

'I was trying to get him and his family to shelter.' Personally, I didn't see anything understandable about it at all.

'Keep your hair on. The world had gone mad. Their judgement was clouded.'

Her Welsh accent was strong today, which was always a sure sign of stress. I saw her wince. Her mood would not be improved by this splice side-effect manifesting now. I went to close the door behind us and, maybe because I had just been thinking of Shuck, I patted my leg and called him to me.

Nothing happened, but Neith looked at me curiously.

'What are you doing?'

I was embarrassed. It had been instinctive, and now I was left looking like an idiot as I explained what had happened after I had been punched.

'So, let me get this right. After we had all been explicitly told to take shelter and sedate ourselves, you brought home a demon dog and let it sleep on your bed?'

Neith's voice was rising. My room opened onto an open corridor overlooking the food plaza. A few alarmed faces whipped their heads around and looked up. The population was very jumpy. I tried to calm her down.

'I don't think this Shuck was the portent-of-doom version. I think he's the saves-weary-souls variety. I guess we'll find out in a year.'

'A year?' Neith's voice was incredulous but quiet as we left the accommodation block and headed towards the food quadrant.

'Yes. If I die, we'll know it was the portent-of-doom version.'

'If you die within the next year, it will be because I've sodding killed you,' hissed Neith. 'What were you thinking?'

'I was thinking that my face hurt, that I don't belong here, and that apparently in your stupid world the gods are real, and no one thought to tell me.'

Neith stepped back and honestly, I thought she was about to punch me as well.

'Now you listen to me. The gods are not real, and they don't exist.' She took a deep breath. 'We are going to have breakfast, make up, and go to work. Is that clear?'

I glared at her for a nanosecond and decided not to be an arse. We headed down to the plaza although there wasn't much in the way of breakfast. No one was cooking this morning, so we just grabbed some pre-packed pots and rations.

There were a few people around, but the quadrant was unusually quiet. Initially, I thought we were being avoided, but I realised pretty much everyone was sitting in stunned silence.

'This is shell shock. They need to get busy.'

'They need to talk to a counsellor,' replied Neith.

'Do you think the counsellors are any less shocked?'

Neith tore open a packet of nuts and started to eat them slowly. Rubbing them between her fingers she removed the thin brown husks, as she looked around the space.

'No, I suppose not. But you're right. We at least, can get busy. Come on, we have a meeting to attend.'

Neith stood up and called out. 'Citizens. Yesterday was dreadful. Today is not. There are street crews out there cleaning up the debris, go and help them. Go get busy. The rest will follow.'

I raised my eyebrow. 'Custodian Salah, is it?'

'What you said, got me thinking. The people need to do something. I'm worried about what too much introspection will bring. We've already had reports of multiple suicides overnight. I suspect there will be more to come.'

I watched as she picked up a fallen chair and tucked it under the table. She tried to move a fallen awning. I could see it was too heavy even for both of us to move but she was trying, nonetheless. She stumbled and fell.

'Stupid piece of crap.' She kicked the blue trimmed sail and started crying. Ugly sobbing tears. Genetically, I was incapable of dealing with tears, but I cautiously walked over to the awning and stood alongside Neith, looking down at it.

'Stupid awning.' I kicked the sheet of fabric. Bending over I pulled up a section of it and slapped it. 'Bad awning. Why are you on the floor? Get up, you lazy sail.'

I looked over at Neith who was wiping her face. 'Is this a dereliction of duty, or turning up for work in inappropriate attire?'

She sniffed. 'Disorderly conduct I'd say.'

'Punishment?'

She looked at me and grinned weakly as she stood up and tucked her hair behind her ears and wiped her eyes again.

'First offence just a warning. Repeat offender, cut up and used as napkins.'

'Very good Curator Salah.' I kicked the awning again. 'Boulevard awning. Next time, it's napkins for you.' I waved my finger at the fallen tarpaulin and Neith laughed.

'Come on sand brain. Let's get to the meeting.'

For a while we linked arms and I'm not sure who was comforting who. I thought I was helping her, but I realised that just being with her and seeing this devastation through her eyes I could feel my anger ebb away.

As we walked along, I began to see more of the damage for myself. Smoke was rising from a fire that had run unchecked through a retail sector. The automatic extinguishers could only do so much without a ground crew beating back the flames.

Teams were sweeping broken glass into the street. Another crew was collecting the glass and loading it into refuse machines. As soon as the street was mostly clear, a second machine came through, blowing air ahead of it.

Two rotating brushes picked up anything larger and whisked the debris into a hopper.

'We usually only see them during sandstorms,' said Neith as she watched it pass us. 'Good to see someone using their initiative.'

We weren't making much progress. Neith was stopping at every crew and thanking them, asking their names, telling them hers, chatting about where they went to school, who their favourite team was. She swapped recipes and top tips for restaurants in Cairo. All the way along she smiled, patted shoulders, and made jokes. None of her previous anguish was now on show. Now she was in full troop-rallying mode. I wore my sunglasses and kept back. People looked at her and smiled. They looked at me and frowned. Neith was trying to raise the morale. I was bringing it down.

'How long have you been up?' I asked as she retrieved her jacket from a café that she must have left earlier in the morning.

'I got up when the sirens stopped.'

'You were awake?'

'Yes.'

'So, you didn't sedate yourself?'

'No, someone needed to stay alert.'

'You weren't worried that thinking about them might keep them here?'

'No more so than letting one of them sleep on my bed,' she said, somewhat sharply.

I decided to change the subject. 'You mentioned lots of suicides?'

She stopped and looked at me. I didn't understand her confusion.

'The suicides. Why?'

'Julius. I'm speechless. Why do you think? I'm barely holding it together myself.'

I paused. Had something else happened? I was missing something, but I didn't know what. Seeing the naked distress on Neith's face, I wasn't sure how to proceed.

'Stop a minute. I don't understand.' This planet had a very different attitude towards death. Clearly they had no associated superstitions or taboos around it and they certainly didn't believe in prolonging a life in pain, but they didn't embrace death. They believed in a life well lived. Making the most of every day.

'Why would last night's incidents cause people to take their own lives?'

Tears welled in Neith's eyes. 'Julius, please do not say anything that crass in public. I get that yesterday wasn't a big deal for you. But, for us?' She paused and looked around at the debris and shambolic scenes. 'Yesterday, our world fell apart. You have no idea how we are coping. Or not. If citizens have decided that they no longer want to live in this world of uncertainty, who can blame them?'

She walked on, and I just stared after her in amazement. Had she really just ignored the fact that less than a year ago I had been dragged through to a parallel universe? It wasn't one night of debauchery and violence, but a one-way ticket to a new world surrounded by strangers, many of whom wanted me dead.

Neith looked back, and clearly my expression said everything I was thinking.

'It's not the same as what you went through, Julius.'

'No, it's bloody well not. I was alone. You all have each other. And you also still have your homes, your work. You still have your bloody planet.'

'But, Julius, yesterday we discovered that we may be wrong about the concept of gods! We built our entire civilisation on that premise. That we were in charge.'

'And now you're no better than the Beta lemurs? In fact, those knuckle-dragging monkeys might know more than you do?' I wasn't angry, I was exhausted. 'You know, whatever we saw yesterday has shocked me to the core as well. Remember, this is my field of study back home. I give lectures on this stuff, but I'm not dealing in realities. I'm talking about belief systems. Yesterday—' I ran out of steam. 'What the hell was that?' I ended wearily.

I ran my hand through my hair, pausing to shake out some bits of debris. This wasn't helping, and Neith was right in one aspect. This was easier for me because I had already dealt with a mind-blowing event. And survived. These guys were trying to cope with the same thing I had, and I felt sorry for them. Whatever the gods or anomalies were, we wouldn't find out by arguing with each other on the street. Lapsing into a difficult silence, we headed towards the civic buildings.

Day Four - Julius

We walked into the council chambers in a subdued mood, which was matched by the individuals within the room. A team of eight red custodians stood at the chamber doors, and we had to be swiped in. It was the most overt security I had seen here, excluding the raid on Alvarez's house. It was a circular chamber with benches around the perimeter and a central atrium. The walls were glossy white, with air con slots, the benches were made of a dark polished wood and the floor had the standard power points for hologram projections. It looked like every council office I had ever been in except this one looked like it had been designed by Luc Besson.

'Why are there so few people?' I whispered.

'This is an emergency session. Once we've got a proper handle on what happened last night the inner chamber will let the larger council know what the plan is.'

Neith left my side and started shaking hands with a few people. Like others in the room their conversations were subdued. There were a lot of faces here that I didn't recognise, and I helped myself to a glass of water. Standing around in chambers with a bunch of strangers, discussing things I had no knowledge of, always filled me with dread. I would far rather be out on the Fens wandering around under the enormous Cambridgeshire skies, or tucked away in a corner of the library, chasing down a footnote. I shook my head; these moments of homesickness came and went. I was about to head over and join Rami when Neith returned and tapped me on the arm. We headed over to sit with Sam.

'Why's Rami with Asha?'

Neith looked across the room and gave him a small wave as the custodians started to take their seats.

'The seating is arranged by departments. Rami was working with the custodians last night so any report he will give will be under their aegis.'

That made sense. I scanned the room, checking off the departments I recognised. Minju was sat to one side with a few faces that were unfamiliar, no doubt fellow archivists all huddled together whispering and looking around nervously. I nodded in her direction, and she gave me a small smile of recognition, but nothing beyond that. Asha's husband, Haru Giovanetti, was here in his capacity as head of medicine. People were gravitating towards him appreciating his confidence and easy-going manner. Reassured, they would peel away again into their own little clusters.

Spotting the engineers, I quickly looked away. I had recognised First and Second Engineer, surrounded by colleagues, although I couldn't see Jack. Each clique was muttering and looking over their shoulders. Every new arrival was watched and then discussed.

'Who's that bunch over there,' I asked, pointing to a sour faced group that were currently giving me the evils.

163

'Civil Affairs,' muttered Neith. 'Bunch of jumped-up, interfering dogsbodies.'

'How come I've not come across them before?'

'They have no oversight into the mouseion or the quantum stepper. Drives them ape. In other cities they have far more influence but not in Alexandria. In fact, I'm surprised they are here at all.'

'A lot of the city was busted up last night?'

Neith nodded and we headed over to join the other curators, I was glad to see Stef stand up and come over and hug me. Even Sabrina looked pleased to see me.

A few more stragglers came in, and then the doors were closed. The atmosphere became even more hushed and oppressive.

The pharaoh stood up and addressed the room. He had been hurriedly voted in after the Alvarez scandal, when it was revealed that the previous pharaoh was up to his armpits in the corruption. This new one laughed a lot, and people took comfort from his relaxed and friendly manner. Whether he was any good was yet to be determined.

'We have many questions, but before answers must come data. Each section head will report. Haru Giovanetti.'

Haru stood up and small hologram projections popped up in front of us to illustrate his statistics. I took my notepad out and started writing. This attracted a few nudges from those who weren't used to this "affectation" of mine. I knew that all information was already downloaded to my personal files, but I liked to handwrite stuff. It went into my brain better. Another black mark against me.

As I jotted things down, Haru went on to describe the casualties.

'Given the number of events yesterday we have surprisingly few deaths as a primary result. So far we have accounted for fifteen deaths, of which only five were deliberate. Electrocution, ossification and incineration. Other deaths were side-effects of falling in water, being trapped under masonry, and so forth.'

I nudged Neith and gave her a hopeful smile. I had expected the death toll to be far worse given the utter chaos we had witnessed, and while fifteen was an atrocious number in the light of what we had seen, it seemed acceptable. Neith stared at me, her eyebrows raised, and I had to pause. This might be a small loss of life to me. For them, it would have been monumental.

Haru continued. 'The figures for subsequent loss of life are unsurprisingly higher. We had seventy-five heart attacks. Due to how overstretched we were yesterday we only managed to locate and save fifty-two. They are all now stable, but twenty-three died untreated. Suicides.' He paused, and the room stilled. I had the feeling this was a number they were dreading. 'To date, we have reports of two hundred and thirteen unexplained non-violent deaths

165

and eighteen violent deaths where the individual was believed to be the instigator of the action.'

I was horrified.

Neith looked at me and whispered, 'Probably threw themselves off a high building. She tapped her screen for a further breakdown of statistics. Yes. Death by gravity. It's the floor that'll kill you.'

She continued flicking through the causes of suicide while I sat there transfixed. I was finding it very hard to understand what had caused this level of death. Now wasn't the time to ask, but I'd be coming back to it. Every time I thought I understood this lot, they tripped me up.

'Bast! Rigaut stopped,' muttered Neith.

Stopped was such a perfect way to describe death if you have no concept of the afterlife.

'Wait, do you mean Professor Pierre Rigaut, of Religious Beta studies?' I must have been too loud as the pharaoh looked over at me. 'Good morning, Curator Strathclyde. Your thoughts may prove interesting later, but for now, could you allow the section chiefs to speak first?'

The tone was curt, but I didn't think hostile. However, I noted that the head of civilian affairs tapped the table in approval, as did a few others. I tried to shrink into my seat. Scared and angry people didn't act rationally, and I felt uneasy as the reports continued.

Minju explained that no exhibits or archived items had been touched. The aberrations yesterday had shown no interest whatsoever in any of the Beta artefacts.

Asha reported how her teams had helped save civilians from various anomalies and incidents. She singled out Luisa Githumbi for her efforts in baiting Medusa while the custodians were able to herd a family to safety.

'It was a good example of teams of varying abilities working together. I understand that the engineers had a similarly successful venture when they teamed up with some curators.'

First Engineer stood up. I watched warily. As yet, I hadn't had any positive encounters with the engineers.

'Thank you. I shall now report on the events of yesterday. Clearly, my report is the most essential, and I have spent some time drafting it. However, to digress for a second. Yes, we did have some interference from curators who potentially could have cost the lives of three engineers.'

Sam stood up. 'As acting head of the QS facility and head of the curators, I would like to hear more of this incident. I have looked over all the footage and saw no acts of wilful endangerment.'

'Curator Strathclyde called one of the anomalies by a name. This empowered it, making it harder for my team to neutralise it.'

Had I done that? Was I responsible for making the situation worse? I wanted to leave the room. So many people were looking at me. The best look was sympathy, but no one was outraged on my behalf. At best, I was a misguided idiot. At worst, a dangerous threat.

'Returning to my report. At sixteen hundred hours, we began to receive reports of anomalies radiating across the city. This followed from a previous incident observed by Custodian Giovanetti, Chief Nymens, and some junior officers.'

Clearly, he was unaware of Arthur's other appearances, and I didn't feel that now was the time to mention them. And, if I was honest, I wasn't much minded to help him at that moment.

'We observed that the anomalies that had the most cultural recognition appeared to have the greatest impact. Those that based themselves on the ancient Greek and Egyptian myth structure demonstrate a greater pull on weaker psyches. In turn, this observance correlates to a stronger phenomenon.

'We began to run some field experiments and noticed that a lack of interaction with the phenomenon actively weakened it, to the point of its disappearance. I am using *disappearance* in a figurative sense at the moment until we fully understand what was occurring. We also postulated that these manifestations were an issue with the quantum stepper itself. There were massive readings coming from the machines, but nothing visible appeared to be coming through the QS. It was powered down at twenty-one hundred hours, at which point we observed no new manifestations in the city. And the readings from the machines displayed no further interactions. Indeed, as the population sedated themselves, there was nothing further for the anomalies to focus on, and they disappeared.'

I loved how everyone kept saying manifestations, anomalies, aberrations. But maybe they were right to? There is, after all, a lot of power attached to a name in folklore. However, in this brave new world, they didn't do folklore or gods. We wouldn't be naming any Carrionites today. No siree. No gods, no aliens, no naming of anything, thank you very much.

The pharaoh stood up.

'First Engineer. Thank you for your report and your strategies in saving lives. We now need to focus on two issues. When can we re-open the quantum stepper? And can we be assured that something like this will never happen again?'

First Engineer hadn't sat down when the pharaoh stood up, and I wondered if it was a power play. For all I knew it could have been a simple act of protocol, but there was something about First Engineer that made me think he believed he was the most important person in the room.

'We will not open the stepper for at least a week.'

He glared over at us curators as we muttered amongst ourselves. We abruptly fell back into silence.

169

'Only when we have analysed all the data will we consider a temporary opening. I do not envisage us using the stepper, for human interaction, for at least a month.'

'Very well. And are you able to offer any reassurances into any further outbreaks?'

'Absolutely. There will be no further incidents of manifestations as long as the quantum field remains closed.'

'Oh dear, does he mean me?'

We all turned our heads to locate the new speaker.

Loki was lounging against a wall, twisting a lock of hair around his finger. He was wearing a black pinstriped waistcoat, trousers, and a pink tutu. It was a curious look, but he pulled it off. In one hand, he was leaning on a brolly that kept shifting its form. Now it looked like a sword, and just for a second, I thought it was a snake. Maybe it was the snake that was distracting me from the tutu? The pharaoh shot back in his chair, and Asha shouted for the reds.

'More shooting, my dear Asha? I think not. Someone might get hurt.' He smiled. 'Although, I can assure you it won't be me.'

'You are a spoilsport, Loki,' said Anansi from where he was sat amongst the engineers, who exploded away from him. 'I think a few of these bodies could do with some perforation. There's an awful lot of hot air in here.'

I was aware of a presence beside me and was almost comforted to see Arthur. Today he was dressed as a Roman soldier.

'What do you think?' he whispered. 'I'm not sure it's me, to be frank with you. Anansi said I should draw on my Roman influence. Apparently, this world loves the Romans.'

I was trying to watch as various dignitaries tried to climb out of the windows or hammer on doors. It was quite a spectacle. They really didn't like people turning up unannounced. I was trying not to smile.

I whispered back to Arthur. 'They hate the Romans. They consider them barbarians. They're more likely to throw things at you than worship you. I think Anansi may be pulling your leg again.' Anansi put his finger to his lips, and the room fell silent. It didn't appear to be a voluntary silence, given the expression of the inhabitants.

'Did you just call me a dick?'

'Might have,' sulked Arthur, who had indeed called him a dick plus a lot worse, beside. 'Julius tells me that this lot hate the Romans.'

'Goodness. Do they really? Silly me. And obviously, you care what they think…'

I grimaced. Now poor Arthur was stuck admitting to caring about what the puny humans thought of him or being stuck appearing as a version that would weaken him. I stepped in and found I was able to speak.

'I imagine it's hard to ignore the opinions of others in Arthur's case. He is not yet as powerful as yourself, or Loki. The path to greatness is a stony one.'

'I never had any problem,' said Loki. 'People just look at me, and know who I am.' In my head I tried to envisage Tom Hiddleston as hard as I could, but Loki just laughed. 'Nice try Julie, but I know who I am.'

I did wonder if I had a hundred people all think of Hiddleston I could force him to change his appearance, but I decided not to voice that out loud. As far as I knew he couldn't read minds, but I squashed the thought quickly. Loki had a penchant for pain. Not his own.

I cleared my voice, as it appeared that I was the only one currently permitted to speak. 'No Lucifer today?'

'Too busy, unfortunately. I do worry about him.'

Anansi snorted. Of the two, I sensed that Anansi was the more powerful. Given the way one or two of the occupants in the room were staring at him in wonder, I realised that an African god would naturally have more power here than a Norse one.

'So, Anansi, yesterday you told us you would provide evidence of the gods' existence. I think you have done that.'

'You would think so wouldn't you, and yet this one—'He gestured towards the First Engineer. '—still denies our reality. Why is that, do you think?'

I was not about to be drawn into speculation with a trickster god. The best way to avoid being tricked was to let someone else do the talking.

'Ask him.' I shrugged. 'I don't know why they won't believe the evidence of their own eyes.'

'Interesting. Which evidence should they believe?'

Every word I spoke, I was aware of hidden meanings, things unsaid, ways in which to trap or be trapped. I was beginning to sweat. I shrugged again, saying nothing this time. So far I had narrowed my options down to two choices. These were people from another Earth with unexplainable powers. According to everyone here, there were only two Earths, so maybe not. The other option was that these were actual gods, which again, *according to everyone here*, didn't exist. Soon, someone was going to have to change their mind.

There was a gasp in the room as all the people present suddenly had the ability to speak once more. Anansi raised his hand, and the room watched him carefully.

'Please do not speak unless invited. Now you.' He leant back in his chair and put his feet up on the table. I could only see two long legs, but the sense of others was almost tangible. Today, he was wearing a hat crowned in tall feathers and, as he tilted his head in the engineer's direction, the feathers swayed in a non-existent breeze. I realised I, and probably everyone else, was being mesmerised by the gentle sway of the feathers. An image of a hundred teeth snapped out of the dark at me, and I

173

jolted back in my seat. Anansi looked across and smiled as the feathers came to a halt.

'Sorry, where was I? Ah yes, quantum anomalies. Particle baggage. That seems a rude way to refer to Loki there. Tell me again how we don't exist.'

First Engineer stood and addressed the pharaoh. 'As I said earlier, these anomalies feed off our attention. I would suggest we simply ignore them for now.'

'You also said that they couldn't manifest without the quantum stepper being operational,' stammered the pharaoh. 'So how do you explain their presence now?'

'Oh, I know this one,' said Loki, waving his brolly in the air. 'Can I?'

All heads swivelled to Loki for an explanation.

'We didn't come through your tickly little gate. We don't need help, but some of our brethren did. Besides which, I think they liked the sensation. You know what Anubis is like. He could easily self-manifest, but I think he was enjoying your stepper. It gives you that little quivery feeling in the pit of your stomach, like going over a bridge too fast. Honestly, he's a wee scamp.'

I could see half the room looking around nervously. The idea of Anubis turning up again was visibly disturbing them. The other half seemed aghast at someone describing the god of the dead as a wee scamp.

'Citizens!' demanded First. 'It is essential that you ignore these manifestations.'

Anansi yawned and looked across at me. 'Do you think he'll believe the evidence of his own existence?'

I jumped up. 'First Engineer. Please, stop talking. You are putting your life at risk.'

'When I take advice from the superstitious ravings of a second-rate angel, that is the day I will step down from my office.' Dismissing Julius, he addressed the pharaoh. 'Sir, I suggest you have the reds remove Strathclyde at once. I propose that it is his febrile imagination that is firing up these—'

He came to an abrupt halt as froth began to foam around his mouth and his body became rigid. It was over very quickly. With a massive spasm, he rocked backwards and then crashed to the floor. His eyeballs leaked blood, and his lips turned blue. I wasn't a doctor, but even I could see he was dead.

Haru ran across the floor but only reached him as he crashed backwards. Pulling a scanner out, he took a quick reading and a blood prick.

'Massive amounts of venom in his system.'

The Anansi I remembered from the tales and legends was a more jovial and happier god. I had forgotten this version. A vengeful spider was not something that I wanted to dwell on.

Second Engineer jumped to her feet and was now addressing both Anansi and Loki. Her voice was shaking but I noticed that she was staring directly at them.

Working in the quantum field on a daily basis bred some very unflappable people.

'Right. Who are you and what do you want?'

Anansi smiled at Loki indulgently, then turned his attention back to Second Engineer.

'That's better,' smiled Anansi. 'And you are?'

'I am First Engineer.'

Well, that was pretty brutal, I thought, but certainly efficient.

'Very well, First Engineer. We are here to help out our friend with a challenge.' He waved over at Arthur who was now sitting, looking noble and regal. He'd reverted to the pre-Raphaelite image of a blond Victorian hero.

'Arthur wants to set up a quest for you all to engage in, and we thought that sounded like an excellent plan. It's just the sort of thing we gods like to do. So, we are going to set you up into two teams and see who wins. Good, hey?' He looked around the room expecting enthusiasm but was met with every sort of silence.

'And what is the nature of this quest, noble Anansi?'

Oh, I liked the new First Engineer. At least she was displaying some common sense.

'The search to find da Vinci's missing codex. Or, How to Build a Time and Space Machine.'

Day Four – Julius

First Engineer hissed and stood. Given how she had just gained her promotion, I admired her bravery.

'That is forbidden!'

The pharaoh looked at her, his face mottled with rage. 'You knew about this?'

Anansi tutted, and they both fell silent.

'Of course the engineers know about this,' Anansi explained slowly. 'They are the guardians of da Vinci's works. They built and now maintain the stepper. They know there is a complete codex out there. They just don't think anyone else should be able to get their hands on it.'

This changed everything. Honestly, I could see their point. So far, the stepper was being used for good, although personally, I think they could have used it better. Instead of saving the artwork and keeping it for themselves, they could save the artwork and give it back to us. Or — and how's this for revolutionary? — they could leave behind the procedures to reverse dementia, cure cancer, rid us of petrochemicals. Even so, the idea of the thieves having their own stepper filled me with dread. They wouldn't be so careful about only taking stuff that was about to be destroyed. They would remove art straight from the wall. Hell, they might even take the artist straight from his bed.

The tension was evident. People were straining against the enforced silence. The engineers looked mutinous.

Minju appeared calm, but her tail was flicking like a car wiper. I gave her a sympathetic smile and glanced at her tail. I knew she was proud of how she was able to still it and not betray her emotions. I didn't want her fear to be exposed. She followed the glance of my eyes, and I watched as her breathing deepened and her body stilled. When she was totally calm, she looked back at me with a slight nod. It wasn't much, but in this surreal situation, I was glad there was something I could do to help.

'There will be two teams,' announced Loki. 'The fuddy-duddies and the funsters.'

Neith nudged me and smiled. I didn't have the heart to break it to her. She would discover soon enough what sort of people Anansi and Loki viewed as funsters.

'Now, you are all muddled up at the moment, so let's make it clearer who's who. At this end of the room, we shall have the fuddy-duddies. Those whose job it is to uphold law and order and — oh god, I can't continue, it's so boring. At that end, we'll have the funsters. Those that know what they want and help themselves using every trick in the book.'

There was an uncomfortable pressure in the air, and my skin felt slightly itchy. As I blinked my eyes, I could see that the seating positions had changed. I blinked my eyes again. The people in the chamber had been divided into two clear groups. I was still sitting with Neith and familiar faces, but as I looked across the floor, I was looking at friends. They couldn't be who we had been fighting against this past year. These people couldn't possibly represent our enemy within.

Asha, who was now sitting nearby, and Sam both jumped to their feet and roared for the guards. Almost as quickly as they jumped up, they sat down again. Although, from the way their feet shot out in front of them, it was clearly not of their own volition.

'Is it all a bit shocking?' murmured Loki sympathetically. 'How would we have ever guessed that the pharaoh was a baddy?' he slapped his hand to his cheek in mock outrage. 'Who would even have believed that Minju the mild-mannered curator was evil through and through?' Loki was laughing openly now. 'Oh, Julie, your face!'

God, how much information had I unwittingly passed along to her?

I looked across at the group of individuals who were looking deeply awkward and defensive. Maybe it was unsurprising, but there wasn't a single engineer over there, and maybe I softened towards them just a little. Some were protesting their innocence. Most looked confused that Minju sat amongst them. It was clear that their identity was kept a secret from each other. As undercover cabals went, it was a tight one.

'Mikel,' said Sam in a broken voice. 'People have died. Curators have been killed, angels disposed of. How could you? What of the oath we took?'

Mikel twisted his lips but looked unapologetic. He wasn't a man I recognised, but his betrayal clearly shocked Sam.

'I'm sorry, Nymens. Truly I am, but you know I was always against any integration with Beta Earth. We need to keep this planet pure. Death to the Angels!'

A few people sitting on the other side of the chamber clapped. For my own part, I couldn't believe that Stef was over there. He looked at me and shook his head.

'It's a mistake, Blue. Honest. Mr Loki, sir, could you check your list again?'

Loki made a show of consulting a clipboard that had just appeared in his hands.

'Stefan Seidel. Pocketed a jade statue of a fawn and handed it over to Soliman Alvarez. Requested another assignment asap. This is you isn't it?'

Loki waved his hand, and we watched as a hologram flickered in silence in the centre of the floor. We all watched Stef use a sleight-of-hand move to pocket the statue as Sabrina's back was turned. He dropped a rock into the lava below and then pointed in horror to Sabrina who looked visibly upset. Then they both smacked their wrist braces and disappeared. Seconds later, the hologram stopped.

'You pustulating shitgibbon!' I wasn't one for swearing, but at this moment I was tempted to join Sabrina. 'When did you turn?' she demanded.

Now Stef shrugged, all pretence at innocence gone. 'Turn, honey? I was never one of the boy scouts. Running around risking life and limb just for the bloody honour of it. Where's the fun in that? Pulling the wool over all your eyes, spying on Julius. That was what made me get up in the morning. The money is just a glorious bonus. You should see my summer house.'

What a mess. I looked across at Minju. 'What about you, then? Are you in this for the money, or because you hate Betas?'

Minju paused, considering my question.

'Hate the Betas? Julius, I'm not a monster. I admire Beta Earth so much. From the rise of the first great empire of Rome, to the British Empire, and the rise of a new Chinese dawn. I watch the strength and power of your mighty nations, and I wail at the weakness and shallowness of my own society. We are working towards a new day. The rise of the Egyptian Empire, and we are so close to a new history for Alpha. An Egyptian dynasty for an Alpha civilisation, and we will use whatever we need from Beta Earth to power that rise.'

So, not a monster then. Just a raving psychopath. Super.

Anansi clapped his hands together, trying to get the conversation back under his control. Which, given that he had just thrown a hand grenade into the heart of Egyptian society, was going to be tricky.

181

'Now, I'm going to give you some space to discuss your teams and your strategy.'

'No, stop.' Asha shot to her feet. 'We can't go haring off on a treasure hunt. We have to deal with these traitors. This betrayal needs to be dealt with immediately.'

Anansi turned and looked at her. The room suddenly felt colder, and we tried not to look in the direction of the previous First Engineer.

'Asha, do you remember Jan Kosgei?'

She paused and frowned. 'The boy in my primary school?'

Anansi nodded.

'Yes, do you remember the time he was pulling legs off a spider, and you bloodied his nose and tried to nurse the spider back to life as you wept?'

Asha nodded slowly. This was such an old memory, and one she had forgotten until Anansi brought it up.

'Your tears, Jan's blood, and the spider's pain summoned me that day, and I watched and approved of you.' He paused, and now his tone sharpened. 'And it is for that memory alone that I do not kill you. But never ever interrupt me again. Is that clear?'

Asha stared him in the eye, and slowly sat down again, glaring at the people sitting across from her.

'Excellent. Right, some quick rules. No approaching Leonardo. We will transport you wherever you want to go but won't help any more than that. Anyone found cheating, we'll just tell the other side where the codex is. Any questions?'

I cleared my throat. It was now or never, and while the rules were being laid out, this was the best time to try and make the most of it.

'What's in it for us?'

The two gods and Arthur looked at each other, confused, and Anansi looked back at me.

'The chance to find and secure the codex. Stop the other side. I would have thought that was enough?'

I shook my head. 'Not if we lose. We may as well not compete at all.'

'But it's fun.' said Anansi with a slight wheedling tone.

'No. I want something if I lose. Otherwise, we're not playing.'

Asha leant across Neith and slapped me on the thigh.

'What are you doing? Shut up.'

I ignored her. If there was one advantage I had here, it was that I knew how the traditional bargaining with a god went.

'Well, what do you want?'

'At the end of this, no matter the outcome, all gods are to leave this planet and never return.'

I felt Asha relax. Across from me, I saw Minju evaluating what I had just said.

'But, Julius, that means I won't see you again,' said Arthur.

'We can always catch up on my Earth.'

He turned his back on me, offended by my lack of concern, and went to join Anansi and Loki who were making a pretence of discussing it.

As I watched them, I wondered how the hell this was happening. How was I actually watching two gods and a mythical king debate the fate of this planet?

'Very well. If everyone is in agreement?'

Unsurprisingly, everyone was. No one relished an existence where all-powerful gods could derail your plans on a whim, and just kill you if they were put out.

'Right then—' began Loki.

'Wait! 'Minju stood up. 'These teams. Do we have to select them from the persons present?'

Loki clapped his hands and laughed. 'Ah. Yes, you're missing someone aren't you?'

I groaned. I knew what was coming and nudged Neith's knee. 'Try not to lose your temper.'

Neith looked at me in confusion, and I watched as her face slowly melted into absolute fury.

Loki smiled at Anansi. 'Well, she's your girl. Do you want to summon her, or shall I?'

Suddenly, Clio was sat next to Minju, staring wildly about her.

Minju murmured something to her, and Clio sat still and watched the room. Glaring at Anansi, she nodded at Neith, who started swearing under her breath. Anansi laughed.

'Hello, sweetie.' He grinned, talking to Clio. 'Cat girl next to you will explain what is going on. Now, if you could all retire to the two side chambers. When the sand has got to the bottom of the egg timer, we will dispatch your teams to wherever you want to go.'

Arthur leant across and muttered something. Loki laughed, and Anansi shook his head.

'Ooh, la la. I haven't given you the clue. Here it is. This is all I will tell you to help you locate the codex.' He paused dramatically. 'La Gioconda has the answer.'

Day Four - Julius

We were sitting in a break-out room. There were giant floor cushions and long benches designed to lie on. Plates of nibbles and drinks were scattered tastefully around the room, and some gentle music was being piped through the speakers. It had all the air of a mid-level management meeting. The only thing that spoilt the mood was the swearing and crying. Shortly after we moved to this room, one of the men declared that he was going to stop. His announcement was met with a few hugs and regrets, but no one tried to stop him, and he walked out of the room.

'Just like that?'

'No, not just like that,' snapped Neith. 'He'll go home and discuss it with his family. If they don't persuade him to stay, he will stop. I sincerely hope that they are successful, but it is his life, not mine.'

I could see she was angry and upset and I should have let it go. But I was also at odds and so, like a fool, I carried on pushing her.

'You treat it like it's a cultural norm. What's wrong with you?'

And, for the first time ever, Neith was properly mad at me. She had been peeling a small satsuma, but now she crushed it in her hand, the wet flesh squeezing out between her fingers, and she slammed it on the table. Several people turned around.

'A cultural norm? Like you have some moral high ground with all your murders and warfare?'

I was embarrassed that we were attracting attention, but I couldn't let her misperception of us go unchallenged.

'That is hardly the same thing?'

'Are you mad? Of course it's a cultural norm, in fact, it's your guiding principle. When aren't you lot running around killing each other, wasting lives and resources?'

'No one wants to go to war!'

'Of course they bloody do, or else you wouldn't always be doing it.'

While we weren't shouting, our voices were rising and those closest to us were stepping away from the scene. I was about to come back with some stupid justification when Rami dashed over to us from across the room. Grabbing Neith's arm, he gave her a quick shake and hissed at her. She looked at him, then me and wiping her hands on her thigh she stormed away.

'Are you alright?'

I looked at Rami and shook my head.

'No. But I will be.'

He squeezed my hand and gave me a quick hug. They were a tactile bunch. It had taken me months to get used to it, and if I was honest, I wasn't completely comfortable with it, but, right now, the hug did make me feel a bit better.

Across the room, Asha slapped the table, and we all stopped talking.

'Right. We are going to have to focus on this. First Engineer and I have been talking, and we have agreed that securing the codex will need to be our top priority. With that in mind, we will have to comply with this challenge we have been set. We have no idea as to the scope of power of these strangers, but we have already seen enough evidence to know that we cannot dismiss them.

'I propose that we send a team of curators to Beta Paris to examine the *Mona Lisa*, or *La Gioconda*, as Anansi rather poetically named it. I propose Curators Salah, Gamal and Strathclyde. We don't know what the nature of the clue we find will be, but for now, we have nothing else to go on. Any questions?'

The room was silent. Giovanetti had spoken and the engineers were backing her. What more was there to say? Only a fool would raise his hand.

'Yes, Strathclyde?' said Asha, and I could swear she sounded weary.

'Wouldn't it help us to know more about the codex?' I watched as First glared at me. 'How big is it? What colour is it?'

Asha looked at First and raised an eyebrow.

'We don't know. It was lost centuries ago.'

'And you never made a copy of it?' I asked, incredulously.

'The contents were too valuable to risk someone else stealing the copy.'

'And yet you lost the original.'

First just glared at me.

'When did you lose it?'

'Centuries ago.'

'And no one ever wrote a description of what it even looked like?'

'No,' she snapped, 'because we hadn't planned on losing it.'

'So, if you lost it so long ago, how come you were able to complete the stepper in the past few decades?'

None of this made sense to me, and I could see from a few faces in the room that they agreed with me. No one had openly questioned the engineers before, and it was clear that her answers weren't stacking up.

'Because, over the centuries, we have worked on the discoveries and advancements of our forebears until we created a working stepper rather than a theoretical one.'

'Well, if that's the case, why the urgency to get the codex back? If it's that basic, it can't be a life-or-death document. Not if what's in there requires centuries of experiments to bring it up to speed.'

Now First looked furious.

'That is not the point,' she said curtly. 'It is our property. The risks are too high.'

'You mean there may be stuff in the codex you had forgotten about? Or stuff you don't want us to know about?'

She fell silent. I knew she was lying about the codex, but I didn't know what about. The fact that she had decided to stop answering my questions suggested I was close to something.

She turned to Asha. 'Custodian Giovanetti, I regret that we are unable to supply you with further details on the codex. I take full responsibility for the failures of my predecessors to secure the maestro's greatest ever piece of work. But it has been the sacrifice of every engineer throughout history to bring da Vinci's plans and ideas to life, and during this search we will assist you in every way that we can.'

A spattering of applause broke out. Once again, I had misjudged the influence these engineers had over society. Oddly enough, I didn't think they were inherently bad. After all, none of them had turned up in the other team. But people working with the best of intentions can commit the greatest of crimes. I sipped my coffee and wondered what they were hiding.

As I watched, the new First was muttering into her brace and a minute later my brace pinged.

Status Update: Resolved. Consideration removed. By order of the First Engineer.

My face flushed. What did that mean? Had I pushed things too far? I stared at First, but she simply looked at me and then turned back to Asha. I needed to find Neith.

'Great Ra. They have come to their senses.' Sam startled me, giving me a massive hug and I nearly collapsed in relief.

'I'm safe?'

'Looks like it. First clearly sees the world differently to her predecessor, plus with these manifestations, you are now our number one expert.'

I wanted to laugh out loud but this didn't seem the right time. Some guards entered the room with a quick report for Asha and then left again. As they did so, she looked after them thoughtfully.

'Arthur? Loki? Anansi?' It was clear she was addressing them, but there was no reply.

'Julius, would you try?'

I imagined the sound a leather cricket ball made when it hit the sweet spot on the willow bat, with a pigeon cooing gently in the background.

'Arthur?'

And, of course, Arthur materialised in front of me. I have to admit I was getting better at not flinching.

'Hello, Julius. Isn't this most excellent? Loki and Anansi are very impressed. They haven't had this much fun in ages.'

'Yes, it's very entertaining,' I said through gritted teeth. 'Look, Asha has a question. Can you help?'

Asha stood up and executed a dramatically deep bow.

'High King Arthur, greatest ruler of the sceptred isles. I have a favour to ask.'

It was perfect, and I once again recalibrated just how sharp that woman was. First Engineer was scowling, but you need to dance with whoever brought you to the party.

Arthur glowed and waved at her to continue.

'I know everyone in this room is fuddy-duddy, but how will I know who is a funster beyond those in the other rooms? When those guards of mine just gave their report, I realised I had no idea if I could trust them. Are you able to make it clear to us?'

Arthur paused, considering, then disappeared. A few moments later he reappeared, and Asha once again bowed low.

'We have conferred, and I persuaded them to grant this boon.'

He waved his arm majestically around the room, but nothing appeared to happen. We all looked at each other, and Arthur stamped his foot.

'You promised!' A disembodied voice laughed. 'Very well, do it again.'

Arthur once more majestically swept his arm, although this time it did seem a little lacking in regal fanfare. Above everyone's heads bobbed a little 3D glyph. They were upside down. Sludgy, little grey pyramids with a sad face on them.

Everyone in the room, except Arthur, had the same little glyph hanging over their heads. I dashed over to the window and looked out on the street where teams were still cleaning up after the previous day's debris. Everyone had stopped working and was pointing to each other's heads and swiping their hands through the symbols, unable to bat them away.

'It looks like everyone is grey,' I said, watching the crowd below.

'No, look over there,' said Neith from across the room, where she was looking out of another window. 'That woman has a golden glowing one.'

'There's another one over here,' called one of the engineers. The rest of the engineers were busy taking readings and measurements of what they could see.

Asha's wrist brace pinged, and she tapped it lightly and spoke into it, looking around the room at us as she did so.

'Hello, Governor Lawrence, how are you? We haven't heard from you in months.'

A man's voice boomed into the room. Asha was clearly making sure that all communications, for now, were going to be open to scrutiny.

'No need for formalities, Asha, my dear. We were just saying the other day that you guys need to come over for the weekend. But look, that's not what I am calling about. Strange little symbols have just appeared over our heads.

Is this something to do with the kerfuffle in Alexandria last night?'

'Yes, linked. We're trying something out.'

'Will it be long? They are very pretty but a little distracting?'

'Pretty?'

'Yes. I quite like the golden crown, a bit archaic but a fun idea.'

We all watched as Asha continued to talk to the Governor of Italy, her face growing pale.

'Yes, the gold ones are nice aren't they? Tell me, does anyone have any other sorts?'

There was a pause as the room waited for his reply.

'No, everyone I can see is gold. No, wait. A courier is down in the reception area. He has a really dreadful shitty grey one. Gosh, what does that mean?'

Asha paused, rapidly trying to think of a quick cover. I scribbled on my notepad, holding it up to her, and she gave me a thumbs up.

'It means he's not up to standard. We're trying a scale of citizen worthiness.'

'Well, I approve of that.' His voice boomed with laughter. 'Although I don't think we need to be quite so explicit about it. Have you run this past the pharaoh?'

'The pharaoh is fully aware of this.'

'Hang on. I can see my grooms. They have golden crowns as well! That can't be right? How can they possibly be worthy?'

Asha looked across at me, and I scribbled on my notepad again. She read what I had written in astonishment, then nodded her head.

'Well, Gianni, we're still ironing things out, but as they are associated with you, your worthiness is conferred on them.'

He laughed loudly. 'I like that. Well, let me know when you are going to refine it or phase it out. And pass on my congratulations to those clever engineers. Chat again soon.'

The room fell quiet as the call ended. Asha tapped her finger on the desk.

'First. Can you patch me into the emergency broadcast system? I want the worldwide network.'

A few minutes later, after some fairly feverish typing on a large computer, First Engineer looked at Asha.

'Speak into your brace. Everyone on the planet should hear it, either from the public speakers or their own braces.'

She turned and looked at us. 'I'm afraid for those in this room it will be noisy, as all your braces will broadcast. Chief Custodian, I suggest you go to the bathroom and broadcast from there otherwise the feedback loop will be atrocious. My apologies for not making a better system.'

'Nonsense. This is just what I wanted. Thank you.'

She turned and walked towards the loos. As she left, Rami rolled his shoulders, flexing out the tension. 'Nubi's balls. This must be so hard for her. How many more personal betrayals is she going to endure?'

I looked at him. 'Were she and the governor close?'

'No, he was a school friend of Haru. These allegiances go back decades.'

'Haru. That's a point. Where is he?'

I looked around the room and tried to remember when I had last seen him.

'Didn't you notice? He was on the other side of the room, crouched down at the back.'

I looked at Rami shocked. 'He's one of the enemies?'

'Makes sense of a lot of things if you consider it.'

He was right. As head of medicine, he was always on hand to tend to injured curators. In the privacy of an examination cubicle, goods could be smuggled across. Angels with messages asking for help could be disposed of. Memories could be erased. Injuries exacerbated. Curators that discovered wrongdoings could suddenly die of their injuries. He was in a perfect position to manipulate events after the curators returned to Alpha. I was about to reply when every wrist brace and loudspeaker chimed an alert.

'Citizens. I am Chief Custodian Giovanetti of the quantum facility in Alexandria. You will have noticed glyphs above your heads. The vast majority will have a small grey pyramid. There is no cause for alarm. We are simply testing out a new system. A small golden crown floating above your head, signifies you are part of a small group of individuals. Those who support Death to the Angels, those of you who are involved in the stealing of artefacts from Beta Earth, and those of you hoping to install a new world empire.

'Do not be alarmed. This is new technology, and I am certain only a few are affected. If you see someone with a crown, record their name, and start compiling lists. Do not attempt to arrest these individuals if you don't have the relevant skill set or authority.

'We will collate the lists and work out how to proceed. If you discover you have a golden crown above your head and believe it to be an error, please present yourself to the local authorities who will work out what to do next.

'We believe this problem is mostly local rather than worldwide, and we ask the world to bear with us as we try to catch up with this new development. We will address you all again tomorrow. Until then I am establishing martial law in Egypt.'

My spine shivered. Twice in three months the custodians had taken charge. The last time they had handed back power quickly and easily. Would it be better or worse this time?

Day Four - Clio

As the announcement ended, Clio held her wrist brace out in front of her and snapped a hologram. Grinning, she examined the glyph above her head. She wondered if she could ask Anansi to make her crown larger. Maybe add some rubies? But then she remembered she was mad at him right now. She sneered, looking at the rest of the room. They were all shouting at each other in the wake of Giovannetti's announcement. So typical. They had the balls to be clandestine villains, rulers of a new world, but they didn't have the courage of their convictions to go public. A bunch of power-mad, craven losers and she was stuck with them.

Only one person in this room worried her, and that was Minju Chen. She had never met her directly. In fact, until Anansi had told her that Minju was the brains behind everything, Clio wouldn't have believed it. Anyone that had kept herself so well concealed was obviously good at what she did. Now was the time to see how she responded. Like Clio, she was silent and still.

Clio picked at the grapes and watched the various groups cluck and panic. There were lots of calls being made. Clio smirked as she noticed how many were voice only. Calling the wife and kids, checking in on mum and dad. Everyone out there writing sneaky little lists, all dobbing on one another. Giovanetti was going to go through the population like rotting meat. Her success

198

depended on how long the glyphs lasted. How long could someone with a crown remain unseen?

She snorted as she watched the pharaoh swat above his head, then put his ceremonial headpiece on. His face was a picture when the glyph simply rose to the top of the hat, still visible. A group of sycophants circled him, all trying to erase the crown and shaking their heads.

'Hello, Clio.'

Clio turned and looked the curator up and down. Tall, blond, well-muscled, this was the one that had been brought on board to keep tabs on the mud fly.

'Sod off.'

Stefan recoiled then tried again. 'Come on now, we curators need to stick together through this. If anyone gives you any hassle just let me know and I'll take care of them for you.'

Now Clio gave him her full attention. It was nice to be surprised.

'Do you actually think I need help from you, little boy?' She smiled, but it didn't make it to her eyes. It barely made it to her lips and, the way her teeth were exposed, made Stefan shudder.

'Don't make me ask a third time, because you really, really wouldn't like that. Sod off.'

Clio watched as Stefan took a deep breath and thought better of it. Nonchalantly, he helped himself to some grapes, as though that were the only reason he had come over and walked back to find a better bet to hitch his wagon to.

Just when Clio despaired of this lot getting their act together, the pharaoh stood up and banged his hand on the table until everyone stopped talking.

'Chief Custodian Giovanetti has exceeded her authority here. As soon as we've found a way to mask these bloody symbols, I will have her arrested and stripped of her rank. Here is what I propose for now. Everyone is to return to their private estates. Use the government heli-cruisers and get to a place of...'

Minju rose to her feet, and the pharaoh looked at her nervously. Interesting, thought Clio. Even the pharaoh was wary of her.

'Sit down, Jim. That's not what we are going to do.'

Clio watched the faces of the room. This assertive Minju was a surprise to the vast majority. She had sat in the middle of the web, quietly pulling strings while everyone ran around doing her bidding. Anansi adored Minju and had been boring Clio with this fact. Clio wondered what Minju would do if she knew she had such a powerful fan. Probably work out how to use that to her advantage. Clio decided not to mention it to her. Change was in the air, and Clio needed to keep her wits about her. In a new world order, she may even be able to come home.

'These people, claiming to be gods, have set us a challenge, and it's one we can't afford to lose. I don't care if you believe in them or not. The simple issue is that whoever and whatever they are, they have more power than us, and they are in control. This is a monumental opportunity. But we are on the clock, and we are running out of time.'

'Yes, but our identities!'

'That isn't important right now. We have one goal only, and that is to secure the codex.'

'But how am I supposed to govern?'

'Jim, do I need to ask the guards to remove you?'

Some very large men in red uniforms stirred and took a step forward. Around the room, people glanced warily at the remaining custodians and saw that they appeared to be answering to a quiet little archivist, not the pharaoh of upper and lower Egypt.

'Once we have the codex, we will be able to build our own stepper and redress the balance. As for our identities, I imagine that can be easily fixed. Clio?'

Clio choked on her grape and scowled at the woman. She didn't want the attention but knew that it was probably inevitable. Still, she'd have rather remained unbothered by all these idiots.

'Yes, ma'am?'

'You appear to have the most knowledge about these entities. In your opinion, are they capable of erasing everyone's memories about our revealed statuses?'

'Probably.' Clio popped another grape in her mouth.

'Can you ask?'

'It doesn't work like that. Anansi is a busy god. I can't just call, and he'll turn up.'

'So, how do you communicate with him?'

'Well, sometimes he's bored and just shows up. Other times, if I'm desperate, he will turn up if I call.'

'And you can't do that now?'

'Nope. I'm afraid I'm not feeling all that desperate right now.'

The pharaoh sprang up and leant across the table, shouting at Clio.

'Have you any idea just how bad this is? Everything I have worked towards has just been obliterated.'

Clio yawned and studied her fingernails. 'Look, I get it, babes. Your life has just gone tits up. You're in dire straits. But the thing is, I'm not. Everyone knows I'm a wrong 'un. My situation hasn't actually changed at all. Sorry.' She shrugged unhelpfully, then made a big act of pretending to think of something. 'I *can* help with one thing.'

He paused, breathing heavily, his temper barely held in check. 'Yes?'

'You've got a bit of spittle on your chin. Not a nice look.'

There was a snigger from Stefan's direction, but by the time the pharaoh turned to look, everyone's faces were blank. His expression was murderous, and no one would meet his eye. Wiping his chin, he sat down and began to shred bits of the flower display.

'Thank you, Clio,' continued Minju. 'That was exactly as helpful as I expected. I should like to chat to you later about your previous encounters with the gods, but for now, we need to locate La Gioconda.'

She turned to Gloria Acardi of civic affairs. 'I seem to remember that the painting went to our friends in Madagascar. Is it still there?'

'No. It went to Russia. I believe the Grimaldis have it.'

Great, thought Clio. Paranoid, gun-toting, lunatics. She had very little to do with criminal elements on Alpha Earth, but who hadn't heard of the Grimaldis? In a world where crime was genuinely low, the Grimaldis were like a cup winner's graduation ceremony. Complete with fireworks and flying monkeys. They would never have flourished in Egypt, but the Urals were a law unto themselves.

'Hmm,' said Minju. 'Not ideal, but at least we have a head start on the others. I imagine right now they are drawing up plans to visit the Louvre in Beta Earth.'

There were a few sniggers, and Minju paused briefly. She didn't care about them. All she cared about was getting to the codex first. Saving artwork, selling artwork. None of it mattered to her. Forging a new empire was what drove her, and she needed the resources her own step machine would bring her.

'We need brains and brawn on this team. The Grimaldis aren't to be negotiated with. The team will need to steal the *Mona Lisa* and get it back to us. Clio, Stefan,

Mo; you three will be the team. Clio, you're in charge. Mo, if you think she's going to double-cross us, shoot her, but don't kill her. We need her.'

'You're not making a girl feel welcome,' said Clio sorrowfully.

'I don't intend to. I know nothing about you, and you have a lot of friends on the other side, plus a very powerful protector. All I can say is that if we win, your record will be clear and, if you want to come home, no one will bat an eyelid. Maybe your god can even wipe everyone's memory of you?'

'If it's alright with you, I'd rather work alone. Those two will just slow me down.'

Minju laughed, surprising the room. It was a genuinely happy sound and one they didn't associate with either the shy archivist or the terrifying architect of a new world order.

'Clio dear, you are not going anywhere on your own until I have some confidence that you won't instantly betray us.'

Anansi appeared next to Clio and, once again, the room flinched. Anansi smiled, enjoying the reactions, and nudged Clio.

'Love your crown.' Grinning he turned to the others. 'Now who's in charge of Team Anansi? I do hope it's Minju. Got to love her, *what* a player!'

Minju sat still, watching him. The pharaoh stood up again, but Anansi snorted.

204

'Zip it, Jimbob, you're not fooling anyone. She got you elected. She got all of you to the positions you currently hold, and she also knows who all your replacements are, as and when required. Ain't that the truth?'

Minju resisted a small smile, but Anansi simply beamed across at her.

'Now then friends. Are you ready? Time's up.'

Minju looked over at the god that was lounging against the corner beside Clio. 'When this is all over can we get rid of these silly symbols?'

'What?' Anansi looked around in fake astonishment. 'Why? They're funny.'

'I'm not laughing. I take it they appeared because the other team asked for them?'

'Correct.'

'So to balance things up, can I ask a similar favour.'

Anansi grinned. 'Of course. What do you want?'

'Can I reserve it until I really need it?'

Anansi chuckled. 'Player! 'He glanced over at Clio, still laughing. 'She's good. I might swap you for her.'

'Whatevs,' said Clio with a scowl.

She didn't mind working for someone who was so capricious, but, frankly, she could do without the jokes. At least, not when they were aimed at her.

'Now, then. One wish on ice. So, where do you want to go and who's going?'

Minju explained what she had in mind and, although she asked Anansi if she was on the right track, he just laughed and said that would be cheating.

'No more clues, or else I'll have to help the others as well.' He clapped his hands together, and it sounded like a whole round of applause, with ghostly spider hands joining in the chorus.

'Off we go!'

Day Five – First Engineer

Hypatia Smith, formerly Second Engineer, now First, ran her hand over the wall of the quantum stepper. She loved being in this room. For now, it was a large solid white wall, but when it came alive it shone and flexed with colours and sounds, infinite possibilities rippling through the dimensions. Of course, now it was silent, as was the rest of the room. She had shut the room down completely and dismissed all personnel. Only engineers had access now, and only those she approved. She had been relieved that all engineers had reported for roll call, and not one wore a golden crown. Further proof that their cadet programme worked, even if it was brutal.

'You wanted to see me?'

Hypatia scowled. She wanted more time to gather her thoughts but Third had arrived quicker than she had expected. No, not Third, she corrected herself, Second. Another example of her sluggish thinking. First had been dead twenty-four hours. She needed to improve her performance rapidly, so far she was not impressed with herself.

'I fear I have miscalculated.' She paused to see how Second would react, but of course, he remained silent. If an engineer at their level believed they had miscalculated anything, then there would be solid reasoning behind the statement. It wasn't a needy plea for reassurance.

'When the teams were dispatched on this ridiculous hunt, I should have insisted that an engineer accompany them.'

'Agreed,' said Second. 'However, as Second I should have also been advising you.'

'You weren't present.'

'No. Therefore you were on your own in a situation with many new variables.'

The conclusion was the same. Hypatia could have done better but given the circumstances, she'd probably done the best she could.

'The curators won't however discover anything,' he said. 'I understand the two teams are searching modern-day Paris on Beta Earth, and modern-day Russia here on our Earth. It would have just been good to have an engineer present to observe how these anomalies travel.'

'Wait to see where they go next? I'm conflicted.' Hypatia grumbled. 'I don't want to overplay our hand. There's little to be gained when we know they are travelling without a chance of finding a codex.'

'But what about these quantum anomalies? What if they interfere, and guide them in the right direction?'

'Then we are in real trouble. Strathclyde is already asking all the wrong sort of questions. We're going to have trouble containing this.' Hypatia admired the speed with which the Beta had spotted the flaws in her story, but then he hadn't had years of subliminal manipulation. That reminded her. 'Incidentally, to prevent further loss of life, the quantum anomalies are to be referred to as Gross, Observable, Dimensional Subjects. Recommend to all engineers that the acronym will be a permitted abbreviation.'

'Sensible.' He paused, again uncertain of how to continue. 'It is chaotic, though. What if they do stumble onto the truth of the quantum stepper and centuries of research and development are exploded in one silly treasure hunt?'

'As long as they think there is some secret leather-bound book out there with all of Leonardo's jottings in it, then we're fine. We have the only codex that *our* Leonardo wrote.'

Second snorted. 'Do you know, they didn't even pause to consider that Beta's Leonardo was utterly incapable of writing a treatise on quantum mechanics. The man was obsessed with waterwheels and wooden helicopters.'

'Never underestimate a Leonardo,' admonished Hypatia. 'But yes, we can be grateful that they won't be successful. But what if all our centuries of study and research are suddenly revealed by one stupid flick of a god's finger? And what if this hunt somehow plants the idea into Beta Leonardo's head?'

'That is my greatest concern at this stage,' said Second. 'What do you suggest?'

'We can do nothing to fix the past right now. We just need to be poised to step in if we feel they are getting close to the truth.' Hypatia considered whether she could confide in Second. He was sensible but able to see the bigger picture. She had even heard him singing which meant he had an untapped creative flair. She decided to risk it. 'In the meantime, things need to change. I think we are destroying our future on our current trajectory. The arrival of the gods accelerates this destruction.'

'This seems an extreme pronouncement. What is your evidence?'

'Our culture is stagnating.' Hypatia picked a satsuma from the fruit bowl and began to peel it. 'There are no new developments. Only the engineers make progress, and our most significant progress we hide from the rest of the world. It is unsustainable.'

'I see stability wherever I look,' said Second

'I see inertia.' Hypatia offered Second a segment of the fruit.

'Interesting,' said Second, looking slightly concerned. 'I will spend the weekend considering this hypothesis.'

'Do. But, in addition, I need you to keep an eye on all team members. For now, I don't want a leak about a codex hunt to get into the public domain.'

'The usual way?'

'No, I think that has to stop as well. No more deaths. If anyone starts talking, cloud their memory and monitor them. Monitor the media channels, as well. Maybe it's time to re-run *The Sopranos*. That should keep everyone busy.'

'After the scenes in the city?' said Second in surprise.

210

'Quite right. *Downton Abbey* instead.'

Second nodded his approval. 'Good choice. We need to pacify the population right now. It's our duty to protect this society and Beta Earth. We all took the vows.'

'I know. I just don't know how killing them cares for them.'

'For the greater good.' Second trotted out the standard justification, but Hypatia frowned.

'I am currently unconvinced of that argument, although it does have merit. For now just cloud them, as I said. We have a lot to think about.'

As Second left, Hypatia lay down on the floor and stared up at the ceiling. She liked to stretch out and think like that. The floor of the stepper's room was as good as any. She kicked off her high heels and wiggled her toes. The future of two worlds lay in her hands as well as those two teams of curators and murderers. If she backed the curators, could she rely on their sense of duty to act how she wanted? Alternatively, would she be able to blackmail and manipulate the other team into a position she wanted? Minju had surprised her, and she realised that society might be in a more perilous state than she realised. Maybe she wasn't the only one who had realised how turgid society had become? Either way, she needed to get it back under control.

Which team would she have more success at neutralising? Which team would she have more success at eliminating? One thing was certain, no one could end up with details on how to build a quantum stepper. That was her domain and her honoured duty, and no one was going to get in her way.

Day Five – Russia - Clio

Clio was skulking down in a marsh and trying to have the time of her life. She was back on Alpha, and finally leading her own team. Ever since being stranded on Beta Earth, she'd had to wait for Anansi to notice or care that she was in the wrong spot. The pair of them had had a fun year playing havoc, but it was so good to be home. She hadn't realised how much until she found herself yanked back and sitting next to a savage Minju Chen.

Despite all the petty drama: the pharaoh shouting and being ignored, Minju fuming, Anansi laughing; in that room, the air had smelt beautiful. She had looked out the window, and admired the clean, graceful Alexandrian architecture. The people walking on the plazas below were free from disease and poverty. Although, admittedly, they were currently looking a bit put out as they stepped over fallen masonry. She would have to fix that. Misery and deprivation made people very whiney. Now she was home, and she was going to find a way to clean her slate. And that started with her current mission.

Granted, Stefan Seidel and Mo Oddy were not who she would have picked to help her in the first stage of her re-assimilation. They would be good at their job; it was just their company was somewhat lacking. She had been spoilt by her previous partners. Running around with a god had been exhilarating and before that, she and Neith had been invincible. She shook her head, no point dwelling.

Now, she was also crouching in a marsh which was sub-optimal. And while her trousers were waterproof, the cold was still making her knees uncomfortable. The midges weren't improving her disposition either as they bit at her skin. The team were crouched down in one of the many ditches that crisscrossed this vast, open landscape, a scrawny bush their only cover. About half a mile ahead sat the Grimaldi homestead, a huge sprawling residence resembling nothing short of an actual hamlet. There were no visible roads and supposedly all access was by air. Nor was there any sort of fence or wall, instead they looked at the range of large stone buildings with red and green domed turrets and long connecting walkways. On top of each flat section sat a rocket launcher, although looking through her visor, they were unmanned. On the far edge of the compound, Clio noted a hangar capable of housing several planes. Sat beside the hangar were two tanks. Nothing said warlord quite like a tank or two.

According to Anansi, there was an underground road that started in the heart of the compound and exited several miles away along a lonely stretch of road.

'I thought you said Anansi gave you the full security breakdown for the compound?' sneered Mo, as he smashed his hands around a butterfly. 'Which part of the camel's arse have we landed on?'

214

'Are we on top of the road? Are we supposed to dig down to it?'

Clio arched her eyebrows at Stefan. 'I'm going to do you the honour of pretending I didn't hear that. I take it you weren't the brightest in your class?'

Stefan picked at the stalks of grass around him and shredded the small leaves, leaving each stalk bare. A minty perfume filled the air, and his stomach gave an audible rumble.

'What do we do if we have to, you know, actually kill someone?'

Mo and Clio looked at each other and shrugged.

'You kill them.'

'Yes, but, I mean, they're Alphas?' He began to shred another stalk of grass.

Clio tilted her head and tried to remember that Stefan had only recently graduated. He was so green.

'Do you honestly think there is any difference between killing a Beta or an Alpha? They are both human.'

Mo snorted and spat on the floor. 'The infamous Clio Masoud teaching ethics! Look Seidel, obviously, if you have to choose to save someone, you save your own kind. Otherwise, just kill anyone who prevents you from doing what you want.'

'Kill anyone who prevents you doing what you want,' mimicked Clio in a guttural voice. She continued mocking now.

'When the queue is too long and prevents you from getting to the front, just kill everyone. Prevented from having seconds? Kill 'em. Prevented from having a drink at a children's party? Kill 'em. That's how the mighty reds do it, apparently.'

Mo narrowed his eyes but didn't reply.

Seeing that she had failed to needle him, she turned back to Stefan. 'You know the drill. We're curators, we do not kill, we incapacitate.'

'Yes, but on our other missions…' Even now he was reluctant to openly admit to stealing artefacts and thwarting missions.

'Well, judge the situation.' She sighed. Being team leader was turning into something of a drag.

'It's the Grimaldi stronghold.' Mo said with a grunt, contradicting her. 'Kill on sight.'

Stefan gulped but nodded in agreement. Clio rolled her eyes. Was he seriously just going along with what the biggest man said?

'Nubi's balls, what is wrong with you, Mo? That's dreadful advice. Do you want to tell everyone you've arrived?' Clio turned to her colleague. 'Stefan, only kill if you have been spotted. If you can incapacitate that would be better.'

Clio was hoping after they retrieved the codex that Minju would find a way to re-integrate her into Alpha. She did not want her homecoming to involve a blood vendetta with the Grimaldis, because she wasn't sure she'd survive the attention of the crime family. If they decided to come after her, she would have to kill the entire clan before she'd be safe again.

The Grimaldis were one of the reasons there was so little crime. It was a contradiction, but governments had noticed that if you allowed a certain criminal element to expand, they would monitor any other criminal organisations and snuff them out. It was a curious arrangement, and one that the custodians didn't like. However, the civil leaders did, and as they controlled a lot of the media output, most of the crimes went unreported. Only a few would be leaked out to feed and manipulate society.

The shadows were beginning to lengthen as the sun fell on the horizon, and the three of them considered their plan.

'What I don't understand,' said Mo, 'is why someone with as much ability as Anansi, who was able to transport us across an entire continent in the blink of an eye, who knows exactly where the painting is and how to disable the security, would put us out here. How does someone that powerful make such a mistake?'

'Because it wasn't a mistake. We are exactly where he wants us to be. It's funny.'

All three of them looked up at the sign again.

'So, do you think that's a joke as well?' said Stefan, pointing up behind him. He was sat on the grass, the bulk of his weight leant against a large metal sign.

'"Keep Out. Landmines" seems completely in line with both Grimaldi and Anansi,' scoffed Clio.

'Only I can't see any,' said Stefan, his visor over his eyes.

They quickly decided to approach the house in darkness. Their suits would muffle any heat radiation, and the goggles would pick out the landmines. Stefan was scanning the land between the stream and the house, and it seemed to be clear.

'Maybe it's just a bluff?'

'Not really the Grimaldi family style,' said Mo.

Clio studied him carefully. As a red custodian, he had greater access to the actual operations of the various criminal factions. Much as it irked her, he did have more knowledge about this scenario. She was supposed to be team leader, but she knew people like Mo. He would try to take control, and she wasn't having that. This was her mission, and it wasn't going to fail because some knuckle-dragging ego on legs wanted the glory.

Mo activated his visor and looked across the land. 'It's not a bluff, the whole area is littered with landmines. Non-uniform placement.'

Clio flicked on her visor, but again the land looked clean to her.

'Are you sure? I'm not reading anything?'

Mo passed over his visor and she patched it in warily. Suits and visors were individually configured. Using someone else's always caused headaches and discomfort, and, after only a short period, nausea. She activated the visor and looked ahead. Even through the swirling double vision she could see all the hot spots of hundreds of landmines. Tugging the visor off, she thrust it back at Mo and rubbed her temples.

'Why is your kit better than ours?'

'Because you curators only deal with Betas and their level of technology, whereas we custodians have to deal with Alpha technology. You fight monkeys, we fight equals.'

'Don't make me laugh. You would piss yourself if you ever had to deal with some of the nutters we face. What do you lot do? Make sure the streets are clean and that everyone is up to date with their donations?'

Stefan cleared his throat as Clio and Mo glared at each other. 'He has a point. We need to upgrade our kit, who knows what else we are missing?'

'And how do you propose we do that?' asked Clio.

'We could— Oh, right.'

Clio tore at a hangnail while she tried to think of a way through the situation. Normally, she would contact a section head from the curators to request the upgrade. But now they had all been outed, they wouldn't be getting any additional help. And Anansi had been crystal clear about offering transportation services only. He shouldn't have given her the security information on the *Mona Lisa* either. Maybe he thought depositing her in a stream by the side of a landmine field redressed the balance.

'Is there an engineer we can contact?'

'Great Ra, Stefan, did you not use your eyes? Not a single engineer had a crown. We have no engineers on or side.'

'That is so unfair!'

Mo spat and ran through another weapons check. 'Nothing is fair. Take what you want. Stop whining.' He continued to clean his gun as he talked. 'You two will have to follow me as we approach the compound. Masoud, you take the back and watch the rear. I'll clear the way to the painting. Once we have it off the wall, you call your god, and we will be gone.'

It was pretty much the identical plan they had agreed on earlier, only now Clio and Mo had changed positions. Frustrated, Clio had to agree with the new strategy. She looked at Mo's superior kit enviously, then shook her head. Nothing could be done right now except proceed.

She decided to take advantage of the stream. A heavy mist emanating from the water would be entirely plausible and would add another layer of cover. The sun had set, and the last elements of light were beginning to fade away.

'Stefan. Deploy some of the smoke gigs along the stream, we'll head off once the mist is properly assembled.'

Mo nodded his approval, but Stefan just looked at her blankly.

'I haven't packed any.'

Clio looked at him incredulously. 'I told you to tool up?'

'I did.' He went on to explain what he had brought.

'That's barely half of what we need.'

'You didn't specify—'

'Sweet baba cakes, why didn't you ask?'

'To think everyone makes such a big thing about you curators,' said Mo sourly. 'I have some, we'll use mine.'

This was going from bad to worse. Mo was taking over the mission, and it was all Stefan's fault. Neith always used to double-check, which Clio had considered a waste of time, as Clio was always fully prepared. She was one hundred per cent reliable. Unless, of course, you were including betrayal. But arriving on a mission with only half the arsenal for you and your partner... What was he thinking? When they got back to base, she would ditch Stefan and re-establish her authority over Mo. For now, she would lead the team to a successful conclusion.

'Let's go,' said Mo. The mist was obscuring the fortress and outer hangars.

'I'll say when we go,' snapped Clio. 'I'm the team leader don't forget.'

'Good luck making your way through the landmines.'

He stood and walked forwards. Stefan looked worriedly at Clio but jumped up and hurried after him. Scowling, Clio got up, brushing the leaves from her trousers. She walked into the mist, carefully following

Stefan's back, contemplating all the ways in which she could hurt him.

Day Five - Clio

Getting into the compound had been relatively easy for Team Anansi. The mist obscured the sweep lights, and Mo's visor showed the way through the landmines. For an Alpha compound, the security was low-key but effective. However, the Grimaldis weren't expecting invasions by actual custodians and curators. If they had, they might have improved the security levels of the biometric keypad that Clio easily circumvented. This was where a curator excelled over a custodian. She was used to creeping around unnoticed. Mo was used to simply kicking in the door.

The three were now fully clothed in their bio suits, allowing them to communicate through the internal speakers, but not alerting anyone to their presence. Even if you couldn't hear them, it was obvious from the body language there was a row going on. Mo's arms were folded. Clio's were flying.

'Of course I'm going to lead the bloody way,' hissed Clio. 'Anansi told me where it is. What are you going to do? Ask someone?'

'That's right. I'm going to ask you, and you're going to tell me. Remember, my visor is picking up more hidden technology than yours. It makes sense for me to go first.'

'But you have no experience in evasion and finesse. We need to get in and out without anyone knowing we're here.'

'And you will now watch the rear.'

The three crept through the door and into a long corridor. Anansi had told her which route to take, avoiding all the major living areas. They entered via the closest door to the painting. Clio had calculated it should take just five minutes to get to the display room.

'I'm not reading any type of motion sensors. Seidel, Masoud. Are you picking anything up?'

Clio tapped her brace. When it proved negative, she examined the walls and floor, gently running her hands across the wall, testing for vibrations or currents of air.

'Nothing. Just heat sensors, which our suits will camouflage. That's curious. Okay, I suggest—'

'Keep moving. Eyes and ears, but at least it's one less thing to worry about.'

Clio ground her teeth. Having to give way to macho heroics was making her lose focus. However, he was right, his tech was better. That said, she beat him hands down on brain power. She brought up the rear and tried to work out why there were no motion sensors. They moved quietly through the corridors, pausing at each intersection, waiting while the visor's prism view confirmed the next turn was empty before they jogged forward. Despite their size, Mo and Stefan ran as quietly as Clio. Their cushioned footwear helped, but both men had trained to approach a target with stealth.

Clio was still worrying about the lack of sensors when the explanation flew past. A flock of canaries filled the air, their small bodies passing her head in a flurry of birdsong and yellow feathers. She called out to the two men. Stefan nodded, but Mo was still trying to work out what *birds* was code for when the first one flew past his head. He drew his laser and shot at the bird, exploding the tiny bundle into goblets of blood and bone. A second after that, a forcefield dropped at either end of the corridor. The heat sensors couldn't track the battle suits, nor could it track the birds' body heat. But laser fire? That it had no problem detecting.

All three drew their weapons and checked the ceiling for escape. They heard footsteps running in their direction. Whoever was approaching was not much concerned with stealth.

Within moments, both ends of the corridor were bristling with security personnel. Stefan and Mo both fired, but their shots simply fizzled out at the forcefield. In return, the guards shot at the floor by Clio's feet. One-way forcefield. Super. Now they were trapped with a flock of agitated canaries, their terrified bodies crashing into the three curators.

If she lived past this, she was going to ditch Stefan and bloody kill Mo.

The guards suddenly parted to make way for a tall man in his forties. He was wearing a smoking jacket over a pair of dark trousers, and a set of monogrammed slippers. One hand held a brandy glass, his other was in his trouser pocket. His dark hair was slicked back revealing a large burn running down from his temple to his chin, the red scar tissue emphasising the blue of his eyes. The scar was remarkable because it was clearly a choice. It was even more remarkable because, if you were going to choose a life of crime, you'd surely want to blend into the background. Unless, of course, you were an apex criminal. Untouchable and terrifying.

'Good evening. I do not remember inviting guests. Who wants to die first?'

His voice was heavily accented, and again Clio decided that was a choice.

'Grimaldi is it?' asked Clio.

He chuckled. Even that sounded contrived. This man was a walking artifice. 'Ah, we are going to play. Yes? Let me see if I can name you. Curator equipment. Tall, black, beautiful and very bad. You are Clio Masoud. I am right. Correct?'

Clio wondered about calling the language police, his speech patterns felt like a deliberate construct, as did the exaggerated accent and broken language. She smiled back at him, remaining silent.

He shook his head. 'Well, this is interesting. This is connected to our crowns. No? You all have them, so I am not going to kill you. At least, not immediately. Put your guns down and let us talk.'

The three looked at each other. Clio spoke through their private channels, ensuring Grimaldi couldn't hear what was being said.

'Right. Guns on the floor. Stefan, the minute they let down the force field, deploy the concussion bang. Our suits will protect us from the worst of it.'

Stefan looked bleak.

'You didn't pack the bangs did you?' Clio hurled her laser on the ground in disgust.

'I do not care for private conversation,' interrupted Grimaldi with a hint of amusement, his broken English grating Clio's ears. 'Please, also removing your hoods and your braces.'

'Braces are integral to the suit,' said Mo with a smirk, which was immediately wiped off his face as he was told to strip.

Standing in her smalls, Clio was trying to decide which of her colleagues she would kill first. She and Stefan had stripped immediately. Nothing was gained by delay. They needed to move on to the next stage. When the forcefields came down, they could re-evaluate the situation. Stefan might be bloody useless, but he knew all the trade craft in getting out of tricky situations. Mo was curiously reluctant to remove his clothes until he was down to his skin and a digital tattoo of two white kittens running across his torso was fully revealed. Grimaldi bit his lip and tried not to snigger. The moment had come, and Clio prepared for attack. She slowed her breathing and flexed her fingers, ready for combat.

'Okay, shields down.'

As the forcefield dropped, Clio lunged for her kit, pulling Stefan in front of her as a shield. Mo reached for his gun, but neither was fast enough as Grimaldi threw in his own gas bomb. She tried to kick it away, but the gas was already venting out of the device as it sailed towards her feet. Clio had just enough time to see the guards and Grimaldi place masks over their faces before she passed out to the sound of canaries singing wildly.

Day Five - Clio

Clio was sitting on a chair. Her head was hanging down, her eyes closed. As she came to, she kept it that way. She would fake unconsciousness until she had a better idea of what was going on. A band around her chest secured her to the chair, but her wrists and ankles were free. Listening carefully to the noise of the room, she decided it was mostly unfurnished. Lots of open floor space. Two people were close by, breathing with their heads down. Mo and Stefan were alive. She'd need them to get out of this.

A door opened and closed as someone entered the room. That helped. She was now able to place the room at roughly five metres square with a high ceiling. She was sitting six feet from the exit. Disconcertingly, there was a small movement of air on the floor nearby, indicating an open drain or sluice.

'Are they awake?' asked Grimaldi.

'Yes, sir. All three, according to the chair's readings. All are currently feigning unconsciousness,' a woman's voice answered with little interest in her captive's pretence.

'Right.' His tone changed as he addressed the intruders. 'You are sitting in volt cloud. I will count down from three for you to lift your heads, open your eyes and place your bodies in comfortable position. Three—'

Clio didn't hesitate. She flicked her head behind and counted two guards by the door. Snapping her head back, she placed her hands on her knees and looked Grimaldi in the eye. To one side of Grimaldi, a woman was monitoring a console, the blue light of the screen casting shadows across her face. The room had no windows and no other furnishings beyond their chairs and the console. The walls, ceiling and floor were made of the same smooth white surface and in the centre of the floor was a drain. Perfect for washing down the waste. In all her years of being a curator she had never been tortured and she had no intention of today being her first experience. She began to sweat.

At least now she knew why her legs and arms weren't restrained. A volt cloud was no laughing matter. Stefan had also moved quickly into a position of attention. On the count of one, Mo had decided to try and fake them out. Grimaldi just nodded at the assistant, who touched the screen and electrocuted the red custodian. Clio noticed the woman's hand shook as she operated the machine but when Grimaldi looked at her to tell her to stop, the operator's tremor was under control. Not a willing torturer then. Or maybe she was past caring. Either way, Clio didn't think she could rely on her to help them and the two guards would likely shoot them. For now, she needed to give Grimaldi anything he asked for.

'Number three. That was lowest setting, yes. You would like to try again?'

Mo sat upright, eyes focused ahead, hands on knees and a small sheen of sweat on his forehead.

Volt clouds used a portable electricity field. Electricity fields had been first used to herd dangerous animals away from habitations or towards safer environments in times of fire, flood or drought. It acted like a small cloak, enveloping an area around the animal and prevented them, through mild shocks, from moving in the wrong direction. Handlers could manipulate the field from a safe distance and gradually move the animal into place.

It hadn't taken long before some bright spark realised it could be used in other ways. Crowd control was mooted and immediately banned. Clio had heard of volt clouds but had never experienced one.

'Understand, you are completely enveloped in the cloud. The first few centimetres of the field around your body will give you mild buzz. After that, it hurts. Try it now.'

Clio wasn't an idiot. There was no way she was going to voluntarily electrocute herself. She winced as Stefan extended a finger. This was going to be ugly. As his finger moved, he flinched in reaction to the first shock. In flinching, the rest of his body moved into the volt zone. In trying to escape the shock, his movements became wilder until he started screaming.

Grimaldi nodded to the assistant who switched the cloud off.

'You have three seconds to get yourself comfortable and still.'

Stefan complied, although now he was panting. 'As courtesy I have extended your buffer zone just a fraction so that any residual spasms don't set you off again. Now you can talk. The buffer around your heads is also a little wider. This is good, yes?'

He pulled a chair forward and sat down a few feet out of reach of any sudden lunges. In Grimaldi's world, it was always best to prepare for the worst. None of the captives should be able to reach him, but why take the risk?

'Now, why has my evening been interrupted by two curators and a custodian? Are you here to kill me? I would have assumed not, given the presence of curators. But you're wearing golden crowns, so who knows?'

Clio was running through scenarios. She assumed the cloud was tied to the chair, so even if she lunged forward, the cloud would travel with her. Could she get to Grimaldi fast enough before the electricity incapacitated her? She had a bladed fingernail. She could use that to cut the belt securing her to the chair. But again, how bad was the charge? Mo and Stefan's reactions suggested it was pretty nasty, and she was certain that Grimaldi would be happy to use a fatal charge if required. For now, her best bet was to talk her way out of this. The truth would work, but how much?

'Screw you!' panted Mo.

Grimaldi nodded towards the assistant, and Mo started screaming as the cloud tightened around him. Stefan was sat next to him, desperately trying to stay still as his colleague screamed and contorted. His arms and legs flapped as his jaw stretched open in a high-pitched scream. Grimaldi pulled out a gun and shot Mo dead. The noise of the gun shocked Clio and she watched as the assistant flinched. Guns didn't exist on Alpha Earth, they had long since evolved to use the more efficient lasers. Guns were loud, brutal, and often inefficient. At a close range though they certainly had a lot of impact.

Mo's body slumped forward, still held by the waistband, his blood flowing down to the sluice.

Clio hadn't moved her head an inch, but she could see the blood out of the corner of her eyes. Interestingly, the chair hadn't tipped over. Clearly, it was attached to the floor, through the leg shafts. She kept running through these little details as she kept her breathing shallow and tried not to smell anything.

'Number one, number two, who wants to talk? I only need one of you.'

'We're here to steal—' began Clio, but Stefan spoke rapidly over the top of her.

'—the *Mona Lisa*. We're here to steal your painting. We were sent by the pharaoh and Minju Chen. We are here with their approval.'

Clio twisted her head slightly to try and make eye contact with Stefan. She began to feel a very slight buzz

233

around her skin. Stefan was sweating heavily and it mixed with Mo's blood on his face. His eyes were blinking rapidly, and he was breathing erratically. At this rate, he would have a heart attack before he got to the end of the story. If only she could signal to him to not mention the gods. They would need some sort of leverage to get out of this alive. Right now, she wasn't worried for her own life. She knew Grimaldi would want to know more, and she was the infamous Clio. Traitor and all-round bad egg. He would want to talk to her. That would be her opportunity to try and get herself, and maybe Stefan, out of here.

'I'm the leader of this mission. I will take responsibility for our actions.'

'Ignore her,' panted Stefan. 'I know everything. We want the *Mona Lisa* because it has a clue to find da Vinci's lost codex that shows how to make a quantum stepper from scratch. If you take me to the painting, I can show you where the clue is.'

'Interesting. And what should I do with Clio here?'

'Kill her. She's officially dead anyway. We don't need her. I know everything she does.'

Clio looked up at the ceiling. Well, maybe she wouldn't waste time saving Stefan after all.

'And, Clio,' asked Grimaldi politely. 'What do you say? Shall I kill you? Yes?'

'Your call. I mean, you don't have to kill anyone.'

'True, but where is fun in that?' Lifting his gun he shot Stefan in the head and smiled at Clio. 'Now then, Masoud, I think you have a new partner.'

Day Five – Beta Paris - Neith

The city stank. Petroleum fumes laced the air, and a cold rain hit me in the face. Why had this civilisation thought that these cold northern countries made for a base of excellence? The Eiffel Tower rose on the skyline behind Julius' head, and I was unsurprised to see his smile. In a minute, he was going to make some asinine comment about the weather. I loved him like a brother, but he really did have a weather fixation.

'Oh wow, Neith, that smells so good. Do you know there's a word for it?'

'Pollution,' I said dourly.

'No silly. Petrichor, the smell of rain.'

A word to describe what rain smells like. I decided to ignore him for now. I had too much to handle right now. An Englishman's obsession with being cold and uncomfortable was not on my list of priorities. Plus, relations between us had been frosty recently, and I was trying to make amends. Seeing him back home and over the moon, I couldn't help but feel bad for how I had been behaving and all that he had gone through. I didn't want to speak now and put my foot in it.

'Ramin, have you found us somewhere?'

Five minutes earlier we had been deposited in the Jardin des Tuileries, a large open space near the Louvre. Next time, I would remember to tell Giovanetti to be more specific with her instructions.

'I've booked a corner table at *Rue Blanc*. We'll be able to discuss our next move there. Come on, it's five minutes this way.'

'Rue Blanc,' said Julius in delight. 'I've always wanted to eat there.'

'This isn't some sort of epicurean jolly, Julius.'

'I know we're going to break into the Louvre and steal the *Mona Lisa*, but it would be an even bigger crime not to enjoy the finest cuisine in France along the way.'

Working with Julius was a lot like working with Clio. Both were very easily distracted. Clio was always off looking for a greater challenge, a bigger thrill or threat. Julius was just incredibly curious. Neither were very good at staying focused. Life recently had become disappointing, and I was trying hard to rectify the situation.

As we were waved to our table, I could hear someone arguing with the *maître d'* that they had most definitely booked and confirmed. I knew Clio would be nudging me right now and laughing. However, I had to grab Julius' sleeve, I wasn't certain, but I had a sneaky feeling he was about to return to the front and offer them the table that we had just nabbed from them.

'Not now, Julius, we need to plan.'

We sat down and Julius looked around the room with a disconsolate air.

'What's wrong?' asked Ramin.

'Nothing.' He picked at his napkin. 'It's just I feel bad. That party has obviously been looking forward to coming here for months. It just feels, ugh, I don't know. Impolite?'

Ramin smiled and poured everyone a glass of water.

'There were three suitable reservations I could have cancelled for this timeslot. There was a party that earned the most money last year but paid the least tax. There was a young couple. The man made a large purchase at a jeweller's last week. Finally, there was a family where the daughter is eighteen today. I chose the party that paid the least taxes. Did I make the right choice?'

Julius smiled and raised his glass to Ramin.

I shook my head. 'That was time you could have spent researching the Louvre.'

He gave me one of his sardonic looks as the waiter took our order. As he left, Ramin replied. 'It was a quick subroutine that I tasked Tiresias to handle. Despite not coming through the stepper, the wrist brace still appears to have a connection to it.'

'Do you think that's the gods' doing, or is there some independent quantum link in our brace?' asked Julius

'You'd need to ask an engineer,' I said, 'but my money is on your gods. Remember when we were abandoned in the fifteenth-century and our braces stopped working?'

'In which case,' suggested Julius, 'download all the information you need directly to the brace. There's no telling how long the link will remain viable. Gods have lots of words to describe them. One of the biggies is capricious.'

I wasn't happy, but we began to do as he suggested. The idea that we were on Beta Earth not via the stepper, and that our recall button wouldn't snap us back to safety, was unnerving.

'Do you think the recall button still works?' said Ramin, echoing my thoughts.

'We'll find out later probably when the Louvre security guards are firing bullets at us.'

It had only been a few hours since we had left Alpha. Back in the briefing room, Giovanetti had quickly taken charge once she announced martial law. It was a proud moment, watching her restore calm. Having established that the most pressing issue was the codex, she assigned the two most experienced curators in the room, and the best Beta expert available to be the team that would step across. Or fly across, or hop, or whatever it was that Loki had done to bring us here. We were either the fuddy-duddies or Team Loki. Neither title suited me. Loki had a soft spot for Julius and Arthur. I wasn't sure how he felt about the rest of us but decided it didn't matter and I didn't care.

There had been various discussions about the clue *La Gioconda has the answer*, but the solution was immediate. The answer would be on the back of the *Mona Lisa*. Only Julius had disagreed, saying that was far too easy, wouldn't someone have noticed a clue written on the back of the *Mona Lisa*? I had suggested it was written in invisible ink, and he'd asked if I'd watched *National Treasure* too many times?

I blushed but was glad that no one else noticed or agreed with Julius. And so here we were. While Giovanetti began to instil some discipline after the gods and the revelation of the rest of the criminal networks, I wondered if she would arrest her husband herself, or leave it to someone else. Personally, I wasn't sure if I'd be able to trust myself. Maybe he would do the decent thing and stop.

The waiter removed our bowls of soup, and I decided it was time to build bridges with Julius.

'How was your call to your parents?'

He poured the water and smiled fondly. 'So good. I can't begin to tell you. Of course, they have been receiving the postcards, but they arrived out of order. And I think some of the curators who delivered them might have had to write some themselves. Maybe they lost the originals? Anyway, it doesn't matter. It was just lovely to listen to them and catch up on all their news. Dad finally won first prize for his carrots so, understandably, he's elated. Mum wants to know if I'm eating properly.' He waved his hand around the restaurant and laughed. 'I'll have to send her a snap of this and some locusts. See which she approves of more.'

'What did she say when you explained you wouldn't be able to visit?' asked Ramin, and I watched as Julius' face fell a little.

'I told her I was a tax exile for the year. She didn't buy it, but I think she's going to go along with it.'

The waiter arrived with the next course, and Julius seemed glad of the diversion. Maybe when we got the codex, there would indeed be more knowledge in it? Maybe we could adjust the stepper, and Julius might actually be able to visit his folks? We hadn't discussed it because I didn't want to get his hopes up, but I'm sure it had occurred to him as well.

'Right, let's get on with things. Ramin, are we good?'

'Yes, static field running. We can now discuss running naked down the Champs-Élysées shouting The French are buffoons and no one will turn their heads.'

'Good, now we haven't had long to plan this, so I'm open to suggestions, but this is what I propose.'

Julius looked at me puzzled after I outlined the plan. 'Are we doing this at night?'

'No, a daytime robbery is easier, as there is more scope for chaos. At night, you are very exposed. That doesn't always hold true, but it does in this case.'

He still looked unhappy. 'I don't understand. The painting is on a wall, not in a store. How will you get past the crowds?'

'What crowds?'

241

'Oh God,' said Julius. 'Look, I'm really sorry to be the one to put the fly in the ointment, but the *Mona Lisa* is a huge deal over here. She's displayed in her own room, and every day that room is crowded with visitors. And I mean crowded, all day long. We probably have five minutes maximum in the morning, when the front door opens and the visitors make it as far as the painting. I came here once on a school trip. It was dreadful. No one saw a thing, really. It was very hot, and everyone was pushing, and they smelt bad.' He shook his head. 'Basically, you will need to not only deal with the security features, but also a good fifty people all standing in a small, crowded room blocking all your exits.' He paused, waiting to see what I would say. Ramin and I exchanged a glance.

Julius put his fork down. 'You're doing your superior Alpha smile again. Unless I've missed something, I can't see how your plan is going to work. There's just no way you can get that painting off the wall and get out in one piece. Even if the security guards didn't shoot you, the mob would probably tear you apart. No way will they permit you to steal the *Mona Lisa*.'

'Good job it's a fake then,' I said and watched as he stared at the pair of us.

'A fake?' His astonishment was priceless.

'One hundred per cent,' said Ramin as I ate my food. 'The real one is down in the vaults in Bay X456, labelled Man in Boat.' He sipped his water. 'Mind you, Neith, I'm not happy taking it. This is actual theft, not curation.'

'I know, butt. We'll just have to make sure it gets returned before anyone notices it's missing. It should all run like clockwork.' I took a forkful of risotto and silently thanked Ramin for choosing this restaurant. 'Just so long as we get there on time. Julius, this time, when we head towards the Louvre, could you not put money in every busker's hat? You're rewarding them all, regardless of merit. You even tipped that dreadful Freddie Mercury singer.'

He laughed at me, and I felt part of me unwind.

'Actually, that was a Cher impersonator,' I said smiling. I hadn't realised how much tension I was carrying. I had a lot of guilt about Julius, and I hated the fact that recently we had been arguing a lot.

'That singer was bloody awful, wasn't she? But God it felt so good to see and hear buskers again. I even tipped the mime artist.'

I couldn't see what had been wrong with him, but Julius had shuddered and made a joke about hell freezing over. Grinning at each other, we discussed the merits of the buskers and the strange Beta habit of public expression and enjoyed our lunch. The day was going well, and everything was under control.

Which is why, three hours later, we were all sat in a prison cell in the bowels of the Louvre waiting for the police to haul us away.

Day Five – Clio

Clio stared at Grimaldi and reassessed the situation. In the past year, she had worked with Anansi, Stefan, and Mo. And now, in her ever-growing list of undesirable partners, it looked like she was going to have to add a murdering psychopath to the list. He waved his gun at her.

'Follow. And please do not kill any more of mother's birds along the way. That is my little game.'

Clio stood up and stretched, stepping away from the corpses of Mo and Stefan without a second glance.

'And do not try to kill me,' drawled Grimaldi, as he looked back over his shoulder. 'I have a little surprise in store for you if you do.'

Clio followed him into the corridor. 'Nah, I'll pass. Let's go look at this painting.'

As Clio took in her surroundings, she looked for exits and gradually mapped out the compound, trying to guess at the floor plan. If not for now, it might prove useful in the future.

'So, that burn on your face and neck? How'd you get that? Looks old.'

Clio figured that despite its obviousness, no one ever mentioned his scarring. Hopefully, she might be able to annoy him. An angry man was more likely to make mistakes. Grimaldi turned and looked at her in surprise, then smiled.

'Ah, no one ever asks me that. It was a gift from my mother. She was having one of her turns. I don't know if she meant to hit me, or if it was wrong place, wrong time. It was always so hard to tell.'

Well, so much for throwing him off his stride. And now it was Clio that was drawn in. Burnt skin was so easily repaired, even fast-growing children's skin. His mother must have been barbarous.

'How old were you?' asked Clio, appalled, despite herself. 'Did she refuse treatment for you?'

'I was eighteen years.' He looked at Clio and leered, the red scar tissue pulling at his lower lip. 'I had full autonomy and insisted that they didn't repair it.'

'But why?'

'Can you not guess?'

'Revenge?'

'Indeed, yes. Every day, that deranged fool has to look at what she did. I laughed and it did have other benefits. People flinched when they saw me. Just my face created fear before I even made a move.'

Clio was thinking like a curator. 'But you would have been so recognisable?'

'Indeed. And so I learnt discretion. To make my moves out of sight. I suppose I should thank her for who I am today.'

He laughed and opened a door. The room beyond was well lit with ambient ceiling and wall lights. There were no windows and no shadows, and the walls were hung with

245

a jumble of paintings. Sitting on a bench in front of the *Mona Lisa* was an old lady. She was twisting and turning, mimicking the posture and expression of the woman in the painting, tucking her long, white hair behind her ear and fiddling with her dress.

'Out,' said Grimaldi in an almost bored tone. A younger woman in the corner of the room jumped up at Grimaldi's command and scurried over to the old lady. Clio hadn't immediately noticed her and chided herself for being so transfixed by the older woman.

'I'm not going.' The old woman's voice was distracted and a little bit lost. 'I'm staying with my friends.'

'You don't have any friends, Mother. You are a mad old witch, and no one likes you. Oh, and one of your birds is dead.'

Tears welled up in her eyes and she staggered against her carer.

'You killed another one of my birds? Bedrich, why do you torture me?' Her voice was tremulous, and she was breathing heavily.

'I will kill them all if you don't get out of this room now,' Grimaldi sneered, and she shuffled out of the room, leaning on the younger woman who had not said a word. Even now she refused to make eye contact with either Grimaldi or Clio, and Clio recognised utter terror when she saw it. She wondered how long she had been taking care of the older woman.

246

'Right,' said Grimaldi, 'let us have a look at this painting.'

Clio watched as his mother took one last look at the paintings, as her carer slowly pulled the door closed. Obviously, kidnapping the mother to exploit Grimaldi wasn't an option. Although maybe he would be cross that someone other than himself was torturing her? Maybe she could free the mother and really piss him off?

'Now. Before we start, you need to understand my level of protection. I am biometrically linked to this collection. Yes? You understand? If I am damaged or, what a tragedy, I'm killed, the nanites in the frames of these artworks will start to dissolve the paint.'

'What about the statues?'

'They are all hot-wired, goes one goes all. You Egyptians don't have a monopoly on clever engineers you know.'

Half an hour later, the pair of them sat on the bench with the painting between them. They had examined it from the back, the sides, the wooden panel itself and found nothing untoward. No hidden message, no code, no *X-marks-the-spot*.

'We need better equipment. My visor isn't picking anything up. We need to go to Alexandria.'

Grimaldi looked at Clio and began to pick at his fingernails. 'I do not think I would be very comfortable there.'

'Oh, I don't know, you'd be surrounded by thieves and murderers. You'll fit in like a cuckoo in the nest.'

He looked at her, frowning, but shrugged with a tight smile.

'Very well. I'll get the plane ready.'

Grimaldi stood up and headed towards the doors. Clio watched his back, trying to work out how best to hide the interference of the gods from Grimaldi. If he came to Alexandria, he would discover what had been occurring. But, for as long as possible, she wanted to have the upper hand. On the other hand, if she had to spend more time than was necessary in his company, she thought she might kill him and balls to the paintings. She decided to make him someone else's problem.

'No need. I have an alternative method.'

'Faster than my plane?' He chuckled as he looked her over. 'I do not think so. Do not worry, I will be leaving Mother behind. Won't that be nice, you and I can become friends.' He licked his lips and winked at her. 'Yes?'

Clio gritted her teeth. Absolutely not. She had to get away from here as quickly as possible before she accidentally on purpose killed Russia's greatest crime lord.

'No.' She started whispering to Anansi. 'We don't need your plane. Just you, me, and the *Mona Lisa*. Our engineers have a few tricks up their sleeves as well. Now, are you ready?'

She smiled to herself. For a man who liked to be in full control, he was about to be very cross indeed, and she called into the air.

'Let's go.'

Day Five - Neith

We sat on a hard bench in the cell in the basement of the Louvre and looked at the floor in dismay.

'You didn't have to break the board with your foot,' I said morosely.

'Come on, Neith. I was trying to put out the flames,' said Julius, equally fed up.

'And how did that work?'

'How was I to know the guard's phone charger was going to ignite?'

It had all been going so well. We'd got into the vaults. First Engineer had given us new proto-suits to wear for this mission. Bit of an upgrade, she said, and they were dynamite. The cloth, for want of a better word, sat under our day clothes like a one-piece undergarment. As required, the fabric simply glided down our limbs, covering our skin, and emitting a perception filter of the attire we wished it to represent. In effect, we walked into the Louvre in the correct security uniform, and the brace took care of all biometric security protocols.

Again, using the wrist brace, we opened the lock on cabinet X456 and slid out the *Mona Lisa*. A small dull picture of a bored housewife that inexplicably had become Beta Earth's most treasured painting. Having secured the image, we called on the gods to get us out and tapped the recall button. Nothing happened.

'Maybe we're not meant to steal it? Maybe we're meant to uncover the clue here,' suggested Julius, and honestly, Ramin and I were both relieved with that idea.

We'd got the painting up on a workbench in one of the many pristine labs and began to study the back of the poplar wooden board the *Mona Lisa* was painted on. It had been reframed so many times that we dismissed that immediately. That was when it all went wrong very quickly.

A security guard doing his rounds saw us working and stopped for a chat. He had popped in to retrieve his phone that he'd been recharging on the sly. Ramin had been taking a full reading of the painting using the scanners in the brace, and Julius had some white spirit on a cloth to dab onto the back of the wood.

The guard reached for his phone but as he wiggled the charger, a signal from Ramin's brace shorted the charging unit and it suddenly ignited. In horror, the guard grabbed the open bottle of white spirit thinking it was water and threw it over the tiny flames. The phone was an instant inferno.

The flames ran to the painting and, within seconds, the *Mona Lisa* was on fire. Julius tried to pick it up but yelled as the flames set fire to the white spirit on his hands. Now the Mona Lisa fell to the floor, her frame breaking as its corner smashed on the ground. Julius' suit instantly activated and extended down to smother his skin. Clamping his hands instinctively under his armpits he now stamped on the flames instead. The wood appeared to be ablaze from within, the fire was spreading in two directions as the oil paint crackled and charred. The guard watched as the flames burnt through the face of the Mona *Lisa*. That's when he realised that the Louvre's greatest treasure was on fire and that's when he started to scream.

Things began to move very quickly. Ramin punched him hard enough to knock him out, grabbed the painting off the floor, and we all ran to the exit. Which is when the fire alarm sounded, the doors locked, masks dropped out of the ceiling, and all the air was sucked out of the room.

This is a great feature for extinguishing flames, but it's also pretty good at extinguishing humans. The proto-suits now came into their own. The fabric slid down, covering all extremities, and the hood section engulfed my head, pumping fresh air into the mask. I took a grateful gulp, then noticed that Ramin's suit hadn't fully deployed. He was having to use a face mask dangling from the ceiling, while Julius was holding a face mask over the fallen security guard.

Loki appeared. 'Time to go?'

A lack of air in the room didn't bother him as he smiled at the havoc. I could have killed him. 'Not now. If we go now, the guard dies.'

'So?' He looked amused. 'Are you saying you want to stay?'

'No. Of course I don't want to stay. Can you save him?'

'Why?' Loki peered at him closely. 'Is he important?'

'Yes, he's important. He's alive! He's a human being. He deserves his place in society.'

Loki yawned. 'So, not important. Now, do you want to go home?'

I ground my teeth and shook my head, watching in disbelief as Loki shrugged and disappeared. Which is how, ten minutes later, the air in the room was stabilised, and we were escorted at gunpoint into a holding cell.

***

'Now what?' said Ramin.

'Now we come to terms with destroying one of the world's greatest treasures,' said Julius despairingly. A tad melodramatic, but, honestly, he wasn't wrong.

'Ach-y-vy!' I jumped up and started to pace. 'I don't know what to do next. We've lost our clue, lost our ride, and destroyed a priceless artefact.'

'We might not have lost the clue, Neith,' said Ramin.

His brace buzzed. It had finished processing its analysis of the painting. I tapped my foot. He couldn't throw up the holo-screen, as that might alarm the locals. Instead, I had to stand and wait as I saw his eyes flick back and forth across the screen.

'Is there any—?'

'Hang on.'

He tapped the brace, read some more, then tapped it again.

'Are you kidding me?' he muttered to himself. I tried to ask him again what he had found, but he just held a hand up, returning to the screen. With each tap, his expression got more and more incredulous. Finally, he stopped reading and sighing deeply, looked up at the ceiling.

'Well, the good news is we haven't destroyed the world's greatest treasure. It's a fake.'

I didn't know whether to weep or laugh. These Betas with their constant fakery.

'Does that mean that the one upstairs is the actual original?' asked Julius.

I began thinking. Admittedly, we had announced our presence rather noisily, but we should still be able to get out of this. I started to think of a plan. Getting out wasn't an issue. We were only sat here to play nice and regroup. The minute we wanted to leave, we would. We'd just pick the locks and use some whizzbangs to create confusion. Once we'd gone, I'd erase any digital records of us. However, they would now be on high alert. Getting a closer look at the painting upstairs would be tricky.

'Are you even listening to me, Neith?'

I looked up. I had been so lost in the plan that I had missed what Ramin had said. Julius was sat with his arms folded and was scowling off into space.

'What have I missed?'

'I said that this fake shows evidence of an actual man on a boat, under the paint.'

254

'So, the Louvre knew it was a fake?' I muttered out loud, trying to make sense of it. 'No, that makes no sense. Why would a forger go to the effort of painting on top of another painting? It would be spotted instantly. Unless someone swapped this painting and knew what the dummy title of this piece was? That's it isn't it? This thief left a fake with a joke wrapped inside.'

'Hilarious,' muttered Julius.

'But this is good news,' I said, beginning to pace again. 'We'll dial into their security system and get Tiresias to analyse the security footage. They obviously managed to mask their entry and exit, but they'll have been no match for our technology. We'll find out who took it, then play chase the lady.'

Neither of the men was smiling.

'Neith, the paint analysis is modern. I've checked, double-checked, and triple-checked. This painting, both the man and boat underneath and the *Mona Lisa* on top, were painted in the last ten years.'

I didn't understand their expressions. This was great news. The trail wasn't completely cold.

'The problem is the carbon dating is wrong.'

'In what way?'

'There's no spike. There's no evidence of the nuclear tests.'

I looked at him in horror. Carbon dating was an extremely accurate way to measure the age of something. On Beta Earth, all the nuclear test explosions in the fifties had left a thumbprint on every single item on the planet. If this fake showed no evidence of the carbon-14 spike, then there was only one conclusion. I squeezed my fingers into my eyes and attempted not to scream at the top of my head. Now I understood Julius' fury.

'The original's back home isn't it? Some snivelling curator came in and stole it!' I was bouncing on the spot. I would hunt down whoever had stolen it, find the clue, find the codex, and return the *Mona Lisa* to her rightful home. But first, I needed to get to mine.

'Loki,' I snapped. The cell remained empty. I turned on Julius. 'Well, where is he?'

Julius looked at me with a raised eyebrow, and I quickly apologised.

'Sorry. I'm just mad. This isn't what curators do.'

He stared at me and unfolded his arms. 'It's what they've been doing for years. But look, that's not the issue right now. We need to get back and find the original, so you are going to have to apologise.'

'I just did.'

He shook his head. 'Not to me. To Loki. He told you the security guard wasn't important, and you told him he was wrong.'

'But he *was* wrong.'

'He's a god. They are never wrong.'

'Actually, Julius,' said Ramin, 'I've been doing a lot of research on gods lately, and from what I can see they are often wrong. In fact, they are deeply flawed, mostly to a psychotic level.'

'Alright. First things first, you can't judge them as humans. Secondly, you need to understand them against the social context in which they were created.'

I interrupted. 'Julius, we don't have time for a lecture. I mean, clearly, we do need to study this, but maybe not right now?'

He cleared his throat. 'Yes, sorry.' He smiled sheepishly. 'Bit of a hobby horse of mine. My point, that I should have made better, is that gods are not wrong, in *their* opinion. You criticised Loki, now you have to apologise. Call his name. I imagine he's listening or will be when you call him.'

I looked at Julius in disgust, but his reasoning was sound. I needed to look a god in the eye, who I didn't believe in, and lie to his face. I took a deep breath.

'Hello, Loki? Clever and smart, Loki.' I glanced across at Julius who was grinning broadly and signalling me to carry on. Ramin was shaking his head. I continued talking into the air. 'I was wrong. You were right. The guard was not important within the parameters of our brief.' Julius scrunched his face up, but it was the best I could manage. The guard *was* important. Hopefully, Loki would accept this. 'I should have listened to you and not argued. You were right.' I looked around. There was still no sign of our ride home, but Julius was gesturing at me to carry on. I was at a loss. I had said all that needed to be said. I tried again.

'Loki, you are clever and brilliant, and sharp, and smart. You are cleverer than all the engineers in the quantum facility, you are even cleverer than all the other gods. I was an idiot not to see that.'

'Yes, you were,' said Loki. I jumped back. Why did he always have to appear so close? He was looking at me in a superior way. 'That's the problem with you little humans. You always think you know more than you do. I wouldn't mind, but you know it is a bit rude.'

Being schooled by a god. My day was not improving. I looked across at the guys for help. I was worried that if I opened my mouth, I might actually say what was on my mind. Ramin clearly recognised my expression as he stepped in.

'Loki. We were wrong. This painting is a fake, the original is back on our Earth. Can you take us home?'

'Of course I can, but can I give you a tip?'

Ramin and I nodded, but Julius narrowed his eyes and cut off Loki before he spoke.

'One of the rules says you are not allowed to help. Is this tip helping us?'

'Good point,' said Loki thoughtfully. I wasn't taken in. I suspected he had deliberately tried to trick us just then and, like a fool, I had almost walked into it. Whatever else we did; we needed a proper session with Julius on how to manage the gods. I watched as he considered his next suggestion.

'How about I update you on the other team's progress if I also update them on yours?'

I thought it through. They already knew this painting was a fake. One of them had stolen it after all. I nodded at Julius to accept the offer. He was clearly better at this.

'A balanced single update seems reasonable. I am grateful.'

Loki smiled beneficently. 'Well, in that case, they have already examined the painting. The real one, that is, and have abandoned that line of inquiry.'

'But you said La Gioconda holds the key.'

'We did indeed. And then, for some reason, both teams went running off after a painting.' Loki tipped his head significantly and rolled his eyes. Clearly, he was trying not to give us a clue while beating us over the head with it.

I watched as the same realisation crossed the guys' faces.

'La Gioconda. We don't need the painting. We need the woman!'

Day Five - Minju

Minju pushed the reports away from her in disgust.

'Nothing. There is nothing in this painting. No clues, nothing. This is a waste of time.'

'Maybe a spectral analysis?' suggested the pharaoh and was treated to a withering expression.

'Why don't we just sacrifice a cockerel and see what the intestines have to say?'

'I was simply trying to help.'

'Well, you're not,' snapped Minju. She had already lost two operatives. Jim was useless, Grimaldi was unpredictable, Clio was a live wire. Haru was still sulking that he'd been outed and had suddenly become terrified of his wife. The problem with her current team was that it had too many factions pulling against each other, or just looking out for themselves. She needed access to more of her operatives. But Giovannetti's little trick had driven everyone into hiding.

'Anansi.'

The god was playing cards with Grimaldi. Despite Clio's best efforts, the pharaoh had actually tried to arrest Grimaldi as he materialised. When Grimaldi asked how he had arrived instantaneously in Egypt, Jim couldn't resist bragging that the gods answered his command. Anansi was furious at the suggestion that anyone commanded him. Minju had promised Anansi that he could kill Jim later, when order was restored, which mollified Anansi, but now left the pharaoh of the combined Niles feeling somewhat on edge.

Grimaldi had a few creative suggestions for how the pharaoh could be disposed of. Anansi cheered up immediately and challenged him to a game of chance. They were betting on the contents of Grimaldi's wine cellar. Double or quits. Anansi put his four aces down and glanced across at Minju. Grimaldi examined his own pair of aces and realised that gods cheat, and he'd just lost his wine. Clio smiled.

'What can I do for you, dear Minju?'

'This painting.' She placed her palms up and shrugged. 'There's no clue here?'

Anansi mimicked Minju, and three pairs of arms suddenly materialised all with their palms facing up in the universal gesture of a disinterested shrug. One of the custodians gave a small scream, then apologised as one of the women sneered at him.

'I never said there was a clue on the painting. I believe I said something like *La Gioconda holds the answer*. Hang on, no, that's exactly what I said. You were the ones that went rushing after the quick solution.'

'The obvious solution,' muttered Clio, and Minju scowled at the implied criticism.

'Maybe we were a bit hasty. But what are you saying? That we need to go and find that actual model? This is ridiculous. There are too many variables involved. Which year do we go to? When do we go? Who goes? How do we ensure we avoid da Vinci?'

'That is easy bit.'

Now that he had everyone's attention, Grimaldi slowly packed away the cards.

'Well?' demanded Minju. 'You aren't here for your charming company. In fact, now that your painting has proved to be worthless, you may as well leave.'

'And miss out on all these new opportunities?' said Grimaldi with a short laugh. 'I don't think so. Besides, Mr Anansi here seems to be the boss man. So, I stay, for now.'

Minju turned her back on him and beckoned the pharaoh and Clio over to her.

'Don't you want to know solution?' called out Grimaldi, his speech patterns already annoying the punctilious Minju.

'No, Mr Grimaldi. If you have figured it out, I'm sure that we will as well.'

'But what if other team figure it out quicker?'

Minju paused and clenched her jaw.

'Fine. What's your idea?'

Grimaldi scratched his neck, drawing everyone's attention to his scar. When he could see they were visibly uncomfortable, he continued. 'You are too hung up on peg about time issue. So, what if other team go now? You go in ten years' time and still you arrive before them.'

'But we still don't know the best time to arrive. Our use of Tiresias is limited and monitored. We can't access the mouseion, most of our contacts and moles are currently being rounded up. So, at the moment, our ability to do research is somewhat bloody compromised.'

'Again, is not issue. Is it, Mr Anansi?' He glanced over at the spider god who chuckled to himself.

'Minju, my dear, I may have a new favourite.'

'Imagine my devastation,' she drawled. 'Well then, what is your very clever idea to get us to the right place without any intelligence?'

'I don't know if it's within Mr Anansi's rules, but if I said, "please take me to whenever/wherever the other team have gone, but take me to three hours before them," would that be acceptable?'

The room started chattering. The solution was so bloody obvious. Cheat.

Day Five - Julius

Hell's teeth. I needed to get used to these steps without a machine. They were so smooth that the change of scene was momentarily disorienting. Still, it was a far more pleasant experience than Neith's quantum stepper, which always gave one a queasy tum.

Having left the smouldering copy of the *Mona Lisa* in the vaults of the Louvre, Loki dropped us back in the team briefing room and disappeared. Asha came running into the room. and Neith brought the core team up to date. And Sabrina filled us in on events while we were away.

Asha had indeed instigated martial law and drawn up arrest warrants for anyone with a crown. Anansi said she couldn't interfere with the quest, so those particular individuals were still at large. That said, they could no longer access the mouseion and while they could use Tiresias, all activity was being monitored.

First Engineer approached us with her hand out. 'Can I have your braces to see how they performed without the stepper being active?'

I slid mine off and rubbed my skin. The others removed theirs more reluctantly. First hooked my brace up to a small diagnostic device slung across her waistband. She frowned.

'Someone's switched off the locator tracker.'

Asha wandered across to look at First's readouts. First was trying to mask her software from scrutiny, but Asha just smiled.

'Not completely switched off. I simply disabled the all-access ability. I was fed up with people stalking my team.'

First looked up from the screen. 'No one should have been doing that.'

And yet, as we both knew, it turned out they did. And they were doing it with alarming consequences.

First returned to the screen, curious to see how Asha had bypassed her security protocols. 'Oh, That's some nice coding there. Unless we were actively looking, we wouldn't have seen the tamper.'

She smiled briefly in admiration.

Asha inclined her head. 'I always said you were the best engineer we never had.'

'Thank you again, but your attrition rate was too high. I wanted to be able to control what was trying to kill me. There's no control in the quantum field.'

'True, it is a tricky field. That's why we need to be precise and repetitive. In a quantum experiment, we do everything we can to rule out all variables. But it takes a toll. That said, I've recently noticed that a rigid adherence to dogma can also result in a painfully venomous death.' She paused, then smiled. 'So, I'm open to some fresh ideas.'

I watched as the two section heads considered each other.

'Very well, First,' said Asha, 'It will be good to see what comes of this if we can get this mess behind us.'

'Completely agree. Let's start with something small. Please, call me Hypatia. It's my name.'

I watched as First Engineer looked over to the rest of us. 'You, however, will still call me First Engineer. For now.'

Looking at everyone's stunned expressions, I figured this was a big thing. I got it. Only a few days ago, this woman had shouted at me for not putting Pi in front of Jack's name. Now she was inviting Asha to call her Hypatia.

'Thank you, Pi-Hypatia—'

'Just Hypatia. We engineers still go on. Maybe with some tiny flexibility. Don't want to get too carried away. Now let me carry on examining the brace.'

Asha turned her attention back to us. Damn it, but I admired her. I wondered how the toll of finding that her husband had deceived her was making her feel. How would I feel? I chided myself. I was a man from a different planet. I doubt we felt the same at all. Still, I think I'd be hurting right now.

In all my excitement of finding there was a missing codex by Leonardo da Vinci, I was acutely aware of what was at stake. If the other team got to it first and managed to build their own stepper, then my planet was about to lose all its treasures. Not just the *Mona Lisa*. Maybe if I could find the codex, I could find a way to take a copy and drop it into the hands of one of my scientists. What would Einstein or Hawking make of it? Could I redress the balance between our two Earths?

I knew I was missing something obvious about the codex and Leonardo, but I just couldn't put my finger on it. Thinking about Einstein just then had snagged my attention, but I couldn't pin it down. It would come to me.

'Right,' Asha continued. 'I just want to bring everyone up to date regarding personnel. Chief Medic, formerly Giovanetti, has been replaced by Alan Kimanzi. Elections will be held once martial law is lifted to replace Pharaoh, Formerly Tarek. We are beginning a recruitment campaign to replace staff shortages caused by the recent arrests. Both the curators and the custodians were the most affected department. We can train up custodians faster than curators. But I anticipate that after this quest, the way we deploy the curators will change dramatically.

'In the meantime, we have a vacuum at the top, following the murder of Alvarez. I have spoken with Captain Nymens, and he will be the new head of the quantum facility. Chancellor Youssef Shan from Cairo Museum will take over from Minju. The two men are beginning to look at ways the departments can work together.

'Finally, with Nymens promoted, we need a new captain. We have discussed this and Ramin Gamal, if you are in agreement, we propose that you take on this role once you have completed this mission.'

Across the room, Neith actually cheered and almost hugged Asha. Remembering herself just in time, she turned and ran over and hugged Rami instead, who was standing shell-shocked. I joined in the clapping and cheers; I couldn't think of a better man for the job. He had stood true to the ideals of the curators, suffered vilification to protect his friends, been banished, and returned vindicated. Rami had a unique point of view and, in my opinion, was the perfect nominee. I was also impressed that Asha and Sam agreed. A new broom was sweeping through the mouseion.

I picked up a glass and joined Rami and Neith. Amongst all this gloom, it was fabulous to have something to celebrate.

'Tell me, *Formerly*, that's not a term I've heard before.'

'It means they're a disgrace,' said Neith, knocking back her beer. Her reply wasn't quite as illuminating as I had hoped.

Happily, Rami as ever correctly interpreted my expression. 'It means their family has officially renounced them, and so they are known as Formerly Tarek. It's a big deal because you need an almost total majority from two generations, extending across cousins.'

'Brutal.'

'Indeed, as you say, brutal. But clear and efficient.'

I shuddered. Imagine your entire family disowning you like that, then making it public. I wondered how many *formerlies* there were out there, and how many more there would be over the coming weeks.

Sam addressed the room. 'Okay. Next steps. I suggest we spend the rest of the day researching Lisa del Giocondo, who was the model for the Mona Lisa. Let's reconvene at my place. Priti will cook, and we'll also celebrate Ramin's well-deserved promotion.'

'And yours,' called out Neith, to good-natured laughter.

'Right,' said Asha. 'Everyone knows what they have to do. See you all at Sam's tonight.'

Day Five - Julius

I made my excuses and headed off to the library to do some research. If I was going to visit Florence, I needed to brush up. The last time I'd visited historic Europe, I had been overwhelmed by the detail, so I knew it would be important not to rely too much on the textbooks. Instead, I would just let it wash over me. It was important not to be too twenty-first century.

The best course of action was to focus on Lisa del Giocondo and Renaissance Florence. A lot had been happening in a very short space of time and, with the speed of the unfolding events, I was convinced we were missing something. I was also very concerned for Neith and Rami. In fact, I was worried for all of them. The recent revelation of the smuggling ring within their organisation had knocked them for six, but now with the glyphs marking everyone out, they could hunt them down.

It was the arrival of the gods that bothered me. We still didn't know what they were, and I knew it was freaking my colleagues out. I was still very wary of the engineers. They were almost visibly twitching, and I was certain it was connected to whatever it was that I was missing. That we were all missing. Our minds were so focused on gods and codices that something was being overlooked in the periphery. My death sentence may have been removed but I didn't feel out of the woods by a long shot.

I sighed. If I ignored it, it might float to the surface. Right now, we were heading to Florence, and I needed to brush up.

An hour later, I had found a few windows in time that I thought might be suitable to visit Madonna del Giocondo. She posed for da Vinci in 1503, but he didn't finish the painting as he turned his attention to a more lucrative commission. At this stage in his career, his income was very hand to mouth, and he often had to leave projects unfinished. In fact, the *Mona Lisa* never made it into the del Giocondo household. It was never paid for, and da Vinci worked on it as a passion project on and off for the rest of his life.

If La Gioconda held the clue to da Vinci's secret codex, then we needed to visit her after they had met in 1503, but before his death in 1519. His will was detailed, and we know he didn't leave her anything. So, whatever the clue was, it had to have happened between 1503 and 1519. Alternatively, he may have told her something or given her a message. Maybe he had entrusted her with a clue or a piece of arcane knowledge?

We also had to visit her when we knew da Vinci was not in Florence. I was betting on 1506. It was a point of public record that he was in Milan and, as it was only three years since they had first met, any message would still be relatively fresh in her memory.

271

***

Over an evening meal and a few more beers at Sam's house, the team got together to discuss strategies. Sam was in favour of a reverse approach. Visit Lisa in 1520, in case da Vinci had left her something in his will, then work backwards through various years, hoping to hit upon something. Neith pointed out that it didn't matter how we travelled; Lisa was only travelling forward in time. Whenever we met her, she would remember any previous visitations.

In Neith's opinion, it was better to start at the beginning of the timeline and cloud her memory each time until we found the answer. Clouding apparently had no adverse side-effects and was a regular tool employed by curators. I wondered if they used it on their own citizens. Rami nudged me as I was drifting off and I realised they were still discussing the issues of temporal paradoxes. I knew it wasn't hypothetical, but equally it wasn't that I didn't care, I just didn't understand, no matter how much I nodded my head sagely.

Finally, it was agreed that either approach would involve clouding. Having thrashed it out, it was decided to be logical and start closest to Lisa and Leonardo's first encounter just in case our interaction did create a temporal knock-on. If we started at the end of Lisa's life, but we had created a disturbance when we "first" arrived in her reality of time, then by the time we arrived, the timeline may have changed to the point that no clue existed anymore. Even as I tried to think it through, my brain began to ache.

'I propose we look at the summer of 1506,' said Rami, as he finished his roasted peppers. 'da Vinci is documented as being in Milan. Lisa's husband is in Venice, and she doesn't go to her family villa in the hills until August.'

'July then,' suggested Sam and Neith almost simultaneously, and everyone laughed. Not least because we all knew how Neith felt about the rain.

I chinked a bottle of beer against Rami's. Our poor friend was notorious for her attitude towards the cold. I was slowly acclimatising to the heat of Egypt. I could probably cope with an Italian summer.

'I can lend you my jacket if you get too cold, Neith,' I said, with a self-deprecating grin. Everyone knew that I rarely wore a jacket in Egypt.

'Are you sure you won't melt as the mercury reaches a sweltering thirty degrees?' Her tone was gently mocking, and the others joined in teasing me.

I held my hands up, laughing in protest. 'If it gets to thirty, you'll have to come and find me in the river.'

'Neith won't be finding you in any river, Julius,' said Asha kindly, but it caught our attention. 'First Engineer has proposed that this be a solo mission, and I agree with her request.'

I glared at First, who simply stared back at me. It wasn't just that I had been looking forward to going. I was concerned about Neith on her own. It wasn't unheard of for curators to travel alone, but it wasn't best practice. And heading into a danger zone alone was unheard of.

Rami cleared his throat. Contradicting both First and Asha was a bold move. 'This step is critical. Neith will be in da Vinci territory. There may be operatives from the other team as well. Who will have her back?'

'It is because of this danger that the fewer people arriving in Florence in 1506, the better,' said First in a tone that brooked no further argument. 'You are visiting a known associate of da Vinci's. The risks in destabilising the timeline are severe.'

It was argued at length, but ultimately it was agreed that just Neith would travel with Loki as protection. The idea of Loki being viewed as helpful struck me as ludicrous, and I tried to make that point.

'Actually, Julius, this is as good a time as any,' said Neith. 'How do I handle Loki? If I'm going alone, any tips would be appreciated.'

Everyone had stopped their conversations to listen to me, so I decided to treat it like a lecture. Although the theoretical part had pretty much flown out the window.

'To begin, there's obviously a lot to unpack with the gods and the whole mythical paradigm, but what I think would be really helpful right now, is to understand, that in many ways they have a lot less free will than we do.'

I sipped my beer and thought how strange it was to discuss gods in the abstract, given that we had spent the day talking with them. 'They are almost walking and talking concepts, with no agency beyond their own descriptions. Take Loki. He will always cheat if he can find a loophole. He will never rise above it. Anansi can be provoked to temper and will always lose if he loses his rag. It's almost a rule.

'Following the same rulebook, we are the plucky underdogs, on account of our mortality. We stand a huge chance of winning, but only if we are the protagonists of the story. Lots of people may die along the way, and we might be part of the dying narrative. It could be Team Anansi that is destined to win.'

'That's ridiculous,' said First crossly. 'We are not characters in a story being pushed around a scene.'

'No, we're not,' I said hurriedly. 'But that's my point. We have free will. The gods don't. They act within a very narrow set of parameters. Study those and you will find lots of ways to navigate them. And honestly…' I paused. 'I don't know how much of this is total conjecture. I am so far down the rabbit hole, the chess pieces are attacking me.'

I took another sip of beer. I'd annoyed the head of the engineers, and I knew what I said next was about to push her further. God knows I didn't want my status reviewed again. I needed some Dutch courage.

'Of course, they may not be gods at all, but powerful people from yet another Earth just pretending to be gods to mess with us.'

275

There was silence in the room as everyone looked at me. I decided to plough on. Every time I raised this subject, I got knocked back. I was beginning to think this wasn't a coincidence.

'What if, instead of just two Earths—'

There was a shout of distress from Priti as First stumbled towards her. Everyone had been looking at me as I spoke, but I had been watching First as she calmly picked up her red wine glass and threw it at Priti's pristine white blouse, pretending to have slipped. Sam jumped up to get a cloth, and people started to mop up the mess. First was apologising profusely, which was disarming everyone as they weren't used to a remorseful engineer. I just sat down and watched her very carefully.

That signalled the end of the evening. As we left the house, Rami, Neith and I walked through the boulevards, expressing our concerns. My brief mention of the gods not being gods but people from another Earth was very carefully and deliberately ignored. Not wishing to discuss this with the others in case it triggered a status update for them, I changed the subject.

'Are you sure stepping on your own to Florence is going to be okay?'

Neith was about to reply but Rami stepped in.

'She's not some Arthurian maiden. She's Neith Salah. Fearsome warrior!'

Neith laughed and punched him on the shoulder.

'Seriously, Julius, I'll be fine.' She linked arms with both of us. 'All I need to do is have a quick chat with her, see if she knows anything, cloud her mind, and return. As assignments go, this couldn't be easier.'

I walked up to my rooms in a foul mood, barely smiling as I said goodnight to Neith and Rami. This was the wrong decision, Neith needed backup.

'I'm sensing some anger?'

I stopped and stared at Arthur.

'Oh yes, lots of anger. What's wrong, Julius. Life not going your way?'

I had decided to be the grown-up but all my worries came to a head as I had to watch Arthur pull silly faces.

'Go away, Arthur.'

'What's wrong? Aren't you having fun? The lads are having a great time. Lugh and Lucifer are taking bets on which side will win, Team Anansi or Team Loki. Obviously, I'm backing you guys. It's brilliant, everyone is talking to me, asking for inside information. Osiris is running side bets based on my intel.'

I shook my head in disbelief.

'This is not a game, Arthur.'

'Of course it is. And the beauty is, whichever side wins I get to be promoted. I can feel my strength growing daily as the more senior gods pay attention to me.'

'And that's all it is to you?'

A head leaned out of a window and told me to keep my voice down. Apologising I returned to Arthur who instantly cut me off.

'Do you want me to silence them?' he said, nodding in the direction of the window. 'I can you know. I'm getting stronger all the time?'

'No,' I hissed. 'I do not want you to *silence them*. I don't want you to do anything. This society is hanging on by a thread because you and your friends are bored. Neith is about to go on a very dangerous mission and her only backup will be Loki.'

'Do you want me to go along? Help out?'

'And have Anansi accuse us of cheating? Handing over the codex to Minju and her bunch of nutters. No thanks, we don't need that sort of help.'

I started walking up the steps to my rooms.

'You want to be a god but the only god you can be is Arthur. The noble and brave warrior king. He who leads and cares for his people. That isn't you, is it? You're acting like a puppet and a fool. There is nothing admirable about you and I wish I had never met you.'

By now I had reached my room. I walked in and slammed the door shut before Arthur could follow me. His look of astonishment had been remarkable, presumably no one had ever spoken to him like that before. I half expected him to re-materialise, but the room remained silent, and I went to bed trying to convince myself that speaking truth to power was a really courageous thing to do. Quite frankly this made me feel worse and I spent a fitful night waiting for a grizzly end and worrying about Neith.

Day Six – Lisa del Giocondo aka La Gioconda

Lisa del Giocondo pushed her accounting books away from her and sighed. Everything tallied, but according to the farm manager, the crops were not going to be as good as previous years. The spring rains hadn't materialised. They had gone from a dry winter straight into a hot summer.

Thinking of the farms made her smile. What she wouldn't give to be there right now, listening to the water pump sloshing into the stone troughs, the laughter from the children, splashing each other as they ran in from the fields. In this heat, she might even join in. There was so much freedom for the little ones out in their country villa. Here in the city, they had to always maintain their propriety. As a mother, she had certain indulgences towards her children. She knew her husband, Francesco, was less forgiving. He viewed his family as scions of the house of del Giocondo, who would bring honour to that name. His family was not as old as hers, and he was always at pains that people should view his line as worthy. To that end, the entire household had to remember themselves at all times.

She rested her elbow on the desk and slipped. Tutting in annoyance, she picked up the paper she had knocked off the desk. Francesco loved a well-ordered and calm household, and she went to great pains to ensure that his daily life was free of domestic encumbrances. As soon as he went away on business trips, she would order the staff to wax and buff all the wood, strip, stuff and beat the mattresses, get the long ladders out to sweep the cobwebs from ceilings. The whole house was usually a scene of chaos.

Right now, he was on a trip to Venice to discuss the financing of a new silkworm farm. It was a project he was very excited about, and she hoped he proved successful. With the master away, the rules relaxed a little. Lisa approved of his high standards, but on such hot days, she was happy to wear her ties a little looser.

Thinking of him and the crops in the farm, she suddenly realised that any new mulberry bush plantings for the silkworms might be affected by the lack of rain. Their roots may have had less time to drink down into the soil and weather any upcoming drought.

Picking up her pen again, she jotted a quick note to her husband. He always listened to her advice, and in farming matters acknowledged that she had the greater experience. With her counsel, he would be able to ask more pertinent questions. From there, the decision would be his alone, but she was always pleased to be able to help and support him.

A flicker overhead made her laugh as a swallow and then a second swept into the room and flew high above her head in the lofty rafters. Another thing she loved about her husband being out of town was that she could fling open all the shutters and try to catch what little breeze there was. In turn, this meant that swallows flitting from room to room were a daily feature. Any mess they left was soon wiped off the tables and chairs, but the wall hangings were a different issue. She always made a point of cleaning those herself. If they were damaged, it was her responsibility for allowing the birds in. She did love her husband, but he would dismiss any staff that failed to clean the house properly. She should probably close the shutters, but now she could hear laughter from the nursery as the children were trying to catch the swallows, their nursemaids scolding the same little birds.

Anyway, swallows in the house meant no moths or flies, which her husband could hardly complain about. Next month, she and the children would head to the countryside to escape the heat and poor Francesco would have to remain in the city, ensuring the business continued to flourish.

A small breeze wafted in from the east, across the gardens, and the smell of roses filled the room. She decided to ask for roses to be set at tonight's table. It would cheer her up as she ate alone.

Deciding she wanted to spend some time with the children, she headed downstairs. Passing the main reception area, she shook her head at the empty space on the wall. Two vases stood on either side of a dresser, and above hung an empty frame. It was Francesco's idea of a joke. It was supposed to be where her portrait by Messer da Vinci hung. But, three years later, he was no closer to finishing it. The empty space in itself was now a point of conversation. *Oh, you know Leonardo…* And their guests would all be made aware of a familiarity that didn't actually exist, and an indulgence on del Giocondo's behalf. It also helped impress upon everyone how he had climbed in his wealth and social standing. His new house, his beautiful wife, his successful business. For her part, Lisa thought it was a lot of silly fuss over a painting. Da Vinci was indeed a maestro. But honestly, when she had seen the portrait in its unfinished form, it just made her uncomfortable. Who wanted to see their own face every day, staring enigmatically at them from a wall?

Smiling to herself, she was heading across the courtyard when she heard the knocker on the front door. Maria went to open it. Lisa continued to the nursery. Minutes later, her housekeeper tracked her down.

'Madonna, there is a lady wishing to speak with you.'

Lisa looked at Maria wearily. She wasn't expecting visitors. And from the way her housekeeper spoke, this lady was a stranger.

'Did she say what it was about? Maybe next week when the house isn't quite so untidy.'

'She is a Nubian lady, Madonna, with a manservant. She says she has a message from the maestro da Vinci.'

Lisa grinned in sudden anticipation. Could the silly painting finally be ready? She nodded her assent to Maria and suggested that she take them through to the solar.

Maria frowned and shook her head. 'The wall hangings are all down in there.'

'Yes, of course, they are.' Lisa tutted to herself, the house was in no state to receive visitors. 'Honestly, which room is currently in order?'

'The study?'

Lisa was conflicted. It wasn't entirely appropriate to invite strangers into Francesco's study if he wasn't present, but it was better than turning away a messenger from the maestro. How wonderful that would be if it were to be hanging on the wall when Francesco returned. He would be overjoyed.

'Right, well this could be good news. Swallows always bring the best omens. Let me get back to the study, then show them up. Could you ask Luca to join me?'

Luca was their steward and an appropriate chaperone. And, if there were any financial transactions to be discussed he would talk on her behalf.

She kissed her children, then reluctantly headed as fast as was seemly back to the study.

Day Six – Beta Florence,1506 - Neith

Normally, a second visit to Beta Earth in as many days was strictly against regulations, but as my mode of transportation was not exactly regulation standard either, there didn't seem to be an issue.

Even before I opened my eyes, I was beaming. The air was hot and dry and smelt honest. I could pick up acrid hints of a nearby tannery, the urine soaking the leather but above that was the smell of roses and lavender and hot stones. It would be centuries before the greasy smell of petroleum fouled the air.

Flicking my eyes open, I saw we had arrived in an empty alleyway. There was no movement, except for two rats scrabbling in the dust over a piece of rotten fruit. Loki was dressed as the pope.

'Very incognito,' I muttered, knowing full well that no one would see him unless he chose to manifest.

'When in Rome…'

'This is Florence.' I looked up and down the alleyway in alarm. 'Wait, this *is* Florence, isn't it?'

He looked at me and nodded his head.

'Yes, Neith, this is Florence. I was simply making a joke.'

I drew my hand to a pocket where I had a concealed laser. Julius had warned me emphatically that Loki had a thing about jokes, and that only he found them funny. Others found them lethal.

'Right. I'm off. Call me when you are ready to go.'

I paused, then decided to be reckless. I had tried to pretend that Loki, Anansi and Arthur were figments of my imagination, and that hadn't worked. After that, I'd tried to ignore them, but I was behaving foolishly.

'Loki? Will we find the answer here?'

Loki raised his gloved hand to his cheek and looked at me in mock alarm. 'Are you cheating?'

'I don't know. The rules were pretty non-specific.'

'Would it be helpful if I told you the answer?'

'Yes.' My shoulders slumped.

'Then it would be cheating.' He smiled wickedly. 'No help from the gods beyond transportation.'

'Fine.' I had been looking around, it was time to get going.

Loki continued. 'I can't tell you if you are on the right track, but I can simply observe that Julius usually seems to know what he's talking about.'

And with that he vanished.

I shook the skirts of my pale blue linen dress and thought about it. *Julius knows what he's talking about.* About what? Very helpful. Julius had wanted to come on this mission. Should he be here? Would I fail to spot the clue without his Beta point of view? He also felt that public nudity was a step too far. Was that what Loki was referring to? It could be anything, or it might be totally irrelevant.

He had also been trying to ask something else last night. Something about another Earth. My head throbbed. A side-effect from last night's oysters, no doubt. Honestly, I could speculate all day. Instead, I checked my body armour was in place and that my brace was linked to the mainframe. I stood in the mouth of the alley, tucked to one side and looked around. It was mid-morning and a market was in full swing.

Traders were chatting with servants swapping loaves and vegetables for money; gossip flowing in both directions. A chicken squawked in protest as it was placed in a sack. The smell of wood burning drifted across from braziers used to cook food on. In this heat, I was certain they could have simply thrown the meat on the baking floor and it would have cooked in seconds.

There was a shout from the other side of the square as a group of young nobles rode through the crowd. They were racing each other and laughing as the people had to part quickly to get out of their way, the noise of the horses' hooves on the cobbles, echoing off the tall buildings. Despite the protests of the stallholders and customers, no one put up any genuine objection. The men were wearing the colours of the Pazzi. Only a fool would challenge one of Florence's leading families.

I was dressed as a household servant. My long skirts and petticoats made a hot day even hotter and I loosened some of the ties on my sleeves. I had a wicker basket for shopping which, if needed, I could also use as a weapon, although this should be a straightforward step. I walked out of the shade of the alley and into the marketplace. The heat of the day radiated off the already baked stones, and I wondered when they had last had rain. There was dust everywhere, and no weeds in any of the cracks. I stopped at a market stall and bought lush red tomatoes and a loaf of bread, immediately picking at the crispy flakes at the end of the loaf. At the next stand, I bought some hard cheese, sniffing it with pleasure. Then, following the directions from my earpiece, I headed towards our safe house.

Florence was a pretty enough town. Last time I was here it was on fire. It didn't seem much cooler now, but at least no one was screaming. So many of my steps involved screaming. Maybe that was what Loki had meant? Julius often asked why we didn't stop to help? When he first asked these questions, I thought he sounded like a child. I too used to think like this, in basic training. However, over the years, I had been properly instructed and had come to see at best, the futility of it, and at worst, the potential devastation caused by our interference. Since Julius had arrived, I was beginning to have those childish thoughts again.

I passed in front of the duomo and cricked my neck up to look at the towering cathedral. A flock of white doves sailed across the blue sky above as little sparrows hopped around my feet and between the two, swallows swept through the sky, grabbing insects out of the air.

It really was a remarkable achievement. Architecturally, it was a bit fussy for my taste but better than the baroque I supposed. Although, to me, they were much of a muchness. As I stepped into the shadow cast by the dome, my eyes adjusted to the shade. I picked out the next alley, leading off the square and set off. A few minutes later, I was standing in a narrow lane, lined by tall stone townhouses. In the heart of the city, this lane was clean and respectable, although its narrowness suggested only a certain level of wealth from the inhabitants. A cat slunk past me but there was no other sign of life. The lane was swept clean of dust and the tall buildings on either side kept the sunlight out. Craning my neck up I could see that the majority of windows were closed and shuttered against the heat.

I knocked on a wooden door and waited for a reply. Soon enough, the door swung open, and a woman looked at me blankly.

'I am here for Messer Bocco. I have news from his family.'

She invited me in and headed off into the house proper. You never knew what you were going to get behind the door to the street. Sometimes it was a large courtyard, before leading on to the various private apartments. Other times, it was a corridor, flanked by guards. This townhouse was more modest. I sat in a small atrium, looking as demure and modest as I could, relieved to be waiting in the shade. These clothes were an utter nuisance, but I knew I'd be able to relax my disguise shortly. I didn't mind pretending to be insignificant, I just loathed the way that when I was noticed, I was looked at. Could they use me? Could they harm me? It wasn't just the men, the women also checked to see who was of the superior rank. It irritated me at a very fundamental level. I pinched my fingers together and calmed myself.

I had never visited the location of a principal before, and so, that morning, Sam had filled me in on the subject of safe houses. There were a few sleepers that protected certain individuals. Hypatia, the ancient mathematician, da Vinci, and Newton amongst others. They never interacted with the principal character, instead, they acted as a safe house for any visiting curators. Their role was to offer guidance and ensure no one interacted with a principal. It was rare that curators ever came to these timeframes, but when they did, they first had to check in with the sleeper and proceed according to a strict protocol. If a sleeper thought a curator might impact upon the principal's timeline, they had full authority to deny the mission and send the curator home.

I had seen an image of the man I was meeting, but he had been here for thirty years and would no doubt have changed a bit. In fact, as I understood it, a "nephew" would be dispatched soon to take over his role. Ostensibly, Messer Alessandro Bocco was a textiles broker. It allowed him to live a modest life in the centre of the city. Not attracting too much attention, but able to travel anywhere without causing suspicion.

An inner door opened, and an older man stepped through. Italian genotype, his dark curly hair was now mostly grey. His clothes were modest, but of a finer cloth than I was wearing. I envied him his dark grey doublet and hose. Under the doublet he wore a simple white shirt, the only flash of colour from the red inserts in the doublet body. My own linen garments looked shabby beside his. Everything about him proclaimed him to be of a higher station. Nearly a gentleman, but not quite.

'Welcome to my home. You have news from my family?'

'I do. And they instructed me to bring cheese and tomatoes but, sadly, there was no fish.'

I don't know why, but a lack of fish had been considered an important element in the code phrase. A silly nonsense, someone had been watching too many spy films. I could just pull on my cuff and he would see the brace. Even so, his eyes lit up, and he asked the maid to prepare refreshments for us. I followed him to a private study.

It was a decent sized room with a desk and bookshelves. There was a rug on the wooden floorboards and a fireplace to one side. The ceiling was mercifully high, and the room was nice and cool. It wasn't so big a room that someone could hide themself but I surreptitiously checked anyway, then set up a muffle field. Once established, I nodded to him that it was safe to continue.

He'd already kissed me in the Italian manner, but now he came over and hugged me as well.

'Are you the first stage of my retirement committee? Because if you are, I want to remain.'

I had been warned that this might happen. These sleepers often went native, despite the obvious disadvantages.

'No, I'm not, although I have been asked to tell you that a nephew will soon be arriving. He was due to arrive next year, but in light of what's currently happening, this may be sped up.' I removed the rest of my basket's contents. An updated brace and updated body armour. Both standalone issues, as Alessandro had to operate without a live link back to Alpha.

'Are you here for a retrieval, then?' His voice rose in surprise. Arriving in Florence, da Vinci's home, was a serious concern. 'What is worth the risk?'

'I'm here to talk to Lisa del Giocondo.'

He stared at me as his jaw dropped open.

'Absolutely not!'

There was a knock on the door. The maid came in and laid the food on a side table for us. She gave me a side glance, but I smiled sweetly, and she curtsied and left again. Almost as soon as the door had closed, Alessandro continued.

'Who authorised this? There is no way I can permit you to access her.'

'Check your brace.'

I drank a glass of lemon water as he read through the instructions from First Engineer. It had been countersigned by the heads of security and the quantum facility.

'It says that the pharaoh has been compromised and that he is trying to kill da Vinci? This is incredible.'

It certainly was incredible, but it was as close to the actual story as we could get without confusing the issue.

'Yes, it's why you'll be getting backup soon as well, in case my presence has an effect. But for now, I simply need to ask Madonna del Giocondo a few questions. I will then cloud her memory and leave. So, what I need is for you to confirm that da Vinci is out of the city and Lisa is at home.'

He got up hesitantly muttering in Italian as he did and pulled some ledgers off the shelves.

'I know the answer, of course,' he said, looking up at me. 'But it's always good to double-check and verify all data.'

He looked worried, but I grinned back. Spoken like a true curator. Sitting, waiting and watching was not a role I could have done, but every now and then a suitable candidate presented themselves to act as a sleeper.

'Yes, here we are. Leonardo has arrived in Milan. More issues with unfinished art. Madonna del Giocondo

293

is at home. Her husband is in Venice. There are four children in the house, between one and seven, with eight household staff. By all accounts, she is a lovely woman but is very proper and dutiful. A true renaissance madonna. She may not permit an audience with a stranger while her husband is away, especially a Saracen.'

I paused. I needed to be convincing, but not upset her or her staff. It always made me grumble when I — an Egyptian and citizen of Alexandria, the greatest city on the planet — was looked down on by a culture that hadn't even managed to harness electricity.

'Any suggestions of the best way to approach her?'

He tore off a bit of bread and dipped it into some olive oil as he thought. 'Actually, that reminds me of something I saw in the marketplace this morning. A tall, Nubian woman asking for directions to Via della Stufa. That's the street the del Giocondo live on.'

I was already on my feet. 'Was she alone?'

'No, she had a manservant with a burn on his neck. Quite striking, they were. I had plans to follow up on them later.'

By now I was at the door. Slamming open the door I sprinted out of the house and across the plaza, my headpiece barking directions. Clio had several hours' head start. Far more than she needed. As I ran, I disturbed a flock of pigeons enjoying the crumbs that had fallen in the marketplace. They flew up around me as I sprinted through them. So much for not drawing attention to myself. I activated my body armour and skidded down the next alley, slamming my hand against the wall of a house to steady myself, and out across yet another plaza. Women running were not a regular sight, and I knew I was creating a disturbance, but it couldn't be helped. Dust was rising up around me as I sprinted across the plaza, its marble fountain devoid of water.

A dreadful feeling began to overwhelm me. As I approached Lisa's home, I drew to a halt at the front door and gently tried to open it. This thoroughfare was far more prosperous than Messer Bocco's and a horse and cart could easily ride along it. For now, it was deserted. The door was unlocked, and I slipped off the quiet street and into the home of Lisa del Giocondo. Putting my hand into my skirt pocket, I wrapped my fingers around the laser.

The family had clearly been doing well for themselves. The door opened into a large open-air courtyard lined by various buildings with walkways looking down into the open space below. To my right lay an overturned stool where a servant would have sat ready to answer the door. A bowl of peas was spilt across the terracotta tiled floor, their small green shapes resting in a pool of dark red blood. The servant whose throat had been cut was now lying slumped in the corner, his hand still clasping a peapod. To the right of the courtyard ran a staircase. Two more servants lay sprawled across the steps. Their open throats gaped up at me as flies began to gather around their eyes.

Ahead, I could hear raised voices and recognised Clio in an absolute fury. Something appeared to have gone wrong. I moved quietly now. I knew Alessandro would soon be arriving and would help me in any way I instructed, but at his age, I wasn't expecting much. The best he could do was make sure no one else entered the house. I had no idea how we were going to fix dead bodies, but for now, I needed to get to Lisa.

The voices were getting clearer. I could only hear Clio and a man's voice. Presumably, her partner from Team Anansi. The rest of the house was silent. No staff, no children, no crying, no protests. Just a massive slanging match. I approached an open door and peered through the crack. There were books and sheets of paper on the floor. A rug was rucked up, and the tassels were lying in blood.

'We go home, yes? Call Anansi. We are done here.'

A stranger was standing on the right-hand side of the room. I was going to have to shoot him first and hope that Clio didn't fire at me while I did. It was a risk, but I knew he wouldn't hesitate if I tried to disable Clio first.

'We can't do that, you pile of camel shit. How many more times? We can't go.'

'We are done here,' he shouted back.

'No, we are not,' she screamed. 'You've murdered the *Mona Lisa*!'

Suddenly, my running across a plaza seemed insignificant. My armour had already deployed to cover my head. I drew out my laser and stepped around the door. Immediately, I fired at the man, my laser emitting its customary whine as a flash of light spat in his direction. I'd ducked out of any return fire, but my aim was good and I'd knocked him out cold. Standing up, I raised my hands. The guy might be out of action, but Clio had her own gun trained on me.

I looked around the room in horror. There were four dead children and two dead adults. Lisa del Giocondo was very clearly dead. She was slumped against a wooden chair, with a curtain tie to restrain her. Her feet jutted out from her dishevelled gown, one slipper hanging off her foot. I couldn't see the other. I winced, imagining her kicking in pain and terror. Her fingernails had been ripped out and bruises bloomed under her now pale skin. Whether she had been forced to witness the murder of her children before or after her physical torture began was uncertain.

'Clio?' I whispered softly. I was sickened. I knew she had a malicious streak and could run towards violence, but torture? And killing children?

'This wasn't me. Neith, I swear to you. He got here ahead of me.'

I was still speechless. This poor woman had died in agony. To say nothing of destroying the timeline.

'Who, exactly, is he?' I didn't recognise him. Was he a rogue custodian or a local mercenary? It was hard to contemplate this level of sadism. The intentional murder of children was incomprehensible.

'That's Grimaldi.' Clio spoke as though I should know who she was talking about, and while the name sounded familiar I couldn't place it.

'Russian crime lord from back home. He got roped into the codex hunt and Archivist Chen suggested he step across with me.'

'But he's killed everyone.' Even to myself, I sounded stupid. We were wasting time, but the enormity of the situation was still rolling over me. Overhead, swallows darted in and out of the windows, feasting on the small flies.

'Why did no one hear the screaming?'

'He deployed a muffler.'

'A Russian crime lord. I don't get it. He's one of us? An Alpha?'

Clio took a break from looking petrified and gave me a snort of disgust.

'Yes, Neith. We too have villains. Why do you think we have red custodians? It's not all about picking up litter and reminding teenagers not to dance on the pontoons.'

I knew we had criminals on Alpha, but they were few and far between. And honestly, I had never paid them much attention. I was too busy focusing on the ones on Beta Earth. Clearly, I had some catching up to do.

'But he's a monster?'

Clio's breathing was now under control, and she gave the room and Grimaldi another look.

'I have a plan.'

I was still staring, trying to get a grip, when Clio repeated herself. 'Neith, snap out of it. I said I have a plan, but you're not going to like it.'

She was right.

Day Six - Neith

I was alone and nervous. I never get nervous on a mission, but I was so far out of my comfort zone I was practically jumping hungry crocodiles with oil on my feet and buckets in my hands. I was back in Florence, but now I was here three hours earlier.

Clio had summoned Loki and Anansi, who had looked at the mess and tutted, but other than that seemed unperturbed. She told them what she proposed, and they both agreed. Even I did, although her plan was terrifying.

Travelling back along a timeline that I was soon going to occupy made me itch even more. And if I got into difficulties, I could completely annihilate the future. Even more than it already was.

I watched as Clio, kicking her long red silk skirts out ahead of her, strode through the market. She had clearly just arrived and was doing nothing to mask her presence, she walked like a Medici, her fine gowns and patrician stare screaming out to be noticed and admired. It felt weird watching her, knowing what her immediate future held. She looked so confident, yet only ten minutes before she had been wide-eyed and panicky, the literal blood of children on her clothes, a destroyed timeline on her hands. But, here and now, she was walking with ease and doing nothing to disguise herself. I watched as people noted her passing. How many times had I told her not to draw attention?

I borrowed a minstrel's whistle and played a little tune from back home. Clio stopped and looked around. As she saw me, she sighed and walked over. I gave the minstrel his whistle back, and he scuttled away.

'Neith?' She looked at me curiously.

'What's occurring?' I said and immediately winced.

'*What's occurring?* Are you still doing that Welsh thing, babes? I read your notes. Welsh and sock folding. You must be thrilled.'

I gritted my teeth. Typical Clio, straight to my weak spots.

'It's almost under control. Just when I'm nervous or stressed. Like right now.'

'The great Neith Salah nervous? Don't make me laugh.'

'I do get nervous, you know.'

'No, you only think that. You are the most together curator I have ever known.'

I almost smiled, but this was not my partner anymore. This was the woman who'd betrayed me and everything I stood for.

'Is Grimaldi around?'

'No, he's—' Clio was about to tell me where he was and then remembered herself. We were not working together. 'How do you know about him?'

'Your little murderous monster in crime? Oh, I don't know nearly enough about him, but apparently, you do. Are you insane? What were you thinking?'

Clio's eyes narrowed. I knew I was taking the wrong tone, the events I had just witnessed hadn't even happened yet. This Clio's future was still blissfully innocent.

'Sorry. Forget that. I need to ask a favour of you. And I need you to say yes.'

Clio relaxed and smiled at me. It was the long lazy grin that I used to love. The one that said *make me*.

'You know we're not on the same team, don't you?'

'Like I'm ever going to forget.' This was oddly more painful than I'd expected. I hated that Clio had betrayed us, but I found the idea of her running around with someone like Grimaldi truly repugnant. I was also having trouble coming to terms with the fact that our noble society had an active criminal underclass. One that we knowingly allowed to fester. Weren't we better than that?

'Listen, in three hours' time, Grimaldi murders Lisa del Giocondo, her four children, and the rest of the household.'

'Are you kidding me?' Clio stared at me aghast. 'Even he wouldn't be that monumentally stupid. Prove it.'

'I can't.'

'You must have a recording of it?'

'I do. It's yours. You gave it to me and said this was the only way to persuade you. But if you think I'm going to show you future footage of yourself, you must be joking. It's bad enough I am even telling you about your own future, let alone showing you.'

She looked up at the sky, as though she expected it to cave in. 'You really shouldn't be doing this. You remember all the lectures we had to attend, all the exams we sat on the dangers of bumping into yourself. I can't believe you are standing so close to your own timeline.' She stopped abruptly and looked me over. 'Do you feel okay? This isn't safe, babes.'

'Safer than murdering *Mona Lisa*,' I snarled. Her concern had thrown me. Would there ever be a moment when I didn't miss her? 'Who knows how this will affect da Vinci? Maybe even as we speak, our pasts are being re-written. Maybe halfway through this conversation, we will blink out of existence.'

She shook her head. She had sat through the same lectures as me. We both knew that murdering Lisa was disastrous, travelling along our own timeline potentially cataclysmic. One would wipe us out, the other could wipe the world out. I was prepared to risk myself if it meant saving everyone else. As I watched Clio, I could see her come to the same conclusion.

'Yeah, fair enough. Well then, tell me exactly what happened, and I'll see if it rings true.' She looked worried. 'And maybe speak quickly?'

I recounted the event and watched as she took it all in.

'Sorry, babes. I really can't believe I would stand by while he killed her babies in front of her.'

'You didn't. You arrived just after he had pulled her fingernails out. But you didn't stop him. Look, listen to the audio.'

She went pale as she heard herself gasp and start swearing at Grimaldi. In turn, he said Lisa clearly knew nothing about any clue. She said nothing when he tortured her, she said nothing when he threatened her children, and when he started to kill them, she just screamed. She was, he said, a waste of time, and then he shot her.

Clio started shouting that now there would never be a clue in the future, as Lisa no longer had one. The shouting continued until I arrived and shot Grimaldi."

'I would have tried to stop him,' she said quietly. 'If I had arrived earlier.'

'I know.' I had the video as well, but I really didn't want to show her. Not just because of the timeline danger, but because I wanted to protect her from seeing the very worst side of herself because she had clearly allowed him to arrive before she did. Maybe deliberately.

She screwed her mouth up. 'So, what do you want me to do?'

'Go home. Now. Before he even meets her.'

Clio started laughing. 'Oh, nice one. You almost got me. Do you think I'm stupid? Go home and leave the field clear for your team to find the codex.'

'There is no codex here, there is no clue. She watched her children die in front of her. If she had anything to say,

304

she would have. Besides, I think Julius worked it out. If I tell you what he realised, you can go first. Get a head start.'

As I had watched Clio's tape and saw Lisa die unable to save her children, I knew that we had raced down another dead end. Loki's words came back to me about Julius, and I finally understood what he meant.

She looked at me suspiciously and fiddled with her skirts, playing for time. I knew she hated skirts, and it made me smile sadly, remembering how often she would swear about them.

'And how do I know that he's right?'

'Because it will make you feel ill. It makes me feel ill. It made Ramin feel ill. Something about what Julius said triggered an actual physical reaction. I don't know what that means, but it can't be a coincidence.'

'But how do I know if you're telling the truth about Julius? What's in it for you to give us a head start?'

'I get to keep the *Mona Lisa* alive.'

'Sounds like all my dices are six. Let's have the clue.'

'Promise you're going to leave?'

'On Daffy the Cat's life.'

I nearly cried. Daffy the Cat was the college mascot. All the cadets loved him and would regularly pet him and bring him bits of food. Swearing on his life was the most solemn vow we had growing up. I took a deep breath. I had to trust that she would leave the minute I told her what Julius had discussed and what Loki had told me. I should have paid attention too.

'According to Julius, there aren't just two Earths, but billions. If that's true, then the codex is probably on one of them. A more technologically advanced version of Earth than ours and invented by a different da Vinci.'

I didn't feel quite so ill now. The more times I thought about it, the easier it became. And, of course, there appeared to be some merit in the idea. Patently ridiculous. But what if? Clio swore and sat down on a small wall.

'That was pretty thick of me, wasn't it? I should have cottoned on much faster.' She shook her head and swore reflectively. 'Well done, Julie.'

I looked at her, bewildered. Was she about to double-cross me again?

'I know all about the other Earths, babes. Where do you think I've been hanging out with Anansi? I've been travelling ever since you shot me on Beta Earth. Girl, the things I've seen. Honestly, I'm embarrassed that I didn't work it out before mud fly, there.'

She stepped away from me.

'You know this means we get the codex first, don't you?'

'Not necessarily. It just gives you a head start.'

'I've never needed one before.'

'We've always been on the same side before. This time you're going to need as big a head start as you can get. Because I will do everything in my power to stop you and bring you before the authorities for your crimes.'

Not that I was planning on giving her a head start. The minute she was gone, I would also return. She'd get a few minutes on me, as we both had to return to the same point in time in the future. She'd simply arrive five minutes tops before me. That was a head start I was happy with.

'Whatevs.' She pushed herself away from the wall she had been leaning on. 'Let me go get Grimaldi, and then Anansi can take us home.'

I watched her as she walked back towards the centre of the square, and I wondered if she would keep her word. I watched her pause, then she turned and smiled at me. I knew that smile. It was the opposite of the *make me* smile. It was the one that said don't mess with me, and never *ever* underestimate me. She threw her hands out wide and called out to the crowd. I began running towards her but my limbs felt like treacle and I knew I wasn't going to get to her in time. Everyone was mesmerised by this tall Nubian woman dressed in brightly coloured silks, staring at them as though she ruled the world.

'Lord Anansi,' she shouted out loud, 'take me and Grimaldi back to Alpha now, please.'

She winked at me and disappeared.

An hour later, I had managed to cloud all the witnesses. It had taken a while to calm the panicked mob, but eventually, I managed. Manipulating the human mind was quite easy. You just had to lean into whatever their greatest fears were. Right now, I was asking if people really wanted to discuss what they had just seen?

Accusations of witchcraft were always tricky. I also mentioned ergot poisoning and plague visions. By the time I was happy that no one was going to remember or discuss Clio's little stunt, I was coming up on my own arrival and needed to get out of there pronto.

Day Six - Julius

It had been ten minutes since Neith had left, and Loki had promised to return her to the same time slot. As the minutes passed, my concern mounted. Rami offered to get a cup of cardamom coffee as it looked like we might be here for a while, when Neith was suddenly standing in front of us. She was alert and scanning her surroundings. She was also clearly agitated.

'Who's here? Is everything okay?' She shook her head. 'That's stupid, you wouldn't know,' she muttered to herself and paused, her wild expression alarming us. 'Julius Strathclyde, are you here?'

'Hello?' I said, hesitantly.

Neith was slightly manic. 'What colour are your eyes?' She sprinted across to me and looked into my face. I smiled down at her as she held my face in her hands.

'Messed up. Excellent.' She spun away from me. 'Sam, what's happening on Beta Earth?'

'Curator Salah,' called First, causing Neith to come to a gabbling halt. 'The quantum field has been switched off. We aren't currently monitoring Beta Earth.'

'Switch it on. Grimaldi killed Lisa del Giocondo.' Neith swung around, looking for Asha. 'Incidentally, Giovanetti, since when do we have criminals like Grimaldi running around?'

'Neith,' barked First. 'Focus. What do you mean La Gioconda's dead?'

'No, she's not. I don't think she is. I think I fixed it. Please, please, please check.'

Neith's panic and pleading had mobilised the room. First sent off a team to open the stepper and examine the timeline. Asha placed the custodians on high alert in case a bunch of gods flooded in, and Rami handed Neith my coffee.

The next few minutes included Neith screaming at Asha for allowing criminals to flourish, and the total hypocrisy of the system, and how in the name of great Ra was First so thick as to not consider a multiple Earth theory.

I decided the coffee may have been a bad idea. I watched as Rami hugged Neith and murmured in her ear. She calmed down instantly and excused herself to go to the loos. Asha told a custodian to guard the door and ensure that she didn't do anything rash.

'What did you say to her?' I asked as Rami came and sat down beside me.

'Told her she was behaving like Clio.'

'Jesus.'

'I know, but I was desperate.'

A minute later, Neith came back into the room. Everyone watched her nervously as she cleared her throat.

'First Engineer, Chief Custodian, Chief Curator,' she said, addressing the three most senior people in the room. 'I apologise. My comments were unprofessional and disrespectful. I know you are working for the good of society. The recent events made me over-emotional, and I won't let you down again.'

With that, she walked over to us as we both gave her a hug. She'd splashed her face with water and was gripping both of our hands as we waited for the results from the stepper. Neith's panic had infected the room, and we were all anxious to see if she had indeed saved the timeline.

First listened to a private communication, then smiled at us all, her relief palpable.

'Zero aberration on the Beta timeline. Well done, Salah. Now please, can you explain exactly what happened?'

As a team we watched Neith's brace replay Clio's footage, and then her own, in astonishment.

Given what Neith had gone through in the past few hours, her extraordinary outburst just now was completely understandable. What I found incredible was that she then apologised for what I considered to have been perfectly reasonable behaviour. Her society had let her down, and she was the one that had been forced to try and fix it.

First Engineer grabbed Neith. 'Salah, these memories are still sharp? You can still remember the events that you prevented from happening?'

'Yes. I called in on Messer Bocco. He had no recollection of meeting me. I also dropped in to the del

Giocondo residence but was asked to return the following week. It seems I am the only one to remember the incident. You will need to ask Clio and Grimaldi if they remember it.'

'This is,' First paused, 'very exciting data.'

'When Julius mentioned the idea that we aren't in a parallel system...'I watched as Neith clenched her fists. 'He said talking about it made us feel sick. And he's right.' She was visibly panting now, and First grabbed a chair for her.

'Ignore that,' said First, reassuringly. 'We will investigate it and report back to you.'

Lots of people around the room nodded emphatically. Best leave this to the engineers. I glared at her and she held my gaze. I blinked first but spoke quickly. I wanted to take control of the situation before she did. I didn't know what First was up to, but I was fed up with her and her sainted engineers.

'For now, let's not think about it, but just accept that there are other Earths. Indeed, Clio's own testimony seems to support this theory. If that is true the codex could be hidden anywhere, so how the hell do we find it?'

I could see that people were honestly trying to answer my question, but at great distress to themselves. Only the engineers were unaffected, but they certainly didn't look happy.

'I have an idea. Loki?'

I called out his name, and was surprised by how quickly he appeared, smiling at Neith.

'Loki. Do you know the location of the codex that we are looking for?'

'Yes.'

'Very well, can you take us there?'

'Yes.'

We looked at each other waiting for the but. When none came, Asha waved at me to continue.

'And that's all there is to it. We ask and you take us.'

'Almost.' He smiled. 'It's in a tricky place. I can't hang around. Also, the codex may be impossible to retrieve.' He laughed at that. 'But yes, happy to take you there and see if you can manage it.'

'And where is Clio right now?' asked Neith to Loki.

As we had listened to the recordings and the video replay of her interactions with Clio, it was clear that there was still a firm bond between the two women. I felt really sorry for Neith.

'She is, as you would say, in the doghouse for leaving you unattended in Florence with no clue.' Loki was obviously delighted to be causing this level of misery.

'Didn't she tell them about the multiverse theory?' asked Neith, hopefully.

'Oh, yes.' He grinned wickedly. 'But they didn't believe her. Plus, it made them all ill. Remember, they don't have Julius or the engineers, none of whom seem upset by the concept.'

313

At this point, First jumped in quickly, keen to distance anyone from the observation that this concept might not be news to her.

'That's simply because we are more used to quantum issues. But that's beside the point. The point is, where are they going next?'

'Not so fast.' Everyone looked at me in surprise. Interrupting the most senior engineer was not the done thing, but I was fast running out of patience with the engineers and their shenanigans. 'We don't care what they are doing. And we now have a location for the codex, remember? What are we waiting for?'

The room was suddenly excited. The codex was within our grasp. Only the engineers looked upset.

'In that case, I insist you take an engineer with you,' demanded First, quickly.

'I don't see how that will help,' replied Asha. 'We need field agents.'

Sam cleared his throat. 'We followed your advice on the deployment of only one curator on the last mission, First Engineer, and look how that turned out. I don't think you are in a position to dictate the structure of agent deployment again.'

'Your agent broke every rule of time travel and nearly destroyed an entire timeline,' retorted First, clearly annoyed at being challenged by someone of her own rank. 'If an engineer had been present, that foolhardy act wouldn't have happened.'

314

'If an engineer had been present and stopped her, then we absolutely would have a broken timeline. Salah's actions were heroic, not foolhardy.'

Sam was clearly settling into his new role of head of the quantum facility quite nicely.

First looked around the room and saw no support. She tried again, this time in a more conciliatory manner.

'I was thinking of Pi-Jack.'

I didn't trust the engineers as far as I could throw them. But Jack? Not that it was my choice, but I could see the same thoughts flicking across Sam's face.

'A team of four is within the rules. We would be grateful for the assistance of an engineer,' Sam said to Asha diplomatically.

Asha nodded. 'Very well. Get him briefed and get him ready.' She turned to Loki. 'And tell Anansi that he can't just follow our team. They have to work it out for themselves this time.'

Loki laughed and bowed. 'As you command. He might even agree. He hates going there even more than I do.'

Day Seven - Jack

Pi-Jack knocked on the door to First Engineer's office and waited. He had no idea why he had been summoned, but if he was going to place bets, it would be something to do with his relationship with Julius Strathclyde. He ran through a few other possibilities, but this appeared the most likely. What he couldn't guess at was what First Engineer wanted from him. Since the incursion of the gods, the quantum stepper had been switched off and the regular night training sessions had stopped. Engineers always had routine night shifts to work on and maintain the quantum stepper. During those shifts, only engineers were present, and the stepper was tested, and experiments were run.

It was exhausting. Not just the lack of sleep. But being constantly exposed to the stepper in its open state was difficult for the mind to be near for any length of time. When curators went through, the stepper was open for a couple of minutes. When the engineers worked, it could be open for a whole hour, pulsing and twisting.

The constant exposure could drive some minds into an echo, and they were usually shipped off to recuperate or die. The rewards, though, were immense. Even in his junior position, Jack had been able to propose hypotheses and play with the maths behind the reality. However, some of his recent equations were beginning to move in a direction that was making him feel ill. He knew he was on the right path, but each time he tried to work it out, he felt anxious and sick. He raised the issue with his tutors who just said that this was evidence of an increasing understanding of the science. He didn't understand what they meant by that, either.

Since the gate had been closed, he'd caught up on his sleep and felt like a camel's saddle had been lifted from his shoulders. With the field closed, he was also experiencing fewer quantum headaches and hallucinations, which were the curse of all junior Pis. Life was beginning to feel normal again.

The door slid open, and Jack walked through. Sitting at a desk were First and Second Engineer. Neither was smiling. Second was furiously writing notes. Jack couldn't resist a glance and saw that they were probability equations.

In front of the desk was a chair with a small table and a glass of water on top and a pill. On the other side of the chair was a bucket.

'Pi-Jack, please sit down.'

Jack sat down and decided to ignore the pill and the bucket for a minute. It would no doubt be explained to him shortly.

'We need your assistance with a situation that is ongoing. What we are about to tell you is classified.'

'Is it going to make me sick?'

'No. That will come afterwards.'

'Something to look forward to then,' quipped Jack.

Second looked up from his calculations. 'Humour?'

'In the light of any other information, I would prefer to fall back on humour rather than any other reaction,' said Jack stiffly.

'In future, please remember that no reaction is the preferred option.'

'Yes, Second.'

First rapped her knuckles on the table. 'As you are aware, the quantum stepper remains closed. Everyone knows this, we are citing ongoing maintenance. The actual reason is that we have been having prolonged interactions with these gross, observable, dimensional subjects.'

Jack was about to smile then stopped himself, simply nodding his head in acknowledgement of the acronym. 'They returned after the stepper was switched off?'

First and Second looked at each other. Pi-Jack had already been marked as the best in his cohort, and probably the best in a few years. The speed with which he had assessed the problem was encouraging.

'They are also responsible for the glyphs we have above our heads, not the engineers, as has been widely reported. This false narrative has been promoted with our approval. They have also challenged some of our colleagues to undertake a treasure hunt to search for Leonardo's missing codex.'

'Why?'

'Because it's incredibly important.'

'No, I mean why issue the challenge in the first place?'

'Oh. The motivation? Actually, I don't understand, but it seems to be focused on the attachment of one of the subjects — a self-titled, Arthur, High King of the Britons — to Curator Strathclyde. As best I can understand, the quest is some sort of dare or bet. I don't understand the dynamics. All I understand is that we are the playing field.'

Jack relaxed. His initial assessment that Julius was the link had been proved correct. And if the gods were still mucking about, that meant he had more opportunities to study them. As far as he could see, this was a beneficial situation. Maybe he was here to observe directly? He could hardly hope for such a break. Studying quantum irregularities was a dream opportunity.

'You are smiling. This is an inappropriate response.'

Jack let his face fall slack and looked at the pill and bucket. Indeed, a smile might be the wrong response. There was more going on.

He raised his hand and was permitted to speak. 'There *is* no hidden codex. We have the original codex that the Alpha da Vinci wrote in our private archives. I've seen it for myself. Nothing about it suggested it was incomplete, or that there was a second codex, so what do we have to worry about?'

'Please take your pill, and I will explain. It is an antiemetic. You may not need it. Your tutors say you are close to breaking through independently, but I'm afraid we need to speed the process up.'

Jack took the pill and waited as First Engineer continued.

'It has been our duty and honour over the past five hundred years to protect humanity from itself. As you rightly observe, there is no hidden codex. We have the only codex that our Leonardo wrote. However, we know that his version was incomplete, and the science that we built our machine on was limited. Even to this day, we know that the quantum stepper is limited, and we have done everything in our power to keep those limits in place.'

Jack frowned. That didn't sound right. Science and engineering were about testing, exploring, discovering. Not maintaining the status quo.

'The quantum field is infinite.' First Engineer paused.

Second Engineer watched Jack for a reaction.

'In what way?'

'In any way. In every way. There is not one parallel Earth, there are an infinite number. We are simply linked to one of them.'

Jack tilted his head to one side, then asked if he could borrow a piece of paper and a pencil. After a few quick scribbles and crossings out, he returned the sheet of paper to First Engineer. He had been spending weeks on a calculation that he hadn't been able to resolve. Having removed the parallel theorem from the equation, the formula fell into place.

'Are my workings correct?'

First Engineer glanced at it quickly and shifted the paper across to Second, smiling.

'Yes, those calculations are correct.'

'Oh, but that means—' he broke off thinking, then resumed. 'Sorry, can I have the pencil and paper back?'

'Later. Right now, we need you to focus. I must say I'm glad that this hasn't caused you any negative side-effects.'

'No, why would it?' said Jack, puzzled. 'In fact, I feel excellent. I feel so stupid that I hadn't got to this conclusion quicker.'

Second looked at First.

'I was twenty-five. How old were you?'

'Twenty-three. And Pi-Jack here is eighteen.'

Jack looked at them both in confusion. 'Why didn't you tell me? Why don't you tell everyone?'

'Because for decades we have been actively manipulating the population to only think of parallels. We start in nurseries. In every health and brain scan, we run sub-routines inducing anxiety and nausea if anyone starts thinking of multiple worlds. Anything from Beta Earth referring to a concept of a multiverse is immediately seized and never broadcast.'

Jack looked at them in astonishment. 'How does Beta Earth know about multiple Earths?'

'Because there is no one there to stop them. Of course, they also don't have the technological or scientific understanding to do anything about their theories.'

321

'Yet,' said Second darkly.

'I still don't understand. Sorry, it's a lot to take in. Are you saying that our QS is broken?'

'No, we're saying that it is limited. And we are still trying to unpick those limits, while at the same time not let anyone know.'

'But that suggests we've developed technology we couldn't have actually designed?'

'Correct.'

Jack fell silent and cleared his throat. 'Is it possible that someone from a different Earth gave our Leonardo da Vinci some idea for quantum theory, but not much else?'

'Correct again. And it's taken centuries, but we think we are getting close to a proper understanding of quantum theory.'

'But I really don't understand the secrecy. If the engineers had been more open, we might have solved it sooner?'

'To what end?' asked Second derisively. 'How well did a partial understanding of nuclear fission work out on Beta Earth? They almost wiped themselves out. Imagine what would happen here if we realised we could travel down our own timeline? If we could simply pick any old time to visit Beta Earth, not just one designated by the restrictions of the machine? What if we could visit any Earth?'

'Chaos and obliteration seem likely,' said Jack, in awe. Imagine just going wherever you wanted, visiting your own past, exploring new worlds. He was itching to start calculating again.

'Which is what previous engineers realised,' said First. 'And so, the quantum stepper was built with an abundance of limiting protocols in place. And any mind bright enough to start spotting flaws in the science was brought in to work in the engineers. Which is where we need you to carry on the honoured tradition.'

Jack looked up; equations placed on hold.

'What on earth can I do?'

'As it happens, it's not this Earth that we need you on.' First was almost about to laugh at her own joke but caught herself in time. 'We need you to accompany the team on their next away mission. They are travelling to another Earth — not Beta — and we need you to do all you can to observe all interactions. The cat may be out of the bag, but we still need to control the flow of knowledge.'

'It would be preferable if none of you were to ever return,' said Second Engineer solemnly.

Jack yelped. 'A suicide mission? No wait, a murder, and a suicide mission.'

'Dear Pythagoras, no. No one needs to die. Don't be so melodramatic,' admonished First.

Jack slumped in relief.

'Just never return.'

Day Seven – Florence - Location
and date unknown

'Team. Report. Loki, where are we? My brace is malfunctioning!'

I turned around, but he was gone. I hated this way of travelling and missed my solid dependable Alpha technology. Swearing, I checked my brace again. According to the readings, I was standing in Florence in the early twenty-first century. The geographical coordinates were accurate, as was the geological age. Despite that, we clearly weren't in Florence. We were standing in a wide-open parkland. There was a river running down to my left, and ahead of me were various ancient ruins. Some were tall, brick high-rises. Others were graceful glass buildings with spires and minarets. As the breeze blew across them, they changed colour, and a ripple of blue ran across all the buildings. At first, I thought there were animals exploring the heights, but on closer inspection, they were just children jumping from window to window using ropes and, I hoped, harnesses. Some of those drops would be deadly.

'Julius? Does this smell like your Earth? Do you recognise it?'

Julius had crossed his arms and was resting his chin on his hand as he contemplated the skyline. 'No, it smells cleaner, if that makes sense? Plus, I can't figure out those buildings. That one to the right with the glass sails? We don't have anything like that, and yet here it's a ruin. This isn't home. I think we're so far from home that I suspect Kansas isn't even on the map.'

He grinned, but I didn't have time for his side quips. I pursed my lips. We were probably going to have to approach the children and find out where exactly we were.

'Ramin, Pi-Jack, any suggestions?'

Ramin shrugged. 'It's nice, wherever it is. Bit too luscious. All this green gets a bit monotone, but you know, bearable.'

'According to my readouts,' said Pi-Jack,' we are exactly where we think we are. Let me find somewhere to sit down.' As he spoke, a bench appeared to grow out of the ground and the air shimmered as motes of dust seemed to build up out of the grass, gaining solidity as they silently coalesced into shape.

We all moved towards the smooth green seat. Pi-Jack prodded it and started dictating notes into his brace.

'That is pretty nifty.' Julius laughed. 'One up on your self-cleaning benches, eh?'

'How is this being done, Pi-Jack?' I asked the engineer. He might have the greater insight.

'I don't know. Maybe some sort of nano structure like our suits? Maybe it's transported in? I'd need to run a few tests.'

Julius cleared his throat and spoke slowly and clearly. 'Please could this bench have a back rest?' One side of the bench began to rise further than the rest, and within a few seconds, the bench had a back rest.

'Interesting,' said Pi-Jack. 'I think that rules out it being transported. It adapts to requirements.'

'Hello, bench, please can you be blue?'

We all looked at the blue bench.

'With yellow stripes.'

And now the bench had yellow stripes.

'Julius, could you focus?'

I was trying to establish command, but now Pi-Jack was wandering around the lawn, summoning tables and chairs at will. I looked at Ramin who was busy using his visor to monitor the local area. 'Do you think we're safe?'

'No idea, but we are definitely out of our depth.'

I agreed and called the team to full alert. We were looking at technology that was far beyond us. At least our suits would give us a few moments grace if we found ourselves in a fight. My worry was that any fight might not last that long. Children swinging through ancient architecture and accommodating park benches didn't seem very threatening, but I wasn't prepared to risk it.

'How many people are in the vicinity?'

'None,' said Ramin, frowning.

'How far are you reading?'

'One mile.'

'Cat's teeth. Those children are closer than a mile.'

'Agreed. Either the reader is broken, the reader is blocked, or those aren't children.'

Pi-Jack and Julius stopped examining the benches.

'If they aren't children what are they?' asked Julius.

We watched as a little group ran across one of the walkways. Their laughter drifted across the park.

'Why don't we ask her?' said Pi-Jack. He pointed towards a woman walking towards us.

'The brace must be broken. She is definitely human,' said Julius appreciatively.

The woman was a personification of nature. Her blonde hair was arranged in a collection of plaits, two long braids fell in front of her chest, and the other smaller braids were arranged around her head. Within the plaits she had woven flowers and cornstalks. Around her flew a cloud of butterflies and small birds. Her rosy, pink gown billowed and while nothing about her seemed sexual to me I couldn't help thinking of adjectives like ripe and abundant. I smiled. She looked like the best day in summer. Full of laughter and promise.

'Welcome. I am Firenze.'

The woman smiled warmly at us and while her dress didn't appear to have any obvious weapons, she rendered the men momentarily silent.

'Hello, Firenze, I'm Neith Salah, and my companions can introduce themselves when they come to their senses.'

In a flurry, they all cleared their throats, then rushed to apologise and introduce themselves.

'Tell me,' asked Pi-Jack, 'how do you get the insects and birds to follow you?'

327

'I cheat.' She laughed. 'I release pheromones that they like. They entertain me, and I like to make an entrance. Do you think that's cruel?'

'No. Well, maybe you are slightly going about under false pretences.'

'You're right. And honest. Thank you, Jack.' As she spoke the butterflies and birds drifted off. 'There, that's better.'

'His name is Pi-Jack.' I wanted to get control of this situation and felt establishing some protocols would help. She looked at me and shook her head.

'Not in his mind he isn't. He thinks of himself as Jack. So Jack is what I will call him. Wouldn't you agree that how he thinks of himself is important?'

Oh good grief. I was standing on an unknown Earth and the first resident we met was siding with Julius' view of reality. I decided to ignore her question and returned t the surroundings around us.

'And are the children here for your entertainment as well as the butterflies?' I asked.

'Very clever, Neith. Yes, they are. As are the fish.' She waved her hand above her head. A shoal of fish and marine life rippled over our heads and swam towards the children, who laughed and screamed and jumped onto the backs of some dolphins. 'They are all just daydreams, but I like to see the movement and hear the laughter. We don't get too many tourists at the moment. Just the occasional wanderer, like yourselves. I can stop it if you like.'

I shook my head. I had no objections, although I was itching to find out what was going on.

'Julius, you looked alarmed when Neith asked if the children were for my entertainment.'

'For a dreadful moment there, I thought Neith was insinuating you were keeping the children to eat later. Like Baba Yaga.'

'How dreadful, which Earth are you from? It's not the same as theirs, is it?'

I wondered how she had so quickly ascertained that we didn't belong to her Earth and that we weren't all from the same one. Julius explained he was from a different Earth and summoned a chair for her. As she sat down, I honestly checked that rabbits and deer weren't about to come and settle by her feet. The brace had finally acknowledged her existence and I wondered if the butterflies and birds had somehow masked her presence. Maybe they were more than just a pretty distraction? A clever cloaking device?

Taking a seat on one of the benches, I decided to carefully interrogate her. 'Excuse me, Firenze, your name, that means Florence doesn't it?'

She nodded at me. 'Yes, this is Florence. I am Florence.'

I wasn't much wiser.

'Sorry, I find it hard to explain this to people that don't already understand quantum states.'

All three of us looked at Pi-Jack who shook his head.

'Honestly, guys, we are in the foothills of quantum technology back home.'

'And yet here you sit, on Firenze.'

'In Firenze?' queried Ramin.

'On, in, at.' She laughed gustily. 'Prepositions can be clunky as they tend to only describe fixed matter. I was at the shop. But how can you be at something when you are something?'

'How can you be a shop?'

'You see. Even asking that question shows you wouldn't understand the answer.' She looked sad. 'And now I've stressed you all. And it is not my intention to make any guest uncomfortable. Why are you here? Maybe I can help with that?'

'We are looking for La Gioconda.'

She smiled. 'Then I can make you happy. I am La Gioconda.'

'La Gioconda?'

'Yes, isn't this wonderful? You were looking for me and you found me straight away.'

'You said your name was Firenze?' I queried. The guys looked as perplexed as I felt.

'Yes, I am Firenze. Isn't this excellent?'

'Uh well, we were hoping La Gioconda would help us find the codex.'

330

'Yes, I am Codex.'

'Uh, which are you?' asked Ramin. We were going round in circles.

'All of them. I am everything. This is fabulous, isn't it? Let's eat.'

Ramin raised his palms in exasperation. 'Do you think the translator is playing up? It's already made a mess of prepositions.'

'Ignore that,' said Firenze enthusiastically. 'Let's go and have food at Haelwyn and Leo's.'

'Who is Haelwyn?'

Firenze looked at me, her bright eyes creasing up under bunched up cheeks. 'I am Haelwyn. Come on. Leo's waiting.'

'You're sure you're not Leo as well?' I asked. Ramin nudged me and told me not to be so sour.

'How can I be Leo?' She laughed and linked her arms between Julius and Pi-Jack and walked ahead. I couldn't bring myself to think of him as Jack. No matter what Firenze said, if I started to call him Jack he would be in trouble back home. Ramin and I brought up the rear.

'I'm a bit worried about the Leo name.'

'Ditto. If it is him, we will have to retreat immediately. Who knows what harm we might cause?'

Theoretically, Leonardo da Vinci was five hundred years dead, but nothing about this Earth made any sense. I wasn't going to put a single ruby on this wager.

We walked down towards the river. A tributary ran down through a lake and onto the river. Between the lake and the river sat a Tuscan villa. It would have looked at home on any Earth, the red clay tiles and brick walls made from the local soil. We walked alongside a small vineyard, and down towards an open tiled courtyard.

'Come on,' said Firenze. 'We're around the back. Leo is probably setting up the food as we speak.'

I could smell charcoal drifting across the air. We turned the corner of the house and an older man, possibly in his sixties, was turning corn cobs on a grill. His curly hair was already silvered and tied back in a low ponytail. He wore a shirt, but it was unbuttoned, and his tanned torso still looked tight and well-defined. He was wearing a short kilt and was barefoot. To one side, a small table was already laid with food, and a long trestle table was set for six people.

He stopped grilling as we walked towards him. Putting down his tongs, he hurried over to greet us.

'Welcome, welcome. Apologies for my delay. As soon as Firenze told me you had arrived, I rushed over.'

He stepped forward and engulfed me in a huge hug.

'Welcome, Neith Salah. I am Leonardo da Vinci.'

Day Seven – Neith

I looked in horror at my living, breathing hero, and pushed back from his embrace.

'Code Black!'

Pi-Jack sidled up to Julius with a worried expression. 'I don't know *Code Black*. What does it mean?'

'It means we have to withdraw from this scenario immediately,' said Julius. 'Our presence has the ability to interfere with the timelines. Code Black is used when there is a risk of engaging with certain principal figures.'

'Code Black also requires immediate silence,' I snapped. There was to be zero engagement or clues. If we felt we were within a mile of one of those key figures or their associates, we were to remove ourselves immediately. Who knew what we would do to the timeline? And here I was, actually hugging Leonardo da Vinci.

'Really, there's no need to worry,' said Leonardo calmly. 'I'm glad your Earth has such sensible procedures in place, but they don't apply here.'

'What! Why?' I stuttered, but I was extremely nervous. I looked around me, checking there were no butterflies nearby. The last thing I wanted to do right now was stand on one.

'Your rules are presumably to protect an Earth of a less advanced nature, yes?'

I nodded. If I could keep my replies to gestures and single words, so much the better. Ramin, Julius and Pi-Jack were all standing to one side. Pi-Jack's eyes were practically on stalks. I could see his hand kept going to his brace to record everything, and then pausing.

'Well then, it doesn't apply here. This Earth is far more advanced than your own. If anything, it's my duty to protect you, not the other way around.'

'I see no evidence that you are more advanced.'

'Are you not a scientist? Do you not have eyes and ears? Everything you see tells you we are more advanced.'

'All I have seen so far is parkland and a ruined city. A woman that can squirt butterfly pheromones, and fabricated benches. I just—' I stopped. I was behaving like a brat. 'Look, it's been a very long year. I have always wanted to meet you, but you are clearly not the Leonardo I was hoping to meet, and honestly, I'm at my wits' end.'

I don't know where it all came from, but the disasters and rollercoasters of the past year all came crashing to a halt at my feet, here in this beautiful Tuscan villa, overlooking a large river with swallows crisscrossing the lawns.

'For heaven's sake, Leo, you've upset our guests. How often do we have people back to the actual house? And now you've made these four edgy and uncomfortable.'

Firenze ushered the four of us to the table. She poured us wine and water and started to describe the side plates of food.

'We have figs and roasted oranges, some honey, and olive oil. I've picked some fresh walnuts, although I think the spiced ones are tastier. Please try them both and let me know.'

She chatted on as she introduced each plate, only apologising to Julius for not having any meat.

'How do you know I eat meat?' asked Julius, bewildered.

'You smell of it.' She smiled politely. 'Your friends do as well, but not so much.'

Unaware that she had caused Julius any mortification, she carried on explaining what was on each platter, then gave a little clap as Leonardo re-joined them with a platter of roasted corn cobs and salted potatoes.

'Do I really smell of meat?' whispered Julius to Ramin, as he sniffed at his shoulder. 'Why didn't you say something?'

'Honestly, I can't smell anything.'

Leonardo looked up in astonishment, then turned on Firenze.

'I make them uncomfortable. *Me?* You told the poor lad he smells unpleasant. Look how distressed he is.'

'Oh stop. Why would he be distressed? He must know how he reeks?'

'You're making it worse.'

'I am not. Julius.' She turned to reassure him, then took in his bright red face. 'Oh, good grief. I am so sorry. How incredibly rude of me. It's just no one here eats flesh, so I suppose we are more attuned to the various fragrances.'

Julius took a big gulp of wine and smiled.

'No, that's quite alright. Your world, your rules. And I apologise if the knowledge of my diet causes you distress.'

Honestly, Julius was excellent at cultural diversity. I was beginning to appreciate just how much of a skill he had at adapting to new environments.

'Do you eat fish? Or crustaceans? Eggs? Milk?'

'Yes,' said Leonardo as he refilled Julius's glass. 'We eat what is freely given. Eggs, milk, et cetera. But not fish or crustaceans. We do not end a life that has awareness.'

'How do you define awareness? What about mushrooms?'

'Julius. Please?'

Leonardo looked at me, smiling. 'Questions are good, but maybe you have some of your own you think more important?'

The way he put that made me stop short. Of course, I thought my questions were more important. We were on a mission with a goal that could put great power into the hands of desperate villains. In the greater scheme of things, were Julius' questions more important than mine? Who knew, but right now this was my mission and my questions. I took a deep breath and decided to engage.

'Please, before I go further, can you supply evidence that this is a more advanced culture than mine? For example, how do you know where I am from? My Earth may be more advanced.'

'The very fact that you are surprised to find a third Earth tells me you are less advanced than us, but a quick potted history for you.' He leant back against his seat and took a sip of wine. 'You understand the multiverse, yes?'

I looked at Ramin and we exchanged a worried glance. Pi-Jack looked concerned, but Julius nodded his head eagerly.

'Not quite. It's a bit new to us, although not to Julius.'

Now Leonardo looked confused. 'How did you get here if you don't understand here? Are you here by accident?'

'May I?' asked Julius, and I nodded. 'On my Earth, we know all about multiverses, but they are purely speculative. We are just beginning to understand quantum physics, we are very much in our infancy there. On their planet... 'He gestured towards us. 'They have built a quantum machine that links them to my planet, and only to randomly assigned points in time. They do not discuss the oddity of this restriction, and they do not discuss the theory of other Earths. I think this has been deliberately manipulated by the scientists, or engineers as they call them, to stop the population looking into the issue. In fact, as you can see, this conversation is making Neith and Rami uncomfortable.'

It was true. My head was aching, and my skin felt prickly. I thought I would throw up and just needed Julius to stop talking. Pi-Jack, on the other hand, seemed fine, if somewhat unhappy. He picked at his figs.

'It's true,' he said. 'The engineers have been modifying society's behaviour for ages. As we began to discover what the quantum machine might theoretically be capable of, we realised it could be used as a weapon, and so we began to limit people's expectations of it.'

'Pi-Jack, how could you?' I was appalled.

'Don't look at me like that. I know it's wrong but look what has happened. We are in a race to stop another faction getting their hands on the blueprints for a quantum stepper because we are so scared of what they will do with it. How much worse will it be if they discover that a stepper can be built with no limits?'

My head was pounding. Ramin looked like he was going to throw up.

'I can help stop that if you would like?' said Firenze kindly. 'I'll make the tiniest adjustment in your memory cortex and undo that conditioning?'

I nodded weakly. I was convinced I was about to vomit over all this delicious food. Firenze laid her palm on my arm and her skin felt soft and pleasant. I was suddenly aware of how gentle her touch was when I realised I no longer felt sick. I looked at Ramin. Firenze leant over and touched him on the face.

'That's incredible. So, in a multiverse,' I spoke and waited for the headache, but there was nothing. I continued cautiously, 'There's no end. It's not binary, it's more like an infinite system?'

'Think of it more like a tree branch,' said Firenze as she topped up everyone's glasses. 'Each branch has a hundred smaller branches, each of them has a thousand twigs. And every single one of them is a unique path.' She sipped her wine and continued. 'Now it's not as chaotic as it sounds as lots of timelines coalesce. They are so close as to make no difference.'

'So, there are other Earths with me on them, doing the same thing I'm doing now?' asked Julius.

'Certainly, but with differences, and sometimes those differences are so slight that the timelines simply merge. In other cases, the changes are so diverse that there are separate realities.'

She leant over and smiled at Julius.

'In fact, there are many Earths where Julius and Charlie are living a happy existence, untroubled by the realities of other Earths.'

Julius dropped his fork and looked at Firenze in painful hope.

'Charlie is still alive?'

'Always. Sometimes. Yes and No. But mostly yes.'

Julius frantically rubbed the end of his nose and looked away from the table. I had to ask, although I was certain no good would come of it.

'And what of Clio? On the other Earths, is she mostly good? She doesn't betray me?'

Firenze paused, as if listening to something, then smiled apologetically. 'There are a few Earths where she's almost good.'

I looked at Ramin. 'Figures,' I said glumly.

Leo cleared his throat. 'Let me explain about this Earth, now that I know it won't make you ill. I'm not going to cast any judgement on a society that has wilfully stagnated its own culture for centuries. I have no idea how much longer you'll last on that course of action.'

'That's you *not* casting your judgement, is it?' asked Firenze tartly.

He scowled and flapped his hand in her direction. She just smiled and drizzled some honey over the figs.

'This Earth, like yours and his,' he said, pointing a bread roll at Julius, 'is four and a half billion years old. All the Earths that went on to produce humans as the dominant life force had a fairly similar evolution. Many Earths blink out of existence as meteors hit them before they've even got going.

'On our Earths, humanity got established around the same time. However, my Earth did not suffer what many cultures refer to as the deluge or the flood or the drowning. So we didn't have that. Nor did we suffer the Yellowstone Catastrophe that many Earths did. Our civilisation has managed to evolve without major interruption, to this point. We have never had to stop and start again. Hence, we are more advanced than you.

340

'And, hopefully, we are now well enough advanced to be able to circumvent any major geological calamity. You see mankind is more greatly affected by geological events than the acts of individuals. Very rarely does an individual make a significant impact.'

'What about yourself?' asked Julius. 'Three Earths, all of which seem to have a da Vinci who's a genius.'

'Good question, and not one I know the answer to. I have travelled to many Earths, and a few people do seem to be locked and persistent. I'm one of them. I am always born in the fifteenth-century, and always in Italy. But sometimes I never make it past infancy, sometimes I'm a drunk, sometimes I'm a raving madman.' He looked at Firenze. 'Am I a raving madman in this one?'

'Only sometimes.'

Julius suddenly jumped up and pushed away from the table. He began to pace backwards and forwards laughing and running his fingers through his hair.

'Of course. That's what's been bugging me this whole time.' He pointed at da Vinci. 'It was you that showed their Leonardo how to build a quantum machine wasn't it?'

'Guilty.'

'It's been bugging me for weeks. I knew there was something wrong with the stepper, but I just couldn't put my finger on it.'

'How do you work that out, Julius?' I asked although I noticed that Pi-Jack didn't seem terribly surprised.

341

'Well,' said Julius, 'when your Leonardo drew up the schematics for a rudimentary stepper, he either deliberately held back the multiverse information, which the engineers have helped to re-enforce, or he didn't actually properly understand it. And if he didn't understand it, then how on earth did he even come up with the primary knowledge?'

'Well-reasoned,' said Leonardo. 'It's one of those chicken and egg things. I developed a stable quantum portal and stepped across into his timeline. As soon as I arrived, I got stuck and couldn't work out how to get home. So, I went in search of the smartest person I knew. Me.' He laughed and slapped his thigh, but Firenze tutted.

He apologised and carried on with a sheepish smile. 'Sometimes, I can be a bit braggy, apparently. Anyway, me and myself spent a few months talking through the problem. Finally, I fixed it and returned. I started to refine and develop my stepper, leaving him with a head full of ideas, but no actual technology. It was his plans and hypotheses that your future scientists seized upon.'

'Wasn't that terribly dangerous?' asked Julius returning to his seat.

'Not really. I've always said that when a society is ready to develop something, it will happen. You'd be amazed how often electricity gets utilised in the same time frame. Give or take a hundred years.'

'But, that all happened over five hundred years ago in our timeline. That can only mean that this is the future?'

342

I said. Honestly, I was confused. Travelling into the future was supposed to be impossible but until a few days ago I'd thought there were only two Earths.

'Not unless he's five hundred years old,' said Pi-Jack cautiously.

It was the first thing he had said since finding himself in the great man's company.

We all looked at Leonardo who puffed out his chest. 'I don't look a day over two hundred do I?'

'Five hundred years! Don't you get bored?' asked Ramin in awe.

'Pah. Only boring people get bored.'

'Leo!'

'Apologies. But no, I do not get bored. I am grateful that our civilisation cracked longevity centuries ago. It's given me so much time to do stuff. Now, enough about me. Why are you here? I'm concerned that if I say too much, my young friend will scribble it all down.'

Pi-Jack grinned apologetically.

'Maybe the time will be right?' said Julius thoughtfully. 'Jack's a sharp mind.'

'All the more reason to tread carefully. I don't know the future after all. Only the past. Jack here may be the next one of us that is a fixed name. Who knows? Very few Earths are more advanced than this one.' He refilled all our glasses and waved one in my direction. 'Now. You. Tell me why you are here while I drink. All this talking has made me thirsty, and Firenze makes the best wine in all of Italy.'

'In the world,' she said reprovingly.

'Sorry, my love. In the world. Firenze worked out how to make the enzymes adaptive to your tastebuds, so it is always perfect, regardless of what you are eating or what sort of palette you have.'

She leant over and kissed his hand as he continued.

'Now, your story. How did you get here? Is it an accident? Are these your first steps in truly unlocking your stepper's potential?'

The four of us looked at each other. Anything less than the absolute truth was going to be found out instantly, so I took a deep breath and explained the entire saga. When I first mentioned the gods, Leonardo scowled, and Firenze shook her head, but she told me to carry on.

'And that's why we're here, to try and safeguard the codex from the other faction,' I finished lamely.

We weren't brilliant engineers and brave explorers. We'd been dumped here at the whim of some gods that were intent on playing a joke on one of their lower orders. Leonardo had listened to my account with increasing exasperation.

'You see? Every time I try to convince the council that the gods aren't all bad, and we should explore them more, they pull a stunt like this.'

He took some walnuts from a bowl and cracked them in his fist, passing the contents over to me.

344

'So what are the gods?' I asked, hoping to finally have an answer.

'I have no idea. They are a feature on a lot of Earths, but not all. And their level of interference and existence is different on each. I take it the gods followed you from your planet?' He looked across at Julius, who shook his head.

'No, we have folklore and mythology about the gods once roaming the Earth. But nowadays no, they do not walk amongst us.'

'No believers?'

'Oh, we have millions of believers. Just no physical, quantifiable manifestations.'

'Hmm, you must have just got an unlucky infestation attracted to your quantum stepper. It's probably pulsing away in the ether and drew their attention. I think they exist as some type of life force within the quantum field itself, but I haven't been able to study them properly. They'll be tricky to get rid of now.'

'Julius made them promise to go.'

'Did he now,' mused Leonardo. 'How did you phrase it? Gods can be terribly literal.'

'At the end of this. No matter the outcome, all gods are to leave this planet and never return.'

'Yes, that seems pretty watertight. And you say you've had no dealings with them?'

'Well, I have studied them and cultural folklore.'

'A scholar. I knew I liked you. In your Earth what am I like?'

'You're a great painter and a frustrated engineer, I think.'

I sat back and watched as Julius chatted with Leonardo. My life had become surreal. Everything I had been brought up to believe was not so much a pack of lies, but heavily manipulated. Everything that I thought my society stood for and represented was about as solid as a sheet of paper. Sitting opposite me was Julius, a man from a planet apparently inferior to mine, full of inequality and deprivation. Yet here he was chatting to one of the greatest minds of all time and both were talking as equals, neither uncomfortable nor careful in the other's presence. I, on the other hand, was tongue-tied and frankly terrified of destroying everything. Exactly what was I fighting to preserve?

'Was I happy?' asked Leonardo as he refilled Julius ' glass.

'I don't know. I think you were driven, but you lived a long and brilliant life, and my world is the better for your presence.' Julius took a sip of wine. 'Sorry, acting like a fanboy.'

'So, you have no gods here?' I asked, trying to get the conversation back on track.

'No, we zap them whenever we see them. We have a quantum disruptor. A little something I rustled up, and it gets rid of unwelcome visitors.' He made them sound like mud flies.

'Explains why Loki didn't hang around,' I said. It was good to know there was something the gods were wary of.

Firenze had been listening to Leo, and now leant over and tapped him on the arm.

'I think we still have a god present. He is tethered to Neith.'

I looked startled, foolishly looking around me. Ramin looked concerned but shook his head. 'I can't see anything, Neith.'

'No,' said Firenze, 'you wouldn't be able to see him, but he maintains a link with her.'

'That makes sense,' I said. 'Explains how he knows when to come and fetch us back.'

'Well, it might make sense, but I'm not having it,' said Leo. 'Firenze, pull him through.'

She stretched out her hand and pulled it into a fist, then tugged it towards herself. There was a fizzle of energy, and the light pulsed before Loki stood in front of us. His hands were on his hips, face tipped to one side, and his jaw was clenched.

'What is the meaning of this?'

'Consider it a polite reminder. You are not permitted on this Earth, even if you remain hidden,' said Firenze calmly.

'I'll go where I like.' He disappeared and reappeared, sitting at the end of the bench, smirking.

'No, you won't,' said Firenze patiently, grabbing at the air again and pulling him towards her. 'You must leave now of your own free will.'

'I have free will and I choose to stay.'

This time he reappeared by the barbecue and threw a hot corn cob at her. She swiped it away, but it was clear she was getting frustrated. Twice more she tried to reason with him, twice more he ducked and dived, throwing stuff and transforming chairs into chickens, the wine into custard.

'Enough,' shouted Leo, who had been watching with increasing agitation. Turning the wine into custard had been a step too far. He had stormed off into the house and had come back with a small box, which he now held out and slapped on the top. Instantly Loki began to roar. His shape pulsed and twisted. The whole time he continued to scream and then he was gone.

'What did you do?' I asked aghast.

'Rid the house of pests.'

'Really, dear,' chided Firenze gently. 'I was wearing him down. He would have got bored and left through his own choice soon enough.'

'Not soon enough for me. Honestly, they are their own worst enemies, whatever they are.'

'Did you just kill a god?!' asked Julius, in shock.

Day Seven - Minju and Anansi

Minju was in the archives reading reports and brewing a cup of black tea. She had a private lift that would take her up to ground level if she needed to, but for now, she was happy to be tucked away down in the quiet corridors; unobserved and uninterrupted and keeping tabs on all the participants in the codex hunt. Her normal channels were heavily curtailed, but she had a few routes that Giovanetti and First were unaware of.

Since being revealed so publicly, she had moved quickly to get her plans into place. She had anticipated another few years of quiet manipulation. Julius's arrival had upset the status quo. He wasn't like the other angels who gratefully accepted their new lives. He challenged and questioned society. She saw his effect rippling out. The disruption of the supply network also revealed a side to the culture that the population was unhappy with. Now was the time to wake the population up, show them what they could be. The arrival of the gods had simply accelerated the process. She wasn't ready yet, but she wasn't going to miss this opportunity.

Frustratingly though, she felt that the other side were ahead. In order to win, she might have to force a full-scale confrontation. If they lost, First would not permit her to live and she had no intention of voluntarily stopping.

A change in the air pressure made her look up, and she shrank back in horror.

A gigantic black spider writhed in the corner of the room towering above her. It was standing on four long black legs, the light shining off the black carapace, the other four were waving manically in the air.

'Loki is dead! Loki has fallen!'

The screeching hurt Minju's ears, and she pressed herself back against the wall. Her tail twitched furiously and sweat prickled her skin. She tried to calculate if she could get to the door before the massive spider. She was still holding onto her teapot, which she now hurled at the creature and ran for the exit.

In a second, the spider was on her. She stumbled and fell to the floor, looking up at a face full of eyes and an open jaw looming over her. In her panic, she suddenly understood who this was and screamed Anansi's name at him. The spider removed one of its thick, hairy feet from her chest and stepped back. As it did, the air around it shimmered and Minju was now looking at Anansi in his man shape. He didn't look any less intimidating.

'The quest is finished!' he screamed at her.

'They have the codex?' asked Minju, as she stood up trying to smooth down her hair and right the items on her desk. Her hands were shaking, and her tail was swinging wildly.

'What do I know or care?' he spat out. 'This was just supposed to be a stupid game, but now Loki is no more because of you.'

'Not me,' protested Minju. Her heartbeat was still racing.

'You, the others, this Earth. Who cares? We will have our revenge on all of you.'

'I can help you with that,' said Minju quickly. The last thing she wanted to be was on the wrong side of an angry god. 'Give me an army. Let me fight alongside you and punish the wrongdoers.'

This might be the moment she had been waiting for. A general never turned away from a battle, and Minju was ready.

Day Seven - Asha

The sirens wailed as Giovanetti ordered an immediate evacuation of the city. After the first five minutes of the gods' return, it was clear that they weren't playing this time. The engineers' theory of pretending they didn't exist was falling short in the face of brutal reality. It was hard to pretend a god was make-believe when she had just set her dogs on your family and torn them apart.

There was no rhyme to the gods' attack. Giovanetti was hearing reports of various gods fighting each other. It was a tide of unchecked rage. She didn't know what had provoked this, but a few hours before a small army comprising of Grimaldi's men and rogue custodians had appeared and launched an assault on the quantum facility. The gods had arrived at the same time, and it was chaos.

Sam ran into the foyer. Asha was using this as her base. If it was overrun, she and her troops would fall back into the quantum stepper room itself. Sam's nose was bleeding, and his jacket was torn, but he had a savage smile on his face.

'It's no good. We're losing quadrant after quadrant. Shit.' He stopped and pointed at her head. 'Look, the glyphs have gone, now we don't even know who's on our side.'

Asha, immediately grasping the issue, spoke into her brace. 'Everyone, remove your uniforms. Retain your armour. Only fire at people wearing a uniform or firing at you.'

She looked back towards Sam. 'It's not much, but it will cut down some confusion. What sectors have we lost?'

Sam flicked up the holo-projection from his wrist brace. Asha looked at it and frowned.

'Why are we doing so badly by the library? We have more custodians than them down there.'

'We only have lasers. They have Beta machine guns.'

'Oh good grief.'

She spoke into her brace. 'All custodians, abandon the library. Fall back to the quantum facility. Sam, where are the gods? The monitors don't seem to be registering them.'

'According to the field reports, they are congregating around the seafront.'

'Is that octopus-monster back?'

'Yes.'

Asha pinched the bridge of her nose and opened her comms up again.

'Hypatia, where are you?'

'Down by the seafront. The quantum anomalies are strongest here. We're doing the best we can but ignoring them is having no effect. We have a few prototype weapons we've been working on since the last incursion, but they are temperamental. Some of the anomalies seem weaker than others, so we are targeting these first.'

'Good woman. I have every confidence in you.'

'Asha. Have you heard from Salah and her team? Do we know why this is happening?'

'No idea. Reports have confirmed Bedrich Grimaldi is leading parts of the army. Clio was last seen with Minju Chen. I heard the pharaoh was trampled by Osiris, but nothing has been confirmed.'

'So, the gods are basically attacking anyone?'

'Yes.'

'Well, it levels the playing field I suppose.'

'That's the spirit. Check back with an update in half an hour. We are withdrawing all troops to the quantum facility.'

'Asha. Defend my stepper at all costs. It cannot fall into the enemy's hands.'

Day Seven - Neith

We all looked in horror at Leonardo, Loki's screams still ringing in our ears.

'I don't think "kill" is the right term,' he said, unapologetically. 'But the Loki manifestation will certainly be curtailed for a while.'

We fell silent.

'This isn't going very well is it?' said Firenze.

She looked so unhappy that I tried to change the conversation.

'Do you get many visitors?'

'Not so much,' said Leonardo, equally grateful to try and cheer Firenze up. 'A few visitors from other Earths who are at a similar standard to ourselves. We are always very careful when we meet not to share unknown knowledge. But if we can help, we do. And of course, we get the regular tourists from this Earth. We have a much smaller population these days. We've stabilised population growth, our planet is healthy, and we are safe and happy.' He yawned and looked up at the sky.

'Leo is itching to get out into the stars.'

'You haven't managed space travel?' said Ramin incredulously.

'Nothing beyond the colonisation of Mars and the Moon. What about you guys?' asked Leonardo archly.

'I take it you haven't worked out how to fold the gravitational field yet?' asked Pi-Jack eagerly, ignoring Leo's put -down.

Leonardo was about to enthusiastically launch into an answer when Firenze coughed discreetly.

'Ah yes, sorry, Jack. Spoilers. Now, what can we do about getting you home? You're more than welcome to stay awhile, but I see Neith here is restless.'

I stopped tapping my foot. Although I was convinced they would know if Clio and Grimaldi made an appearance, I was still worried. I could hardly take the codex, and it was clear that he wouldn't let me have it anyway, given that I came from a backward civilisation, but I needed to make sure it was safe.

'We do need to go, but can you reassure me that the codex will be safe from the others that try to get it?'

'I can do better than that,' said da Vinci with a mischievous grin. 'I can send you back with it.'

I put my wine down and shook my head regretfully.

'No. We're not taking the codex. We don't deserve it.'

'Neith.'

'No, Pi-Jack. I know you are here to represent the engineers, but what you have been doing is wrong. It has clouded our judgement until the citizens of Alpha Earth have become arrogant, greedy parasites. I'm team leader, and I say no. If any of you disagree with me, you'll have to fight me.'

356

Pi-Jack smiled at me nervously. 'All I was going to say was that I agree with you.'

'So do I,' said Ramin. We all turned and looked at Julius who shrugged.

'Your call, but I agree with you. And although I think your self-assessment is a little harsh, it's nice to hear some sense of contrition.'

'When we get back the first thing I am going to do is recommend repatriating all stolen art to your Earth.' I had been thinking about this for ages now, and it felt good to finally come out and say it.

'What about saved art?' asked Julius.

He had a point, but maybe we could take the revolution one step at a time.

'It's definitely something to look at,' said Ramin. 'For myself, I'm going to start pushing for greater inter-collegiate workings. Being out in the field with an engineer has been very rewarding, if eye-opening.'

'I really am sorry, guys,' muttered Pi-Jack again, but Julius told him no one was cross with him personally. I kept my mouth shut.

Instead, I moved the conversation back to Leonardo and Firenze. 'We're grateful for your offer, but we'll make it on our own. Although, if you have a way to get us home...? You ditched our lift quite spectacularly.' I laughed. For the first time since I had dragged Julius back through the stepper, I felt properly at ease. I knew that by refusing the codex, I was trapping him on our side for longer, but it was better than risking his whole planet and others being plundered. He raised a glass to me as though he had read my mind.

'It's the right decision, Neith.' He smiled at me, raising an eyebrow. 'And I really do like you, as you put it, *arrogant, greedy parasites.*'

I gritted my teeth. That was going to be something he was going to bring up time and again. I could already feel it becoming a thing. But as Ramin laughed, and Pi-Jack joined in, I knew we had made a good decision.

Firenze stood up and brushed the bread seeds from her skirt. 'You misunderstood. We're not giving you the codex. I'm taking you home. If you all stand to one side. That way I don't pick up the table as well. Leonardo will be cross if I deprive him of his supper.'

I looked at Leonardo and Firenze. 'I don't understand.'

'No, I don't suppose you do.' da Vinci shook his head. 'Firenze is the codex. She is a modified human with a heart and a brain. She can live and breathe as any organic matter, but she is also a database and a functional quantum engine.'

'Engine makes me sound a little mechanical,' she teased.

I still didn't understand.

'How have you done it?' asked Pi-Jack, coming to my aid.

358

'Have a guess?' said Leo as though coaching a favourite pupil.

'DNA storage?'

'Oh, very good.' He clapped his hands in delight.

'I'm sorry, I still don't understand.'

'Well, neither do I much,' said Pi-Jack, 'but it is possible to store knowledge on DNA. Obviously, I don't know how they've done it, but between them, they turned Firenze here into a quantum stepper. Which explains how she is Lisa del Giocondo, Florence, and Firenze all at the same time.'

I looked at her in amazement.

'How do you focus?'

'I just do. How often do you focus on your knee? Or what you had for lunch yesterday? It's the same thing. If I choose to consider something: my city, my childhood, this Earth, that Earth, your friendship with Clio, these are all things I can focus on or ignore. And you know, I've had two hundred years at this. I was a bit of a mess at the beginning.'

'Somewhat,' said Leonardo. 'I have to confess, I did think I'd ruined things early on.'

'But I worked it out and balanced myself. Now we live like Darby and Joan.'

'Do you use it much? Your skills?' Pi-Jack was clearly trying to find a way that didn't make her sound like an object.

359

'Utilise the world's most powerful weapon? Not likely. I just like making wine and helping Leo with his equations for travelling across the universe. Now, shall we go? Stand together. And think of something nice.'

'Why?' asked Julius nervously. 'Is this going to hurt?'

'Of course not. I just think more people should think nice thoughts. Won't it be lovely to see all your friends again? Now, here we go.'

I wanted to say goodbye to Leonardo, but suddenly the world was filled with sunshine and the smell of roses and a soft, warm breeze.

Day Seven – Alpha Earth - Julius

We landed in a bubble. Neith and Rami had drawn their lasers. Jack took a step towards me, and Firenze's face grew dark.

'Your Earth is infested!'

Beyond the wall of the bubble that Firenze had thrown up around us, I could see a battle taking place. We had arrived in the concourse between the seafront and the quantum facility to the edge of the city, away from the library and other mouseion buildings. As I watched, a god flew over our heads in a chariot drawn by Pegasus. He was firing arrows down on the people below. Firenze flicked a finger, and the arrows disappeared.

'What's happened?' shouted Neith in alarm.

Firenze looked around furiously.

'I will stay long enough to clean up this rot, but I cannot interfere in non-quantum issues. Those people shooting at each other, they are your affair. Take care.'

With that, she ran towards the seafront, growing taller with each step. I gave her one last glance as Neith tugged my sleeve and pulled me over to some park benches, which we ducked behind.

She tapped on her brace for Sam and, after a moment's welcome, he patched her through to Asha, who brought us up to date.

Taking advantage of the rioting gods, Minju had seized her chance and launched a coup with the added reinforcement of Grimaldi's men, and more. Anansi had presumably just transported them.

'Why didn't he just transport them into the facility?'

'Maybe he thought this was worse? Create more conflict.'

'We are hugely outnumbered. Neith, I need you and your team to make your way to the quantum facility. We cannot let Minju take control.'

At this point, Jack, who had been looking particularly dreamy, smiled and joined the conversation. 'They can have it. I've worked out how to build another. And this time it will work properly. Firenze and I were talking as we travelled home.'

Rami, Neith and I looked at him in disbelief.

Asha shouted down the line. 'Enough. This is not a secure line. Retreat immediately.'

Neith clicked her fingers in front of Jack, trying to get him out of his reverie.

'Not another word from you. Right?'

We were surrounded by small conflicts. Behind us were gods with mythical but effective weapons. Between us and the stepper were insurgents with guns and grenades fighting custodians and curators with lasers. We were outnumbered, but this was our home turf, and we were using it to our advantage. Craning my neck, I could make out a curator on one of the upper walkways, lying on their belly, firing down on the army below. Never missing, they picked off the insurgents one by one. The

362

shots aimed to incapacitate rather than kill. As I watched, the door onto the walkway opened behind them, and a woman with a gun crept out behind the shooter.

I placed my hand on the cold marble bench for balance and aimed at the second shooter. I had never shot a woman before and felt strangely embarrassed as I watched her crumple on the floor behind the marksman.

'Great shot, Julius,' said Neith. 'Ramin and I are going to get Pi-Jack to safety. Cover us until we're out of sight. Then break free and get to the facility.'

I nodded but didn't trust my voice to speak without shaking. I wanted to protest; all around me was chaos and I didn't want to be on my own. I flinched as a nearby window shattered. Making myself as small as I could, I hunkered down beside the bench and focused my laser on Rami and Neith's path. Rami on close shield, Neith to one side, shooting as she went. Any shooter that fired in their direction was instantly shot by me. I missed the first person, as my hand was still shaking. Neith looked back at me and gave me a thumbs up, and I swallowed down my bile. She needed me, and I wouldn't let her down.

They had almost made it to the corner when someone kicked my arm, and my laser went flying. In my efforts to protect the team, I had failed to keep an eye on my own surroundings and was now facing an unarmed man. He was a brute of a man, standing easily over six foot, his sleeveless vest revealing arms the width of telegraph poles. Tattoos ran up his biceps, across his face and up into his shaved scalp. There was blood on his forehead and it wasn't his.

He grunted at me and swung his arm back. I rolled away, all of Neith's training flooding through my sinews. I knew how to do this. I would knock him into next week. I sprang up into a crouched position and immediately jumped to the side. My assailant was now pointing my own laser at me. I'd been stupid, and he was faster. He had worked out that my laser was biometrically locked. I had forgotten and had wasted time in defensive manoeuvres. As I realised, I charged at him. At the same time, he hurled the laser in my face.

Temporarily stunned, the next thing I felt was a blow to my gut, and I collapsed to the floor. Wheezing heavily, I waited until he got closer, then grabbed one ankle and shoved on the other, flinging my body around so that this leg stumbled backwards. He crashed to the floor. I flicked my eyes, looking for a weapon, and reached out for a large stone that had been placed for decoration around one of the plaza's olive trees.

It felt good in my hand and, swinging forward, I punched him in the nose with it. In a spray of blood, he collapsed backwards, hands clasping his face. Running for cover, I jumped behind an upturned bench as he staggered off. I searched desperately for Neith and Rami, but the team had disappeared. Hopefully, they had got to safety, but I could no longer follow their footsteps, that route was now overrun with people fighting. I needed to find a better route to re-join them.

I ducked as I heard a scream overhead. A giant tentacle was waving a human in the air above me. He was wearing a uniform but even so, I wouldn't wish his fate on anyone. The air was lit up with lasers and gun flare as they shot at the tentacle, and I prayed that they missed the man himself. The shots enraged the beast who hurled the body across the rooftops. I followed it until it fell out of sight. The tentacles shot back down to ground level, and now four more people were held aloft.

A shadow momentarily darkened the sky and I looked up to see a massive eagle sweep out from the position of the sun. It was so huge that it had to be one of the gods. Were the eagle and the kraken going to fight over the bodies of those screaming victims? I prepared to shoot the people, better that they were unconscious than what was about to happen. As I took aim, the eagle pulled back on its wings, thrusting its legs forward and piercing a tentacle with its talons. A second later the kraken was gone, and the people appeared to be slowly drifting back down to Earth in defiance of gravity. I smelt the sweetness of honey in the air and let out a sigh of relief. Not a god then. Firenze.

Day Seven - Julius

I was still crouched down under the stone bench and knew I needed to get out of here. I was dangerously exposed and needed to get back to the quantum facility. Firenze was handling the gods and arrows, but the stray bullets kept zinging past and causing damage to those nearby. The Alphas were more used to fighting with lasers. Guns may be more lethal, but the shooters were inaccurate. I was more likely to be hit by a stray bullet or ricochet than someone actually aiming at me.

I peered around the other end of the bench and found myself looking at a startled Charlie.

'Bloody hell, Julie, what's going on?'

I was momentarily stunned, then a tsunami of joy overwhelmed me. I couldn't speak and just hugged him. My fists bunched up as I wrapped my arms around his chest.

'Steady on,' he laughed. 'What the hell is this? One minute you and I are on the sofa playing Call of Duty, the next minute I'm in the middle of an actual battle. Did you put something in the food?'

I laughed back. It was so good to see him. So sodding excellent. 'No idea. The gods are fighting the codex. I think the walls of reality are breaking down.'

Charlie gave me a double-take then shook his head. 'Whatever. Whose side are we on?'

'The scientists.'

'Righty-ho. And those Romans, goodies or baddies?'

God, I hadn't noticed the Romans. When had they arrived? Things were getting out of control. 'Baddies. I think'

'Right, come on then. Cover me. "Armed only with my trusty sword".'

I laughed again as he quoted our favourite phrase as young boys, play-fighting on the school field with twigs and branches. And indeed, as I looked at him, he was now holding an actual sword. We both grinned at each other.

He jumped up and ran towards the soldiers, sword aloft like some daft kid.

I shot at anyone who even looked in his direction. It would help if he wasn't yelling as he advanced.

'Charlie!' I shouted, and he ducked behind an olive tree, looking back at me. 'I bloody love you.'

'Course you do, bro,' he shouted back, 'and I love you too.' Grinning, he ran forward again and swung his sword into the side of a Roman who had just struck a custodian. As the Roman stumbled, I watched him fall and then disappear. So did Charlie.

I cried his name like a bloody fool, waiting for him to reappear. Around the plaza, people and creatures were winking out of existence as Firenze began to get angry. Whoever the gods could summon, Firenze could dismiss.

I stood there, amongst the screams and the fights, watching as shots were fired, as people fell in an explosion of blood and gunfire, or vanished, their opponent left floundering, and I had never felt more alone.

Day Seven - Arthur

Arthur looked about him in irritation. There were fights all around him, but this was not the scene of a well-measured battle. As a seasoned warrior he knew the joys and challenges of a well-ordered fight, but this was something far worse. It wasn't even a melee, it was a full-on riot with no clear sides and no sense of organisation.

In the distance, he heard the baying of hounds as Artemis set her dogs upon Isis. Artemis and Apollo were engaged in a full-on fight with Isis and Osiris. These sibling pairs would stop and fight at the drop of a pin, but usually calmer heads would prevail and separate them. Mostly their paths didn't overlap. But here they were lunging at each other, piercing and mutilating their opposite numbers with no intervention. Arthur moved away; he could fight mythological creatures and lesser gods, but he didn't stand a chance against the upper echelons.

Glancing around he saw a group of soldiers dressed in red armour moving in a cohesive manner towards a group of defenceless civilians. At least someone was trying to instil discipline and save the citizens of this city. As Arthur watched, a trader stepped forward clearly ready to request assistance. The lead soldier appeared to say something jokey to his men and then punched the citizen in the face.

Arthur didn't hesitate. Here was a situation he could resolve. Running forward he drew Excalibur from its scabbard and stood between the soldiers and the citizens.

'These people are under my protection.'

The soldiers looked at him in astonishment and then laughed.

'What, you and your sword are going to save the day. Be the hero? There's ten of us.'

One of the civilians tried to run and a soldier lunged forward. Arthur stepped to the right and swung Excalibur up, blocking the red custodian.

'Yes, me and my sword.'

'There's ten of us.'

'Yes. You mentioned that and I appreciate that this does put you at a disadvantage. If you wish to leave now and stop molesting these citizens, I will consider the matter closed.'

Arthur took a deep breath; he knew they wouldn't leave; this sort never did. Not when they sensed an easy victory. It would be better if he stepped forward now and ended this, but he had offered them a chance and honour forbade him from acting before they replied.

'Arses to that! We'll kill you. Then we'll kill those snivelling cowards.' His mates laughed along with him. 'Better yet. We'll kill them in front of you and...'

His words were cut short as Arthur swung Excalibur's blade edge across his throat, arterial blood gushing up in a bright red bloom. As the blade arced, he took out a second soldier who had stepped forward to see what was happening. Now Arthur lunged to his left, the sword made no distinction between the custodians' armour or their flesh and after two more had fallen, the rest turned and ran. Arthur looked over his shoulder and was pleased to see that the civilians had also legged it.

Grabbing a cloth from his belt he wiped the blood off his blade and re-sheathed it. Everywhere he looked was anarchy. He didn't feel responsible. It simply wasn't an emotion that he wasted any time on, but he did have a niggling sense of suspicion that he might be partly to blame. Julius' admonishments from a few days before had been weighing heavily on his mind. Reflection however solved nothing. Action was what was needed.

Recently he had been chatting with Mithras and he felt in him a kindred spirit. They shared similar opinions and motivations and Arthur wondered if in hanging around with Loki and Anansi he may have chosen unwisely. Again, speculation gained nothing.

'You have free will!'

A woman's voice rang out across the skies. Arthur turned and headed towards the harbour. The command held the promise of justice and authority. Its clarion call echoed around his thoughts. Reaching the water's edge, he gazed up at a mighty goddess fighting both Zeus and Thor and holding her own. She was incredible but still she was outnumbered. Arthur ran towards her, growing in stature as he did so. He pulled out his sword and stood alongside her, looking up into the skies at the towering rage of Zeus and Thor. In the face of their fury, he knew this wasn't a battle he could survive. If this were to be his death it would be a fitting one. Not defending this goddess would be the greater failure.

'My lady. Step aside and let me protect you.'

She turned and smiled at him, and Arthur was transported to a time of bliss and perfection.

'My lady Guinevere?'

'Firenze. But I am grateful for the compliment. Also, I'm fine here and you need to go home.'

A shaft of lightning hurled towards them, and Firenze knocked it aside before returning her attention to Arthur.

'King Arthur I presume?' said Firenze still smiling at him. She was taller than him but after a moment of reflection, she shrank until she was slightly smaller.

'Does this make you more comfortable?'

Arthur looked down on her and considered. For a moment, he had felt a surge of pride in protecting this smaller woman and then he laughed at his pomposity.

'My lady Firenze, please choose whichever shape pleases you most and permit me to fight alongside you.'

Arthur had no idea who she was but had already established she wasn't a goddess. Standing next to her, he could simply tell she didn't have the same essence as himself and his companions. She was also infinitely more powerful than he was and also, he suspected, Zeus and

Thor. That said, he still couldn't bring himself to abandon her.

'Arthur. You must leave. The citizens have stated their desire that this Earth be free of your kind. I am here to enforce that request.'

'May I assist you until your task is done?'

'No, Arthur. If you wish to help me, leave now.'

'Very well.' The king of the Britons prepared to bow when Firenze interrupted him.

'Before you go.'

'Yes?' he asked hopefully. Maybe she would permit him to join her in battle, after all.

'I am glad to have met you. I understand now, the appeal you have to Julius.'

It was not what he had hoped for, but he felt a surge of pride, nonetheless. Arthur bowed deeply and was gone.

Day Seven - Julius

Firenze stood on the seawall. Behind her, the waves rose and crashed as she pulled the elements towards her. The sky turned dark, and energy crackled. She was growing in size. Her blonde plaits were now unbound, and her hair was streaming out around her face.

'You have free will,' she bellowed.

I ran to the olive tree that Charlie had ducked behind and took aim at some of the red custodians.

Looking back at Firenze, she was now trying to deal with each deity on an individual basis. She would point at one, and they would either disappear voluntarily, or she would throw out a swarm of hornets that would sting them. They still disappeared, but this time screaming.

A shower of lightning bolts flashed towards her. Thor, or Zeus, or both, had entered the fray.

Out of nowhere, Arthur ran forward. He had grown to the same size as Firenze and was using Excalibur to draw the lightning bolts. As if Firenze needed saving, but this piece of chivalry had not gone unnoticed. She smiled sweetly at him, and I noticed that he became more real with every passing moment. He changed from a vain, insecure idiot into a hero and a true high king. The way he stood filled me with hope and inspiration. They spoke a few words, and then he bowed and disappeared. With him gone, Firenze grabbed the lightning and flung it back at Zeus and Thor. They screamed and writhed across the sky.

It was time to leave. I could do nothing here, but the curators were vastly outnumbered by Minju's forces. Firenze wouldn't help us, but if we didn't find a way to win, all our Earths would be in a worse state.

As I legged it towards the stepper facility, small spiders scuttled past me. Ahead, troops were falling back as the street darkened with tiny spiders rushing towards the facility. Those that stood in their way were soon bitten, those that ran away, or moved in the same direction, were ignored. I sprinted towards the facility, although I was shivering with revulsion as I ran through a sea of small spiders. At any moment, they could turn and engulf me. We broke into the plaza in front of the facility, and I saw heavy gunfire shattering the glass and marble walls of the entrance. Laser fire was being returned, and the air was hazy with dust and discharged particles.

My ears were still ringing from being punched in the head, but even I could hear the gunfire.

A grenade sailed through the air. I screamed out a warning. It was shot mid-flight, but the explosion still rocked the airwaves. The spiders continued to pour in until they started to coalesce into the figure of Anansi.

My brace beeped, and I heard Neith's voice.

'Julius. Stay where you are. Reinforcements from Cairo are on their way. If we can survive the next thirty minutes, we're home and dry. Take shelter.'

I looked across to the barricades, but I couldn't see her. Thirty minutes. They needed every minute they could get. I stepped forward.

'Anansi.' The god turned and looked at me, and for a second I couldn't speak. His fury was terrifying. In my ear, Neith was shouting at me, and I swore I heard Charlie laughing at me across the ether. I pictured Arthur standing in front of Zeus and Thor, protecting Firenze. I was only Julius Strathclyde, but what the hell. I checked my hands, but no mystical sword had suddenly appeared. Just two sweaty palms. I wiped them on my shirt, tugged at my cuffs, cleared my throat and stepped forward.

'You have broken the rules of the quest. We found the missing codex and now you must leave. All sides agreed.'

'All sides?' he shouted at me, his voice echoing off the walls. All gunfire ceased, as everyone waited to see in what particular manner I would be destroyed. 'You made a promise with Anansi and Loki, but Loki is no more, so the pact is broken. I am going into your pathetic little building and will rip open your doorway. All the myths and monsters can have direct access to this Earth, and no one can stop me.'

I wracked my brains. How could I out-trick him? Was there a way to push him through the stepper and trap him on the other side? Could I apologise on behalf of humanity? Did he have a better side that could be appealed to? Could I offer an enraged god a diversion?

Maybe all I could do was sacrifice myself? Try to buy time for the others.

Across the plaza, a small figure stepped from behind the temporary fortress that Grimaldi had erected and walked towards Anansi. As she did so, she smiled at me.

'Lord Anansi. Do you remember my request?'

I watched. Did Minju plan to save the day or obliterate us?

'And you want it now? When you are about to win?'

She inclined her head respectfully. 'I would live to fight another day.'

'Sounds like cowardice to me.' He smirked. 'I will not lose.'

'Even so. I call it a tactical retreat. If you please?'

'Very well.'

I watched as she glanced my way, saluted, then ran off down one of the smaller lanes towards the mouseion complex. I didn't know what had just happened, but it didn't feel like it had been in our favour. However, it had gained us a few minutes.

I took a deep breath and tried again. It felt like a final roll of the dice.

'Anansi. This is wrong. You must leave here.'

'I WILL NOT.'

His voice thundered across the city. I fell backwards under the shock wave of the sound, as chunks of glass fell around me. Touching my ears, I felt blood on my fingers. I couldn't see, and my fingers traced the blood on my cheeks as well as around my nose. Deaf and blind, I scrambled back to where I thought a wall was, the debris cutting my hands. My suit had protected me from most of the impact, but I could smell nothing but blood and dust. How were the others doing? Had their barricades offered protection, or had I just destroyed my own team as well as Grimaldi's? The pain in my head was intense, and I realised I was probably dying. The suit could only do so much. My blood was pounding, all I could hear was the beat of my heart when I smelt honey and sunlight. I blinked as Firenze strode past. A summer storm walking into the plaza.

With my sight and hearing restored, I could see others peering out over the barricades, watching as Anansi and Firenze squared off against each other. It looked like I had suffered the greatest brunt of the damage, or Firenze had healed all as she had passed. The suit was now running through a garbled list of issues I was suffering from, but I ignored it as Firenze began to talk.

'You will leave now,' she commanded. Anansi wasn't a total idiot and took a step back, but the temptation of a power source just beyond his control was swaying his judgement.

'You have no authority over me. Or any god.'

'I have no authority. But I have power, and you have free will. Leave now, or I will destroy you.'

Anansi lunged towards the facility entrance and began to disintegrate into a thousand spiders. Firenze roared like a clap of thunder. She flung her hand towards him. Fingers splayed out, and the air was full of swallows. The small blue birds darted through the air, eating the tiny spiders or plucking at Anansi's half-formed body. Everywhere I looked, birds swooped overhead, attacking the arachnids. A small spider ran across my leg, trying to flee Firenze's relentless pursuit. I went to slap it, but before I could, a swallow swept between my hand and thigh and the spider was gone. With each second, Anansi's screams became more frantic until they finally sputtered out into silence, and the last of the gods was no more.

Turning to face us, she tipped her head.

'I have stayed too long. Think nice thoughts.'

And she too was gone.

Day Seven - Julius

For a second there was silence. Anansi's screams had filled the air and now there was nothing. For a moment I thought we had won. Then the guns started shooting again.

It was so unfair; I could have wept. We had vanquished the gods, but Grimaldi and Clio were still advancing. Reinforcements hadn't arrived, and if Grimaldi seized the stepper he would win. I didn't know why Minju had quit the field, but I didn't think it was to help us.

I sat with my back against the wall. The floor around me was covered in lumps of mortar and I tried to steady my breathing. The air was full of dust, and I was exhausted. Grimaldi's men charged forward, all attempts at a stand-off were now gone. We were in the desperate stages of the battle, but from my position, something looked wrong.

'Asha,' I called into my brace, but my message was cut off. I tried again. On the third time, she shouted down the line at me.

'We are under attack; I don't have time.'

'It's a feint!'

'What?' The sound of shooting around her faded. She must have retreated to hear what I had to say.

'The way the troops are moving forward. It looks like a ruse from where I'm sat. Something is happening on the far left, but I can't see what. I—'

The line broke again. Asha's forces surged to the left. In horror, I saw the double bluff revealed as Clio and Grimaldi ran to the right and grabbed Jack who had been left unprotected.

'All channels! Grimaldi has Jack.'

I struggled to my feet and leant against the wall as I hobbled after them. Firenze had healed my brain from the concussion, but my ankle was still buggered. I saw Neith peel away from the fight and sprint across the concourse, jumping over the debris towards Clio and Grimaldi. I shot at both of them, offering Neith cover as I limped towards the park. Asha had warned us that the frequencies were being monitored, and now Grimaldi must have decided to take Jack instead of the machine. With whatever knowledge Jack had gained from Leonardo and Firenze, he was now our most valuable asset. Who knew what they would do to him to make him share his knowledge? Jack was a lovely kid, and I knew he wouldn't share the knowledge willingly.

Neith and I were closing in on the trio, but Neith was gaining. I watched as Clio and Grimaldi came to the same conclusion. On the horizon, a small heli-cruiser was approaching, with a ladder hanging down. Dragging a semi-conscious Jack along, Grimaldi ran towards the open park. Clio stood behind to halt Neith.

381

'They have a helicopter,' I shouted down the brace to Asha. 'We need air support.'

'On its way, Strathclyde. Neith, make sure they don't get on the cruiser.'

Across the concourse, I saw Neith nod her head in agreement with the instructions, then shield as Clio fired at her. From my line of sight, I could target both Clio and Grimaldi. I chose Grimaldi. It was the trickier shot, as he was moving and getting further away. However, it didn't matter if I missed him and hit Jack. My laser would only incapacitate them rather than kill. If I hit Jack, it would only make it harder for Grimaldi to get him to the pickup site.

Moving into open ground I ducked and zigzagged, wincing and swearing as I went, firing at Grimaldi. He stopped and returned fire. We were unmatched. He had a gun and, unlike some of his contemporaries, he knew how to use it. I felt a flare of pain in my arm as something hot tore past it. The suit must have helped deflect some of the impact of a glancing bullet, but I wasn't certain if it could stop a direct impact. I continued firing, but my ankle was slowing me down.

Asha was clearly watching the fight as she shouted now at Neith, who for some reason wasn't returning fire on Clio, just dodging and shielding from Clio's laser fire.

'Salah. Shoot Clio! Strathclyde isn't going to reach Grimaldi in time.'

382

Neith shook her head. I could hear her over the brace. 'Can't do that. Dropped my laser in the fight, I only have a gun.'

'So, kill her. Neith Salah, that is a direct order. Kill Clio. Save Jack.'

'She's my friend.' Neith's voice was small and heartbroken.

'I don't bloody care if she's your mother. Kill her.'

I continued firing at Grimaldi from behind the fallen statue of a mathematician. I was leaning on his abacus and firing through the counters. Grimaldi was pinned down but returning fire. I looked across at Neith to see what she would do.

'Sorry, boss. It's all about priorities.'

'Salah, that is a direct order. Kill Clio,' roared Asha.

I opened my intercom as the scene played out in front of me.

'Asha. Neith has removed her earpiece and thrown down her gun. She can't hear you.'

I probably didn't need my brace to hear Asha swear. Taking a deep breath she stopped shouting.

'Julius. Shoot at Clio. Protect Neith. Protect Pi-Jack.'

Which is when one of Grimaldi's bullets hit my laser out of my hand, breaking my fingers into the bargain. I felt sick and buckled over in pain. Gasping, I shouted to Asha. 'Lost my laser. Going for Jack.'

If I could get close enough without being killed, I could try and stop Grimaldi. At some point, he would have to reload, and that would be my moment. Anything to stop him getting Jack on that helicopter.

Grimaldi turned his back on me. Even dragging Jack, he was faster than me. My arm and hand hurt like hell, but my ankle was really causing me problems. The foot had swollen in my boot and now every step I could feel pain ripping up my leg as the shattered bone ground against itself. The suit had been administering analgesics into my bloodstream throughout the battle but now it was running low. I fell again and looked around for something to act as a crutch. Across from me, Clio and Neith were engaged in hand-to-hand combat.

Both were silent, and while Clio had the advantage in height and skill, she was only blocking Neith rather than trying to hurt her. Even Grimaldi could see that Clio was not prepared to shoot Neith.

He raised his gun again.

I needed to do something stupid and heroic. I grabbed a stone to throw at him as I scrambled upright. My plan was to call out his name and see if I could distract him long enough for Neith to neutralise Clio. I stood up, then watched my world shatter.

Grimaldi fired at Neith. This time, his aim was perfect. In disbelief, I watched as her head flipped back and a spray of blood bloomed into the air, splashing onto Clio's face.

Clio howled and turned, firing blindly at Grimaldi. For a second he looked at Jack, but Clio was screaming

384

towards him. Ditching Jack, he ran off with Clio in pursuit.

Even as Neith had started to fall, I began shouting for a medical team. I stumbled and slipped across the grass towards her. When I reached her, she was lying on the grass. The blood from her forehead splattered her face. One blue eye and one brown eye open, both staring sightlessly at the sky. I shouted at her to stay alive until the medical team arrived via air support, and I don't remember much after that.

Day Thirty - Minju

Minju Chen uncrossed her legs and stood up, returning to her desk. She had been attempting to meditate but she was too agitated. Three weeks had passed since the Battle of the Gods, as it was being referred to and so far, her lie had held. In the dying moments of the battle, she had been able to see her side was losing. Grimaldi was used to violence and overwhelming force, but he had no discipline or battle strategy. The custodians who were fighting under her command were struggling in the light of fighting their own comrades while also trying to fend off attacks from homicidal gods.

She had been so close but even as the battle started, she'd known her troops were unprepared. How many years had this put her back? She had spent decades cultivating her plan and it was all destroyed in a matter of hours. Her proto-empire lay in tatters and for now, her only goal was to survive.

Her deal with Anansi had proved her smartest move. She had been reading up on gods and played her last card hoping it was an ace. Challenging Anansi in the middle of the battle had taken nerves of steel but he remembered his promise and asked what her request was. She could still see his mocking smile as she asked him to erase her actions from everyone's memory, but he had complied.

Even as she began to run away, soldiers were ignoring her, no one was shouting to her for instructions and commands. Grimaldi had looked straight through her as she sprinted past him.

Down in the archives she had reset Tiresias and sighed in relief as all commands regarding her were obliterated. For the next three weeks, she'd played the part of a terrified survivor, and everyone had bought it. Today would be her greatest test. When she had asked the god to erase everyone's memory, she had said "all of Alpha".' Now she was preparing to see if Anansi had found a loophole.

Day Thirty - Julius

'And then what happened?' asked Minju, almost breathlessly.

It was the first time I'd had a chance to catch up with my friend.

I sipped on the cardamom coffee and raised my cup in salute to her. Seeing her dimples cheered me up. God knows, few things right now made me happy.

'Grimaldi made it to the helicopter, but as he climbed the safety ladder, Clio managed to shoot him, and he fell to the ground and broke his neck. No surgery. Game over. Clio was, of course, arrested. Her list of crimes is quite significant, but she might just get a medal for killing Grimaldi and saving Jack.'

Minju shook her head. 'Grimaldi was a stain on our society. I flew out there last week to oversee the retrieval of his art collection. We found an old lady living there who has been taken into care. The rest of his staff were turned over to the Russian authorities. Relations are a bit tricky between the two countries, and frankly, we have enough on our plate.'

Plans were being drawn up to return anything stolen to Beta Earth, although Russia had tried to make a case for keeping the art.

'How did you get them to hand the art over?'

'Reminded them of who I am.' She smiled sweetly and I laughed. 'In fact, I was going to talk to you soon,

388

officially. I think you would be the perfect ambassador to return stolen art. Just as soon as the engineers can build young Jack's modifications to the stepper.'

My hand shook, and I put my cup down. The idea of being able to return home and take back some of its purloined items was overwhelming. It would also be honouring Neith's wishes.

'And Neith?'

Minju smiled at me kindly, but I just couldn't trust myself to speak.

Shaking my head, I changed the subject. 'And how are you doing? I can't believe you spent all this time hiding down here?'

'Hardly heroic, was I?'

'You were protecting your exhibits. I think that's pretty noble.'

She pursed her lips in disagreement. 'Well, there's plenty of food and water down here. When that weird grey pyramid appeared over my head, I knew there was trouble afoot and so I dashed down here. I know people probably view me as being cowardly.'

'Hardly,' I spluttered. 'You know, I see through you Minju Chen.'

Her eyes blinked in alarm, but she said nothing.

'You hide down here and worry what people will think of you. Well, let me tell you. I think you have the soul of a warrior. You knew your skill wasn't in fighting gods or thieves. You knew that the best way to deploy your talents was in protecting the mouseion.'

She appeared to relax. It had been really remarkable. She had been hidden down here for weeks, scurrying along the corridors, keeping them locked down and safe from the thieves, the insurrectionists, and the gods. She had only been discovered three days after the final battle where, according to rumour, the indomitable Minju Chen had burst into tears of relief that we had won.

'And these gods,' said Minju, 'this Anansi, spider creature. He really existed? It wasn't a quantum malfunction?'

'Absolutely real. According to what Jack learnt from Firenze, they are some sort of quantum creature. They exist in the quantum field itself.'

'How is that even possible?'

'No idea, but you can bet the engineers are on it.'

We sipped our drinks in the quiet hum of Minju's office.

'And this Anansi, you said he could alter memories and do magic?' I think she must have thought I was pulling her legs; she was watching me so intently.

'No it's true, they could all do incredible stuff.'

At that moment, a swallow flew through the room, and Minju recoiled in alarm, her tail swaying wildly.

'It's nothing. Just a bird.'

I knew I would never look at a swallow again in the same way and I was surprised at Minju's alarm, but then she hadn't witnessed the incredible power of Firenze.

'It's not that. It's just these corridors are hermetically sealed for the protection of the exhibits. How did a bird get in here?'

We watched as the bird disappeared into an air vent.

'You'd better fix that. Looks like you might be compromised,' I said and again she gave me an odd look. 'Tell you what. I need to catch up with Rami and the others. I'll leave you to sort out the air ducts.'

She looked relieved, but I decided to double-check.

'I can stay with you if you want?'

She raised an eyebrow, and I was reminded that while I might view her as a lovely lady, the majority of curators viewed her as a terrifying guardian of the archives.

'Very well, I shall see you next week.'

With that, I headed upstairs and out into the sunshine.

All the debris had been removed now, but the scars were still visible. Some buildings were still unsafe to enter, others were riddled with blast holes. A team of workers were replanting some of the flowerbeds, and I gave them a wave as I passed.

'Looking great.'

'We change!' said one of the women, smiling, although she didn't start digging again until I started to walk on. She was quoting the motto of the newly formed

Department of Adaptation. Asha had put out an instant broadcast to the citizens of Alexandria to not commit suicide, but instead, to help her rebuild the city. She gave them a focus and began to hold daily group and solo sessions. People could talk about the recent changes and discoveries they had endured as a society. The classes were swamped. Asha increased the classes, and soon nearly everyone had attended at least one session. This was a whole population desperate for guidance, and she was trying to lead the way.

I entered Pygs and waved to a few people sitting around. I headed out onto the veranda and joined the others.

A flock of swallows chittered overhead as they swept across the beach. I wondered if I would ever look at them again without thinking of Firenze.

Rami was already at the table, chatting with Jack and Luisa. He had been shot in the shoulder and suffered some facial scarring as shrapnel hit his cheek. He'd decided to keep the scar. As he said, he was never going to fill Sam's boots. He was hoping a scar might make him look convincingly scary. I thought he was going to be excellent, with or without the scar.

He also said it made him more attractive down at the bar, but I suspected that wasn't the real reason either. We were all carrying scars. Some were more visible than others.

'What is Luisa saying no to this time?' I asked.

She turned and laughed at me. 'Jack here was suggesting Julia Cleeve for pharaoh.'

I didn't know the woman, but Luisa clearly had strong reservations.

'She says yes to anything. She'll be rubbish.'

'Well, we need someone. Giovanetti has threatened to go on holiday if a working structure isn't quickly imposed. This morning I heard her say she was going to make it Cairo's problem.'

The three of them shuddered.

'What about Chen?'

I could see them all considering my proposal as I sat down.

'Not an insane idea, Blue,' said Luisa. 'But nothing could persuade her to leave the archives.'

'Her sense of duty might,' suggested Rami, and we all nodded.

Jack clinked his bottle with Rami's, and we all sat watching the swallows.

Since his return, Jack had re-joined the engineers but now was known simply as Jack, or *Just Jack* as he was fond of saying. Every now and then, he would stop mid-sentence and start scribbling equations, but Sabrina would just nudge him and remind him it was his round. She was late, and I looked around, wondering where she had got to. In the past few weeks, I had found her company easier to tolerate. She seemed less keen to trip me up or show she was better than me, and it made her more relaxed.

I heard my name being called out and saw her threading her way through the tables towards us. She looked anything but relaxed right now, and Rami and I looked at each other in surprise. Sabrina was a nice girl, but she wasn't the sort to wave her arms in the air. She reached our table panting and Jack offered her his bottle, which she waved away in disgust before taking in a big breath and exhaling with an even bigger smile.

'She's opened her eyes. Neith is awake.'

Coming Next

Book Four
The Quantum Curators and the Untitled Manuscript

Available for pre-order now

Thank you for reading

Getting to know my readers is incredibly rewarding, I get to know more about you and enjoy your feedback; it only seems fair that you get something in return, so if you sign up for my newsletter you will get various free downloads, depending on what I am currently working on, plus advance notice of new releases. I don't send out many newsletters, and I will never share your details. If this sounds good, click on the following:

https://www.thequantumcurators.com

I'm also on all the regular social media platforms so look me up.
@thequantumcurators

Author's Note

Writing about the gods has been great fun. Anansi has always been a favourite of mine and it's been a pleasure to work with him. I have also loved spending time with Arthur. Rather than base him on his original stories, I wanted him to be a reflection of modern interpretations. If gods and myths are created in our image then they need to move along with us.

Most of the gods and mythological creatures in this book exist in our cultures but I threw in a few of my own.

With Thanks

As ever, this is a team effort and I have had some great conversations with friends. Who would win in a fight between a god and a genius? How many Earths can exist at the same time? If you stand on a butterfly, do you really spark a hurricane? And so on. Many bottles of wine and cardamom coffees were consumed in the pursuit of truth. Or wild speculation. One or the other.

In particular, I need to thank Alexandra for reading through my first draft and not laughing too loudly at all the wrong bits. The manuscript was further knocked into shape through various rounds of edits, and I'd like to thank my editors, Mark Stay, Melanie Underwood and Anna Gow. Finally, my excellent ARC team went over it like the most diligent archivists on this side of the two Earths.

I also want to say thank you to my family. It's fair to say that this has been a mad year. Again. And I have so much to be grateful for, they have put up with many crises of faith. I owe them.

And finally, thank you. You have followed Neith and Julius for three books and I hope you will continue to do so. I plan to throw in a few curve balls over the next few books.

Made in the USA
Las Vegas, NV
07 September 2021